Baking Secrets

&

Otherworldly Mysteries

Daisy Hans-Burrell

Ooopsie Daisy Publishing

ISBN: 979-8-218-57131-3

First Edition: 2024

Dedicated to those who supported me in my writing journey thus far, and to those who will support it in the future.

Special thanks to Kent, my love in every lifetime.

Another special thanks to Jade and Jameson, my furry friends who made hours and hours of writing much more snuggly.

Baking Secrets

&

Otherworldly Mysteries

Chapter One

"Alright, your total is \$37.64." I smiled and swiped my card. It was about time I got a new one since my chip didn't work anymore.

"Thank you, have a nice day!" The cashier handed me my receipt. I grabbed my bags, and then I was on my way. The warm sunshine kissed my pale skin as soon as I stepped outside. The strong breeze paired with the smell of freshly cut grass made today feel absolutely perfect.

I fumbled to get my keys, but eventually got them out of the black hole that is also known as my purse. I tossed my groceries to the passenger seat and made my way home. Well, home adjacent. I had a stop to make first.

I live in a small town in north Georgia, almost Tennessee, about forty-five minutes away from this grocery store. There were other ones closer to my house, but this one has the best selection of meat and produce. So, a longer drive was worth it. More scenic as well, which is a win in my book. I passed through bright blue, gurgling rivers and gorgeous mountain valleys that seemed surreal when the sun hit the peaks just right. I get lost just looking in them. Maybe not the best thing to admit while I'm driving.

I turned left onto a long, narrow, dirt driveway. There were loads of overgrown wildflowers framing my car in so tightly I could reach out of my window and grab a bouquet if I wanted to. Azaleas, coneflowers, daisies, black-eyed susans, geraniums, milkweed, rhododendrons, bluebells, asters, and I'm sure many more beyond my field of vision. I pulled up to the house, which was not visible from the street, grabbed my groceries and stepped out of the car. No need to lock it when you're this deep and hidden in the countryside. The wildflowers stopped where the medium-sized, chocolate brown house started, and had a perimeter of mammoth sunflowers surrounding it. The backyard was pretty well maintained as well, thanks to me. It had six, bountiful, raised flower beds overflowing with fresh vegetables and herbs. Some fruit bushes and trees were back there as well.

The house was old and the paint was chipping pretty bad when you looked closely. I felt that was part of its charm, though. There was a quaint patio out front, just large enough for two chairs with a coffee table in between, and some flowers in colorful pots on either side. I approached the patio, pebbles crunching beneath my feet. I hopped up the few steps and wiggled the screen door open to knock on the door.

"Ivy! You're here!" I was greeted with a warm, toothy smile, and an even warmer hug.

"Hi, Mrs. Carmine!" I stepped inside and wiped my shoes on her welcome mat.

"Honey, how many times do I have to tell you to call me Elsie? I know I'm old, but at least don't make me feel old. Mrs. Carmine reminds me of my wonderful mother-in-law, god rest her soul," She chuckled. Elsie is my neighbor, we live about a mile away on Jade Street. She was in her 80s, and unfortunately her husband of about sixty years passed away last year. Ever since then, I have been popping in once or twice a week to spend some time with her.

Frankly, I wish I started doing this sooner because she is quite possibly one of the coolest people that I have met.

Directly to right of the entryway is an archway to the dining room. To the left, a wall plastered in pictures. Following the hallway down leads to a huge kitchen on the right (which attaches to the dining room), and on the left, there was a super inviting living room with the most comfortable sectional I have ever sat in. The whole backside of the house is windows, and a back glass door, that you could see the beautiful fields and forest from every angle possible. That would freak me out at night, but I suppose that's where curtains come in handy. Behind the living room is Elsie's bedroom and bathroom, which shares the wall with the hallway. Against the back wall of the living room lay a small flight of stairs that follow up into the loft. The guest bedroom and bathroom are up there overlooking the rest of the house. That's technically the master bedroom and bathroom but Elsie and her late husband Ernest moved into the downstairs bedroom as they got older. She uses the upstairs bedroom mainly for storage now. I placed the grocery bags onto the kitchen counter and started to unload them. "Alright Elsie. A while back you told me you would teach me how to bake sourdough bread, and today is that day!" I pulled out bags of different flours, sugars, yeasts, and all different kinds of different toppings we could use. Elsie chuckled.

"Sourdough starts pretty simple," she began as she pushed the yeasts aside. "It actually begins with a sourdough starter, which is just fermented flour and water." She reached for a large glass jar, similar to a mason jar but triple the size, that was sitting on her counter full of a dough like substance. "This right here is Audrey. She's been in my family for generations. Starters will live forever if you take care of them right. You'll have to take care of Audrey for me one day when I'm gone." She shot me a joking, but hopeful smirk. "The way this works is you discard half everyday before you feed it. You don't have to, but I do to make room in the jar. You feed it with equivalent parts of flour and water. You measure how much your starter weighs, let's say 400 grams, so then you feed it 400 grams of flour and 400 grams of water. If it looks runny or too thick, you can always add in a little more flour or water. I just use an old kitchen scale to measure everything out. You mark the jar where the substance in there is with a rubber band or hair elastic. The starter should rise up, and once it doubles in size, it should be ready to use. Luckily for you I fed Audrey this morning and she has definitely doubled in size." Elsie gestured to the old hair tie around the jar and motioned upwards to the bubbly domed top of the starter.

"So it's ready to use? We can make sourdough today?" I questioned.

"Yes and no…first we do the float test." She removed the lid off the jar and placed it on the counter. Elsie grabbed a bowl and spoon out of the drying rack beside her kitchen sink, and filled the bowl with water. She scooped a small amount of starter out of the jar and plunked it into the bowl. We both peered inside. "Yay, it floats!" She cheered. "If the starter floats, it's ready to use. Most people don't credit this test, because it really just depends on the amount of bubbles or air in your starter, but it has always worked for me. It should look full of bubbles, and honeycomb like inside. The cool thing about sourdough, is that you don't need any yeast since it already has the fermented starter. It is simply flour, water, and salt. Now open up that bag of bread flour you got." I did as she asked, while she grabbed out a big mixing bowl. "We just whisk together a cup of Audrey with a cup and a quarter of water. Once that's dissolved, add in a couple teaspoons of salt and three cups of bread flour. You can of course adjust this recipe, but this is what I do. Now you do what I told you, and I'll make us some sangria. I've been itching for some wine today!"

"So what now?" I asked inquisitively as I sipped my sangria. Elsie took care in juicing lemons, limes, oranges, and grapefruit to go in our delicious cocktail. I think she added some peach schnapps and brandy too. We moved out to the front porch to soak up some of the late afternoon, or early evening sun.

"Well, we let the dough rest for an hour or two so it rises some. Then every half an hour for two hours, we do a series of stretching and folding the dough. Next comes another couple hour rest, then we shape it and keep it in the fridge overnight and we bake it tomorrow. It's easy, but just a long process." Elsie carefully explained and took a big gulp of her juicy sangria. "You know, you don't have to babysit me. I know my husband passed, but I'm okay. We had a perfect life together. You should be out dating instead of spending time with a little old lady!" She cackled.

"I'm not babysitting!" I exclaimed argumentatively. "I like spending time with you. And I'll start dating when I find someone worth my time." I fiddled around with a big elephant ear leaf to my right, rubbing the silky leaf between my fingers. "Tell me a story about you and Ernest."

Elsie sat there for a second and paused rocking in her chair. She then continued swaying in her antique wicker rocker. Her silvery white hair almost looked like it was glowing under the bright orange sunset. She really was a beautiful, older lady. Elsie was average height, slender, pale-skinned with blue eyes and rosy cheeks. She had lips that were always turned upwards in a fragile smile. "Have I told you how we met?" I just shook my head no. She gave me a longing smile. "It was early 1960…"

"Elsie! There's someone up front!" My mother yelled as the bell alerted her. She was in no condition to greet any customer right now, despite her beauty. She had a full head of bright red hair pulled into an intricate updo, that matched her lipstick. Sandi was a very tall woman; slim, but curvy. She has dimensional olive green eyes beneath thick black eyelashes, black eyeliner, and a silvery teal eyeshadow that accentuated the color of her eyes. She had overly plucked eyebrows that left her with a lot of eyelid, but it worked in a strange way. The harsh contours and angles of her face made her look like a fashion model. She was in the back of the bakery piping elegant swirls of frosting onto her last batch of lemon cupcakes like a mad woman. She was spattered in a rich, blueberry buttercream and had remnants of flour of cupcakes passed dusted on her face and throughout her silky hair.

I licked the excess chocolate off my fingers and washed the rest off in the sink. My mother owns a bakery, and it is her entire world. I love it, too. We have so much fun here together. If I'm not at school, this is where you'll find me. The back of the bakery was private, and a swinging door led to the front. The bakery was about double the size of the front. The front just consisted of three smaller, cream tables with their respective cream filigree chairs, a display case where we presented our baked goods of the day, and a register. The floors are rich, brown tile that complimented the baseboards and the rest of the wood up front. Walls are full of bright swirls and waves of orange, yellow, red, pink, and cream. The whole front of the shop is glass with warm toned wood shutters. We are located right in the heart of our town on Main Street. There's a grocer, a linen store, a hotel, a couple clothing stores, a diner, a gas station, a laundromat, a toy store, and a mechanic all on the road we are located on. We're right by the school too. Perfect area for hub all the time.

"Hi, so sorry about your wait, sir." I greeted the handsome young man who was standing at the register. "What can I get for you?" I asked with a welcoming, charming smile on my face.

"No need to apologize, miss. I was admiring all of these lovely desserts you have in the display case. I know it's last minute, but I was hoping I could get a birthday cake made for my brother by Wednesday?" My god was he attractive. He had slightly tanned skin, which I think was primarily made of multicolored freckles. He had melty, caramel brown eyes that I could get lost in. He had full lips, arched eyebrows, and defined cheekbones.

"Uhm yes. Of course," I struggled to get out coherently. Did I mention he was tall? "What kind of cake?"

"Carrot cake with cream cheese frosting would be wonderful. Could you write happy birthday Danny on it too? It's for my little brother. He's turning eight."

"Of course. Did you want us to deliver it or will you be picking it up?"

"I can pick it up. Could I get it around 5:30?"

"Absolutely you can. That will be $4.05." He fiddled in his pockets for the money and gingerly placed it all out on the counter with a smirk. I counted it out and popped the register open.

"And lastly, can I get a name for the order?"

"Ernest. Ernest Carmine."

"Alright sir you are all set, we'll see you Wednesday! Have a blessed rest of your day."

"You as well Miss…" He trailed on.

"Elsie. Elsie Buford."

"Miss Elsie. I look forward to seeing that beautiful smile on Wednesday." My heart fluttered with his words left on my lips, as he gracefully strolled out, bell chiming merrily by the front door. Wednesday couldn't come soon enough.

It was Wednesday, 3:30. My mom was working on a wedding cake delivery for tomorrow, and I was frosting the cake for Ernest. Well, for Ernest's little brother. My mom moved so precisely and delicately when she worked. Always taking care in every stroke of the icing spatula and the mild spins of the cake stand. I was nowhere near as talented as her, but I was learning, and I was pretty good for my lack of experience. One day I knew I'd get to her level of expertise.

I lathered on a crumb coat of cream cheese frosting already, and that had just finished cooling down in the fridge. Next was the pretty and generous layer of cream cheese frosting. I piped on delicate flowers, along with the requested lettering, and a carrot (that I thought was clever) for good measure. I was so startled by the ringing of the phone that I threw my piping bag across the room, which made my mom laugh a boisterous laugh that filled the room. I approached the phone and picked it up from the base. "Sweet Sandi's Bakery, how can I help you?" My mom spelled her name Sandi with an i, and that helped to stand out from all the other Sandy's with a y around town. Her real name is Sandra, but she always says she's too young to go by Sandra, it reminds her of her grandmother. That's who she was named after.

"Hi, it's Ernest. I came in and placed an order to pick up a cake on Monday, to be ready for today. I was wondering if it was too late to get delivery?" I could tell he felt nervous asking.

"I think we can drop it off. Can I get your address?" I fumbled to grab a napkin and a pen.

"937 Summit Road. It's about ten minutes from the bakery right by the old church. Thank you so much for accommodating my last minute request, ma'am."

"Not a problem, we will be there in a bit." I placed the phone down and spun around to see my mother staring at me with a raised brow.

"There is no we, only you. I have to finish this whole wedding cake by tomorrow morning!" She threw me the keys. "Your father can pick me up when I'm done." She quickly went back to work placing fake pearls along the tiers of the snow white cake.

The clock read 5:12, so I grabbed the cake and my school bag. My dad will surely shit a brick when my mother tells him she let me borrow her brand new Firebird. I think she knows I'm overly cautious enough about everything that I would never do anything stupid in her car. We can probably chock it up to the fact that she trusts me a lot, or just that it's the new company car.

I made my way over to the address. Luckily this town is small enough you can practically figure out where anything is if you're given a landmark. I passed through the clutter of Main Street, going five under the speed limit of course. I took a right at the second stop sign I passed. It took me up a grassy hill that became more and more rural and covered in oak trees the further I went. As much as I like the sunlight, I appreciate the shade that the canvas of the trees gifted to me even more. As I passed the old church, I was just surprised that damn thing hadn't fallen down yet. You can only put a Band-Aid on things for so long.

A shiny green sliver poked out of the dense shrubbery about one hundred feet from where I was. I squinted and made out Summit Road. I threw on my left blinker and started looking out for the appropriate street numbers after I turned in.

Lucky enough for me, I didn't have to search too hard. A minimal, beige house with balloons attached to the mailbox kind of gave it away. I slowly creeped up beside the house, giving myself extra room from the curb—just in case. You can never be too careful.

Approaching the house I heard thunderous laughter of children; they must be in the backyard given how loud it was. Before I even had time to shift the cake to one hand to knock on the door, it was swung open for me.

"Elsie! Thank you so much again!" Ernest snatched the cake quickly from my unsuspecting arms. I could feel the heat rising to my cheeks, which I'm sure gave me a baby pink blush. Wait a second, why was he wearing an apron? "Please come in, the least I could offer you is a drink or a snack for helping me out." I accepted his invitation and followed him inside, taking care to shut the door behind me. It was strange. I saw kids running around everywhere, but no parents. There was a clown making balloon animals in the backyard surrounded by kids in awe, a trampoline that had probably hit max capacity, a group of kids seemingly playing an unfair game of freeze tag—zooming in and out of the house, and a couple kids fighting over who gets to play Spacewar. It was a total zoo. Ernest led me to the kitchen—where you could tell he had about five different things in the works. "What can I get for you?"

"I'll just take a glass of water, thank you. Not to impose...but can I help you with something? You look a little overwhelmed." I took a gracious sip of the water. I wasn't exactly thirsty, but my heart was racing and I felt hot. Am I excited, or anxious to be here? I suppose a bit of both.

"Oh no ma'am, you don't need to help me with anything, thank you though." Ernest turned around to smile at me, and then was startled by a pot of water boiling over. I grabbed a wooden spoon that was out on the counter and placed it over the top of the pot. The water stopped overflowing. He looked at me with a dropped jaw.

"I know a thing or two about cooking." I replied slyly with a smirk.

"Alright, maybe I will take a helping hand, as long as it isn't inconveniencing you. I'm boiling some pasta right now to make the kids some mac and cheese. I was going to make some sandwiches too and cut up some fruit and vegetables, I just didn't get around to it yet. It's kind of a madhouse out here if you haven't noticed." Ernest cackled awkwardly. He showed me the ropes of the kitchen with a couple cracks of jokes, and I got to work making bologna sandwiches.

"Alright, I think it's time to feed the little monsters." I presented a tray of sandwiches, cut apples, strawberries, celery, and carrots to him. I didn't forget the ranch either, of course. He turned around with a messy pot of mac and cheese. I couldn't help but laugh at the partially melted cheese chunks I could spot.

"Be quiet! You're a guest in this home!" Ernest sputtered out jokingly, which just made me laugh harder. Suddenly, a door from the inside of the house slammed open, which made everyone jump. An older fellow in subpar shape came stumbling out of what I could surmise was a bedroom, wearing only his boxers and a stained white tank top. He stumbled into the kitchen with a hand rubbing his head, only making his bed head worse. He pushed past both of us, either blatantly ignoring the chaos or maybe just not aware of it. His shaking hands pulled open a cabinet above the fridge and seized a bottle of what I assumed was scotch. Without a glass, he staggered back into his cave, clutching the bottle to his chest, without even as much as a glance at anyone or anything going on. I poked a curious eye at Ernest, which he rejected with a foreboding frown. I thought it better not to mention to him right now. When the chaos resumed, Ernest and I set the table and let the kids go to town. Shortly after that, Danny opened up his presents and we all sang an off tune and off timed happy birthday to him.

I glanced at the clock at saw it was 7:30. As much fun as I was having, I knew I needed to wrap things up. I started cleaning up and Ernest joined me shortly after.

"You don't need to stay here and clean up."

"It doesn't look like your dad will be helping you tonight, so somebody should." I didn't mean to say that. Women shouldn't speak like that, especially to men. He looked at me blankly with wide eyes, like a deer in headlights. "I'm sorry. I shouldn't have spoken that brazen." I could feel heat rising to my cheeks again, but out of embarrassment this time.

"Nó, no. It's okay. You're right." No explanation. He just continued tidying up. "Mom has been pulling doubles to feed the family. I dropped out of school my senior year, two years back, to start working overtime since my dad...he got hurt at work, you see." He cleared his throat, as if buying himself more time to carefully piece together what to say next. "He got hurt at work and really let it affect him."

"I'm sorry to hear that. It seems like you care a lot and do a lot for your family."

"Danny and Sissy are young and impressionable still." Ernest motioned to an adorable girl with curly brown pigtails in a red and white plaid dress. "She turns five in December. They need to see a hardworking man to have as a role model." I fell silent as we wrapped up the cleaning.

"Well, I need to get going. Thank you for your hospitality." I said as I made my way to the door.

"Thank you for your hospitality, not even in your house. You didn't need to do any of what you did. Especially for someone you don't know."

"That's not true, I knew your name was Ernest." I smirked. "So, I'm pretty sure I would say we're friends now."

"I can't believe you went into a strangers house!" I guffawed.

"Ivy! Times were different back then. You didn't need to worry about all the shit you kids do now." Elsie smiled, clearly reminiscing.

"I guess you're right. So what happened when you went home? What did your mom say? You left me with a cliffhanger!"

"My parents were up still with my older sister Goose, playing a round of Sorry. That was the number one board game in our house. We had such a loving family. My parents were pretty relaxed about things. Something I always loved was that almost every night we would unwind before bed with a family game and some sweet dessert that was either about to go bad from the bakery, or something that was made in excess. Or even an experimental recipe to try out on us. Well, I walked in mid round. My mother was smoking a cigarette, and my father scolded me for staying out so long. Especially on a school night. He had a point I guess. Delivering a cake ten minutes away from the bakery doesn't take three hours after all. Anyways, when he walked out of the living room to put on a pot of tea. My mother laughed and said she let me borrow her car for a reason. My father was a religious man, and my mom was too, to some extent. My mom was really big on believing in fate and how everything happens for a reason. After all, she left her umbrella in a diner when she was out having milkshakes with her friends one day. They went and saw a movie after. It started pouring while she was walking home and a man came running up behind her with an umbrella. *Her* umbrella. And that man happened to be my father. To this day, he claims he had no clue it was hers. He said he just happened to go out with his cousins for milkshakes and it was on the floor beneath the booth they were in. He didn't even live in the town my mother did. He lived in California. He was visiting family and got lost on his walk home."

"Really?" My eyes were huge, I could feel it.

"Mhm. Anyways, she said she thought it was fate that he called and needed a last minute delivery. She wanted to see how it would play out. I think part of her was hoping things would work out in fear of me never getting married and living with her forever. I didn't date anyone before Ernest."

"Well, how did you guys start dating then? How did the client turn into the husband?"

"The dough is resting for tonight and so should I. I get tired early. Come over Saturday whenever you can, we'll bake the dough, and I'll tell you more about my darling Ernest." Elsie took a final slurp of her sangria, cleared off both of our glasses, and stood up. "Get home safe, dear. I know you live right up the road, but you can never be too careful." Elsie bent over, gave me a peck on the cheek, and then made her way inside. I suppose it was time I made my way home for dinner. I had an early start tomorrow because I had a shipment coming in.

Chapter Two

After I pulled out of Elsie's driveway, my ride home was short and sweet. I was the next house on the right. I've lived here for the last four years, and I had no intention of leaving anytime soon. My house was nowhere near as breathtaking as hers, which I was fine with. I love my quaint and cozy space. It leaves less to be afraid of in the dark. My short, gravel driveway led up to a modest mahogany house, enclosed by thick sugar maple and white oak trees. I, too, had a flower bed that lined the front of my home. Of course, it didn't hold up anywhere near Elsie's fantasy garden. I didn't have any pets *yet* so having a little garden gave me a sense of responsibility. I wanted pets, but I just don't have enough time to take care of them. There was a stray black and white cat that came around most nights. I called him ZZ. As in ZZ Top. As in sharp dressed man, because it looked like he was wearing a suit. Get it?

I strolled inside my house and plopped my purse on the table in the mudroom. My house was very open, and I preferred it that way. You could see the dining room, living room, bathroom, kitchen, back porch, and the door to the bedroom all from the front door. I wasn't feeling like making an extravagant, time consuming dinner tonight so I settled on some pasta. I put a pot of water on the stove to boil and started on my sauce. Garlic cloves, red onion, grape tomatoes from

Elsie's garden, fresh basil, oregano, and olive oil. I pan seared a chicken breast in loads of butter to go on top.

I opened my own small plant store and apothecary a couple of years ago when I was 24 downtown where I live. Ironic that my name is Ivy, huh? My parents, lots of books, and living in the countryside gave me a broad education in holistic, spiritual, and homeopathic medicine. I'm decent at foraging, too. However, most people who come in want sage for cleansing, mint for stomach aches, eucalyptus for their showers, chamomile for relaxation, echinacea to prevent getting sick, etc. Nothing too exciting. After tomorrow, I have Saturday and Sunday off. After work tomorrow, since I'll already be downtown, I plan on meeting up with my friends. Saturday I'll see Elsie, and Sunday my parents are stopping by for a visit. They live in central Tennessee, but right now they are road tripping all over the country.

I settled down on the couch with one of the many books I was reading, and a glass of Cabernet. I wrapped myself up into a burrito with the fluffiest blanket within arms reach. Some of the simplest things in life make me happy. Strong wind, the smell of an old book, soft blankets, a spring rainstorm. Luckily for me I could just start to hear the rain come down and kerplunk on my tin back patio roof. Suddenly a faint scratching noise snapped me out of my book and back into reality. Peering through the window nearest to me in the living room was ZZ scratching to come inside, away from the storm that was brewing. Obliging his wishful pawing, I sprung up to open the window and let him inside. I always kept a small bag of cat food in my house for wandering fur babies. I know you aren't supposed to feed strays, but I couldn't help it. I have a soft spot for them, I guess. I think it's because I relate to them. ZZ gratefully chowed down on some kibble and then joined me on the couch. I spent the rest of the night reading aloud until we both dozed off to the peaceful rain droplets tumbling on the roof.

I awoke with a start from a crack of thunder right before 7:00. Perfect. For whatever reason, I found waking up right before my alarm so satisfying. I left the window cracked that I opened for ZZ last night, and it seems like he must've escaped during the night. Early bird gets the worm, as they say. Or I guess early cat gets the mouse in this situation. I closed the window and wiped some of the stray raindrops away from the sill with my sleeve. Luckily for me, the inadvertent drops watered some of my houseplants, too.

I decided on a medium length black dress that came just above my knee on one side. Casual enough for work and cute enough to go out in tonight. Paired with emerald green velvet shoes and a matching quilted purse that made my rich sage eyes stand out against my freckled olive skin. I applied some natural looking makeup and touched up the curls on my long, silky, black hair before giving myself a once over before stepping out into the elements. The sheet of rain cascading from above did not forecast a smooth drive to work. Luckily, there's never any traffic, but you needed to be extra careful on the twists and turns of the pavement.

The rain really wasn't lightening up on my drive. My windshield wipers were on full throttle and I could still barely see. At least I had the subtle tunes of *The Moody Blues* to wash me away to work. I pulled into a parking spot right in front of work. In retrospect, I probably should've brought an umbrella. I guess no mom/dad/umbrella romance in store for me today. Nobody coming to save me with an umbrella.

Ivy's Apothecary was nestled in between *Paw Prints,* a pet supply store, and *The Mindful Mug,* a quaint little café. Luckily for me, *The Mug,* as I call it, opens around 7:00 so they are up and running by the time I get to work. They have the corner lot with a drive through on Main Street where all the hub is. They're essentially slammed from open to close. I became friends with all of the workers there since day one, so we send each other business. Small, local businesses need to help each other out!

I scurried out of my car as quickly as I could without slipping. I had about thirty minutes until my 8:45 shipment came in, so I figured I'd kill some time at The Mug. Their drive through was slammed, however the inside wasn't.

"Ivy!" Hazel, their overly caffeinated barista boasted while motioning me to the countertop "I have this new drink I came up with I need you to try! If you like it, I'll put it as our special today." Without giving me a chance to answer, she got to work crafting my mystery drink. "Here, try it."

I took a big gulp. It was delicious. "Hazel, I think this is one of my favorite specials so far. What is it?"

"Really?!" She chirped excitedly, clapping her hands like a seal. "It's a lavender white chocolate blonde roast latte with cashew milk." I couldn't help but laugh at her enthusiasm at my satisfaction.

"Yeah, I'll be needing another one of these later. What do I owe you?"

"Oh nothing…Unless maybe you want to make me that fancy paste for acne and oily skin? I've been breaking out so badly and I can't control it! The only thing that helps is your fancy potions!"

"I can totally do that!" I reassured her. "I'll bring it by once I'm ready for round two." I gestured to my coffee cup as I backed up to the front door.

It was still raining pretty bad out. The narrow awning covering our block provided just enough shelter from above to disperse the vast majority of the rain into a fine mist. I fumbled getting my keys out of my purse to unlock the front door.

I turned the lights on, eyeing all of the plants for changes. Not much except I could see a lot of new shoots coming out of my *Heart of Jesus* plants and a new leaf was about to unfurl on my *Swiss Cheese* plant. The walls were a deep, forest green with walnut floor. Cream accents in the molding made the shop seem brighter, and dainty fairy lights strung all over the shop seemed to bring upon the ambiance of twinkling stars in a fantasy realm. All of the house plants were up front by the windows, and then the rest of the apothecary containing crystals, solutions, dried herbs, dried flowers, and everything else I needed for holistic medicine was in the back. My register was also in the back, along with a door leading to a meager office with an accompanying door to the left of the office which was a bathroom. Most of the house plants I have organized by amount of light needed. Over time, I've memorized all of their watering schedules. However, I do have cheat sheets made for my customers to remember. Yesterday was watering day for most of my plants, so I decided to focus my time on restocking for the new day.

I took a scoop of turmeric out of a clear jar and combined it with honey, witch hazel, tea tree oil, rose water, and aloe vera. This should take care of Hazel's acne, excess oil, and inflammation. The honey should help too, given its antimicrobial and antibacterial properties. I packed this paste in a small plastic tub and put it aside to give to Hazel on my next caffeine run. Just in time too, because I saw a delivery truck parking out front.

My favorite delivery man, Dean, trotted inside, careful to wipe his feet on my *Beware, There's a Pot Head in Here* doormat. "Hey Ivy! I got some goods for you today." He handed me a large box marked with a fragile stamp.

"Thanks Dean. Drive safe out there, would ya? It's really coming down."

"I always do, Ivy!" Dean spun around with a smirk and began strolling out.

"Oh wait! I think the supplement for your mom should've came in!" I grabbed a pair of scissors off the counter and sliced the tape on the box. Sure enough, right on top were dried Ginkgo Biloba leaves. I tore the bag open and divvied up enough for Dean's mom to have a two-week's worth supply. "Here, make her tea with this. This ration should last her for two weeks, if you give her two cups a day. Let me know if it works." I tossed the bag of delicate, dried leaves his way.

"Thanks Ivy…I appreciate it." Dean wiggled the bundle in his hands, his eyes shiny with what I could only imagine were tears. He made his way back out into the storm and took off. His mom got diagnosed with early onset Alzheimer's a couple months ago. I can only imagine how hard it is knowing that the person who brought you into this world is eventually going to forget about you. Gingko Biloba is supposed to help with memory loss and increase blood flow to the brain, hopefully helping her diagnosis.

I sorted through the rest of the goodies—Kava, St. John's Wort, Valerian, Feverfew, Ginseng, Goldenseal, Milk Thistle, Elderberry, Sage, and so much more. I put everything away in their respective places and prepared for my day of work.

Closing time was 6:00. Ideally, I wouldn't mind closing at 5:00, but I know a lot of people get off work around 4:00 or 5:00, so I want to make sure I'm open long enough for people to be able to stop in. Today was a steady day. A lot of people coming in for sickness prevention with the changes of the season, and headaches today. Succulents weren't doing so great recently, but more niche plants like variegated *Monsteras* and *Pink Princess Philodendrons* were a big seller. I gave Hazel her medicine around 3:00 in trade for my specialty coffee swap. After that, another employee from The Mug swung by a little later to buy a *Calathea*. Now I had about half an hour to make it to *The Witch's Brew,* a fancy cocktail bar by me. I applied a nude shade of lipstick and powdered my shiny skin, and I went outside into the moody sunset.

It wasn't raining anymore. It was gloomy out and the skies were dark, but it was dry. I might as well get my steps in and walk. It was only a few blocks away, and our downtown area was very safe.

The Witch's Brew was lit with green and purple lights. It had a thin layer of fog escaping from the corners inside. None of my friends seemed to be there yet, so I snagged a table on their rooftop bar area.

"Hi, I'm Amber! What can I get for you?" A charismatic girl with fire orange hair greeted me with.

"Hi! Can I get a portobello burger please? And for a drink, I'll take the Amethyst Aura." I knew my friends probably already ate, since we were meeting for a girl's night happy hour. The cocktail was made from Empress gin, lavender, coconut simple syrup, lemonade, Prosecco, and topped with a lemon twist.

"Absolutely!" Amber obliged cheerily. "Be right back!" And shortly enough she came back with my drink. My stomach growled, wanting something other than just liquor right now.

"Hi, honey!" I saw my friend Angelica come in. Her hair was a deep, blood red color and had dark makeup on. That was combined with a white crop top and some flashy, blinged out bell bottoms. I popped up and gave her a kiss on her cheek. A short petite blonde, Missy, and a very casual looking brunette, Steph, followed in like an entourage behind her. These have been my best friends since high school. We all exchanged hugs and took a seat at the table.

I focused my energy on my portobello burger while Angelica kicked the conversation off by talking about the pros and cons of the rotation of men she has in her life. Missy followed up about an update about her wedding planning. She had us all give opinions on which flowers are best suited for her and Mark's wedding. Steph recently started seeing this girl Stacy, who would potentially be meeting up with us tonight. This was kind of a big deal, especially to Steph, because she had just recently come out to people other than the three of us. They met at work, an emergency veterinarian clinic.

Those three friends of mine really loved to talk, and it worked out great because I liked to listen. It also helped that I didn't have much of a personal life. Sometimes I wished I could meet someone too, that actually made me want to talk to my friends about, but I never did. How do you even meet people? I can't meet anyone at work—because I am my only employee. If I'm not there I'm either at home, with my friends, or with Elsie. God knows you can't trust dating apps. I figured my time will come at some point.

I ordered my third and final drink of the night, The Black Cauldron. Black charcoal vodka, blackberry simple syrup, homemade hibiscus tea, along with a splash of seltzer water. I think there were muddled blackberries in there, too.

All the ladies took turns recommending people for me they thought they could see me getting along with. While I didn't deny that, at this point I didn't think I had the time or mental capacity for such a thing.

Close to ten, we all decided to call it a night. We said our goodnights and walked outside with each other. The street lights casted a pale yellow glow upon the sidewalks and made it seem more welcoming. Not that it was scary outside, but the dark, empty streets always seemed to portray a mysterious ambiance of the unknown. And the unknown is scary.

I made it to the car and checked behind both shoulders, just in case. Coast was clear. Now, in just twenty short minutes, I would be home in bed. Hopefully with ZZ.

The road on the drive home seemed exceptionally empty tonight. No headlights glaring in my rearview mirror, no bright LEDs making me squint coming towards me. I saw a lonely deer on the way home, and that's about it.

Pulling into my driveway I saw a cat sprawled out on my front door mat. He jolted on his haunches when he saw the blare of my headlights. Once they cut out and I stepped out of my car door, he seemed a little more at ease.

"ZZ!" I greeted at a pitch so high all dogs within a mile could hear. He meowed happily and raised his tail high above his head. I approached him and scratched his head happily. Once I opened the door, he made his way to the bedroom and curled into a tight ball on the foot of my bed.

I started the shower and began to take my makeup off. I twirled my hair into a tight bun and swung the shower curtain open once I saw steam pouring over the rod. The balmy water traced over all the curves of my body and coated me in a blanket of serenity. I was clearly ready for bed. I stepped out of the shower, dried off less than I should have, threw on a baggy tee shirt, and crawled into bed. ZZ crawled up to my chest, and I cuddled him tightly. He made biscuits on the comforter to the side of him and we both faded away into a deep sleep.

Without an alarm, I awoke around 10:00. ZZ was meowing loudly with angst and pawing at the window to be let out. I sauntered out of bed to appease my little monster, and made my way to the bathroom. I washed my face and dressed casually in a band shirt and some spandex shorts to get ready for a day with Elsie.

I made myself an omelet complete with onions, peppers, spinach, mushrooms, cheddar, and sausage. Of course, hot sauce had to go on top too. I made my way towards Elsie's and turned into her curved, jungle of a driveway around 11:30. Instead of going directly inside, I started off by watering her vegetable gardens, and picking through the vegetables that needed some TLC. A variety of bell and hot peppers, tomatoes, okra, kale, green beans, parsley, cilantro, garlic, and a giant, ripe, sunflower head.

I collected my harvest in a basket I left outside previously, and rapped on the back door.

"Ivy! Look at all the goodies you picked today!" She snatched the wicker basket from me and went briskly to the kitchen to give everything a good wash. She must've seen me pull in because the oven was already preheated to a toasty 450 degrees, with a dutch oven warming inside. She directed me to pull our dough out of the fridge, plop it on some parchment paper, carve some designs in it with a razor blade, sprinkle it with water, and put it in the covered dutch oven.

While the bread started its first baking cycle, I caught her up on my day yesterday. She seasoned the sunflower head until it was a completely different shade, then grilled it to perfection. She topped it off with an herby romesco sauce made from ingredients from the garden, and crispy kale chips she baked alongside the bread. Once everything was done, we settled comfortably on her front patio, and it was about time I got another story.

"Alright, Elsie. I want the rest of the tea!" I bit the sourdough. It was chewy inside with a crusty exterior. It was slightly softened by the mass amounts of butter and honey I topped my slice with. It held in all that goodness, like a sponge.

"Tea?!" She replied, unknowingly. "I'll put a pot on!" Elsie hopped up.

"No!" I couldn't help but giggle. "Tea is a term for gossip. Tell me how the customer became the husband." She sat back down with a laugh.

"You kids and your new-age words. Well, I knew from the first date we had that he was my forever." Her misty, ocean eyes looked at me with a sparkle. If eyes could smile, hers were.

Chapter Three

"Darling! He's picking you up at 6:00! That's in twenty minutes! Get your butt in gear!" My mother Sandi yelled from the bottom of the staircase. I think she was as excited as I was. If not, more.

I didn't have my mother's earthly green eyes, but my red hair was natural. She dyed hers a deep, bright red and mine was a natural strawberry blonde. I wore a blue dress that had cream flowers printed all over it, finished with a blue ribbon around the waist and some buttons up the top. It had a small lace collar that framed my neck just perfectly. I accessorized with some blue flats, a cream purse, and some off-white pearl earrings. I curled my hair so it came just below my shoulders, and topped off the outfit with a headband that matched the ribbon on the front. Ernest was taking me to see She Loves Me. The premise is about two coworkers who can't stand each other at work but are both each other's secret pen pals who met on a lonely hearts ad. Romantic comedies are my favorite.

Just as I was giving myself a once over, a rap at my front door caused my heart to start racing. I flew downstairs to answer it before my parents or Goose could. Turns out, they all had the same idea in mind because the four of us almost all ran into each other. My father opened the door and Ernest's bronzed eyes grew wide looking at the greeting committee awaiting him. He put his hand out to my father.

"Ernest. Nice to meet you, sir. Thank you for letting me take your daughter out on this fine evening." His whole demeanor seemed to loosen up and grow comfortable to all the eyes on him.

"I'm Michael Buford, Elsie's father. This is my wife Sandi and our eldest, Goose." Everyone exchanged handshakes with Ernest, but not me. His eyes seemed to shine golden when he looked at me, though. "I have to say. Thanks for getting this one off our hands tonight." My father clapped me on the back. "Goose is going out with her friends so the missus and I are going to have ourselves a date night." My father shot a loving glance at my mother and she pecked him on the cheek. My god, they're so in love.

"Oh, the pleasure is all mine, sir. I'll have her back by midnight." Ernest said with a wholehearted chuckle at the end.

"Alright kids, you two have fun. Don't do anything I wouldn't do! Jesus is watching!" My mom hollered to us as I was already halfway out the door.

"Your parents seemed very welcoming. I felt like JFK with the welcome I got from everyone!" I couldn't help but laugh at his comparison.

"Yeah well, they're excited to see I'm excited about a date. Really, I guess they're just excited for me to have a date in general." Ernest pulled open the passenger side door for me. I tucked my dress under myself and took a seat in the beige leather interior.

"So, have you seen this play before?" Ernest inquired as he started the car and shifted into first.

"I haven't! I have read the book, though. I absolutely loved it."

"Are you a big reader?"

"I am! Are you?"

"Not too much. I used to be. I'm sure if I had more time I would fall back into it. I normally find my solace now in wood working."

"Really? Like tables?"

"I've made a few tables…not really my thing though. I like crafting little pendants and figurines. Stuff I can really be creative with and express my artistic eye in, you know?" Ernest shot me a glimmer of a smile.

"Oh, totally. I bet you'd be great at cake decorating if you're as artsy as you say!" Ernest laughed.

"I don't know about all that. My color balance is kind of iffy and I'm iffy about changing textures. With wood, I know what I'm getting into. I can create a texture by carving. If I had a runny frosting, I wouldn't even know where to begin!"

"I guess you have a point. So, what do you do for work then?" Look at that…small talk was flowing easy, like a river rushing downhill.

"I work at Dan's Mechanic Shop in downtown. Maybe about a mile away from your mother's bakery."

"Woah, right by me then, huh?"

"Yes ma'am." I suppose that isn't something I would have known. I had no reason to ever step into a mechanics shop, and we had no mutual friends of any kind. "So, you graduate in a few months, right?" Ernest prodded.

"I do...I was considering college, but I think it would be more realistic for me to continue my mother's business. I love it, really, I do. And I know one day she'll need someone to keep it going. Lord knows it can't be Goose, she doesn't have a bakery bone in her body."

"Noble of you."

"Noble how?"

"Noble in the sense of wanting your mother's pride and legacy to carry on. If she hadn't opened a bakery, would you make that your career choice?" I pondered this for a second.

"I suppose not...but if she hadn't had a bakery in the first place I never would've had the opportunity to try it out and realize it's my passion."

"Oh, touché. Good point there, Els." I didn't know we were on the nickname stage now.

I didn't even realize how fast that drive into town went by. I saw cars of all colors, makes, and models swarming to get towards the theater. You had to drive through the bustling part of town, then through twists and turns to make it to the secluded theater nestled and resting on the outskirts of town. The theater in town opened last year and had been the hot spot ever since. I found it odd the parking lot was all dirt, considering how much money had been poured into this place.

Ernest pulled into a parking spot a few rows back from the front, and a little to the right of the front door. Ladies adorned in exuberant dresses with bright colors and patterns of all sorts were hanging on the elbows of gentlemen in dark suits. They filed into the front door, two by two. A gentleman in a tall cap and a bright red suit was

*checking everyone's tickets. I wonder how much these events cost?
Ernest exited his seat and before I could even reach for the handle he
was already on my side of the car, opening the door for me.*

*An exuberant, booming, building stood before me. Beautiful, warm,
toasted browns, golds, and reds made the theater seem to glow
against the harsh, dark, looming background of the deep green forest
encasing us all. Thick, girthy, intricate cream columns lined the stairs
to the entrance. They reminded me of Greek or Roman architecture,
but a little more modern.*

*"If I didn't tell you already tonight, you are the most beautiful
woman I have ever laid my eyes on." I knew he was nervous saying it.
Heat rose to my face thickly, pasting ruby on the apples of my delicate
cheeks. I took his hand in mine and stood up from my carriage.*

*"Why, thank you." I twirled in my dress. He chuckled merrily. Why
did I just twirl? More heat came to my cheeks. "You look awfully
handsome yourself." I copied all the other ladies present and held
onto Ernest by his elbow. I could feel his comforting warmth seeping
through his suit. It made my hand sweat, or maybe that was just
nerves.*

*Ernest followed the crowd in front of us and we began up the
stairs, into the looming doors that opened up into a lobby filled with
intricate wooden structures. He had pre-purchased our tickets in
advance to ensure they didn't sell out. The ticket usher gleefully took
our tickets and bid us an almost robotic "Hope you enjoy the show!"
My jaw dropped as I got a better look at the inside. Bathrooms were
on either side of us when we first walked in. Swirls of golden, beige,
cream, and eggshell twinkled all along the interior, making the lobby
seem even bigger and brighter than it was. Expensive, glistening,
chandeliers illuminated the room so brightly that it almost looked
magical. Too fancy for people like us. Accents of crimson and hunter*

green were ever so strategically placed to add enough depth and darkness that your eyes had to travel every square inch of the place. It didn't make the place look christmassy at all, either. My growling stomach interrupted my racing mind and told me I needed a snack. I pulled Ernest's arm back a smidge. "Wait! Do you think we could get popcorn or something? I'm starving!"

"Oh, of course, I'm so sorry I didn't offer." Ernest turned briskly around. "I haven't taken a girl out in a long time…I'm bad at this whole first date thing. I think I overthink the big picture and I forget little things like that." His voice trailed off.

My blush came back. I was almost relieved to know he wasn't some sort of player. Word normally travels fast in town anyways, but sometimes you can never be too sure. "This is actually my first date." I sputtered out. Ernest looked at me surprised.

The right side of the lobby was a bar/snack/lounge area with tables, couches, and chairs. To the left of the lobby there were more chairs, and what looked like another small ticket booth.

"Hi, what can I get for you folks this evening?" A chipper girl in a red collared shirt chirped.

"Can we get a large popcorn please?" Ernest replied and looked at me.

"And some M&M's!" I added in, a little too excited.

"Of course. That'll be thirty-seven cents please!" Ernest reached in his pocket and counted out the exact change. My mom told me to always let the man pay, but I didn't believe in that, so I brought money too. The red lady handed Ernest our goods and we made our way back to the next set of French doors, leading into the auditorium.

"Would you like some money?" I offered, but he looked at me with a raised brow.

"What?"

"You bought the tickets to the play and you got us snacks. I think I should pay for something you know." I insisted, returning the arched brow. He laughed.

"I intended to pay for our night out, including milkshakes after and hopefully our next date, too. If you'll have me, of course." My smile grew so damn big. "Also since this is your supposed first date, I'll have to be the one who informs you that the man should always pay." He threw me a big grin too.

"Supposed? Are you saying this isn't my first date? And also…I would really enjoy milkshakes after, and a second date too." We strolled merrily into the theater.

"I'm not saying this isn't your first date, however a girl as bright, kind, caring, intelligent, and as beautiful as you should have men lined up out the front door begging for a chance."

"Who says I'm all of those things?" I rebutted.

"I do. I picked all of that up and more the day you went out of your way to not only bring me a cake, but to also take on Danny's birthday party with me." I couldn't argue with that.

"Well, it looked like you could use a helping hand."

Never ending rows of comfy looking chairs lined up in front of the beautiful, enormous stage. Heavy red curtains with thick golden ropes hung along the length of the stage, with matching pleats on some sections of the perimeter. Alternating artwork, posters, and carvings decorated the all the way up the towering walls to the ceilings.

Ernest and I took our seats and the chatter amongst us sounded like buzzing bees. I took a handful of the buttery popcorn and put it in my mouth, wiping the oil from my lips with my forearm. The lights in the theater dimmed slowly and spotlights began to appear upon the stage. Once the curtains were pulled back, I can't tell you how the play began. What I can tell you is the sheer intensity of heat building in my body that rose when Ernest slid his hand down my arm and wrist and how it felt when his fingers locked in mine.

Booming applause, flying popcorn, and people hopping up from their seats jumped me to a start. I was so caught up in the play it felt as though I was watching a television right in front of my eyes. Ernest's damp hand interlocked in mine pulled me up and out of my chair to give the cast a standing ovation as well. I pulled my hand away and applauded the cast vividly. After all, they did incredibly. The row we sat in began to usher out, and we did the same.

"So, what did you think?" Ernest placed my hand comfortably back onto his elbow once we were in the aisle.

"That was wonderful! I mean, I've never seen a play before, but I can't believe how amazing it really was! I felt like I was watching it on TV!" I exclaimed. Ernest let out a laugh.

"This is the second play I have seen. The first I barely remember. I was a kid and my mom took me to see South Pacific. My mom was excited to see it because there were nurses in it. But this one, was outstanding. Maybe the acting was just phenomenal, but I think my present company provided an even better experience."

"Wow, you are such a charmer. I'm really enjoying my night with you, Ernest. This is the most fun I've had in...ever. The most fun I've had in ever!" We walked through the doors to go outside and I spun through, like I was in a movie myself. What has Ernest gotten into me? He laughed, held my hand, and made me spin again, bracing me at my waist to slow me down. Nobody has ever touched me there. I think he felt the overwhelming spark go between us too. At least I wanted to believe so.

"So, Miss Elsie, would you like to get a milkshake with me?" He opened the passenger door for me.

"Oh, Mister Carmine, I would love too!" I replied gleefully. He shut my door and slid across the hood of the car, almost tumbling to the ground. I let a burst of laughter escape.

Small talk on favorite colors, biggest fears, favorite animals, dream homes, and everything else filled the car up with joy and giggles. We pulled in front of a local diner, Mel's Diner, and he opened the door for me to exit.

"What a beautiful night we picked to go out!" I looked up at the stars. I feel as though I've never seen them so bright.

"A beautiful night for a beautiful date with a beautiful girl!" Ernest earnestly swung the door to the diner open. We strolled up to the counter.

"Hi there! I'll take a chocolate malt shake please and whatever the lady would like too." He threw a wink my direction.

"Can I get a strawberry shake, please? With extra cherries too, if you could."

"Certainly ma'am. That will be seventy-five cents, please." The incredibly young man at the register informed us. Ernest and I both fumbled into our pockets in the race of who can find the coins first. Ernest won. "You two lovebirds can take a seat and we will bring those out to you when they are ready."

"I told you, you aren't paying and you won't pay, honey." We found a booth in the corner, and both slid across from each other on our respective sides,

"I'll get you next date…or maybe the next one…or the next one…" I added.

"Wow so how many dates are we having? Should I write them in my calendar?"

"Yes, you should." I chuckled. "I see some more dates in our future." The gentleman came by with our shakes. Ernest took a long draw out of his straw. "Can I ask you about your dad?" He choked a bit on his shake. "I'm sorry to be forward. You don't need to answer."

"No, no. I will. With you, for some reason…I feel safe. Like I can talk to you." He took another long draw. "What I told you was the truth. My father, Lars, was a coal miner and he got hurt bad at work. Dad took a nasty fall. He did get better, though. Because my mom is a nurse, she was able to help subdue his pain for a while, but you could just tell it started to drive him mad. He stopped sleeping, he got angry, he built up a tolerance to pain pills, and he wasn't happy. Not too long after, he discovered booze solved all of his issues. I think he got addicted to just feeling like he was normal again. Then he stopped being able to function without drinking and he got fired from his job. Now…we're here." He started to avoid eye contact with me. I could tell opening up about something that made him so vulnerable was outside of his comfort zone. "My mom Charlotte works her life away to take care of the family, and it's still not enough."

"I am…so sorry to hear that Ernest. I can't imagine what that is like to deal with. Especially with two young siblings…nobody wants to see their family in a situation like that. What are you going to do?"

"My boss Dan is planning on retiring soon, and I'll be running the shop. He knows I'm young, but he's been a family friend for years and he's been teaching me since I was very young. I'm learning more of the business aspect now. I will be working more, but I'll be making enough money to get my own place, and still financially take care of my family and hopefully get my father some help. What's the story with your family?"

"Well, my parents are quite the lovebirds. My father Michael works in a bank, and you know what my mom does. Goose is the opposite of me. She's three years older and has too many friends to count. Even more boyfriends!" I chuckled. "She has no interest in the family business, either. She wants to go to New York City and become a big name in fashion. We aren't sure if she's serious or not, but she says next summer her and her best friend Sally are leaving to pursue their fashion dreams. They met working at Dillard's." I slurped the last of my shake.

"Well, what about you Miss Elsie? What's your plan?"

"I want to keep working at my mother's bakery. One day I'll run it. I love the work, and I love this town. I'm not much of a city girl."

"Good thing. Wouldn't want you running away from me to New York City next summer!" That evoked a deep laugh. I like that he laughs at his own jokes. He glanced at the clock and finished off his shake. "I think it's about time I returned you home. Can't be having *our chariot turn into a pumpkin, what do you say?"* Ernest slid out from the booth and reached for my hand. Every touch gave me goosebumps.

He escorted me out the door and led me to the car. The singing of crickets and frogs deep in the woods filled the air around us. We let the nature speak words we couldn't say, and we just listened.

The car ride home was filled with laughter, and memories I didn't realize would be marking the beginning of the most important chapter of my life—Ernest.

I could feel the anticipation building up in the bottom of my stomach when we started getting closer to my house. His car crawled into my driveway and came to a halt.

You could tell he was nervous just by how clammy his hands were when escorting me out of the car, and by how his lip had a slight tremor. Approaching the doorway to my house, I could see a pale blush start to color his cheeks. He turned to me and took both my hands. "Miss Elsie, sorry if this is too forward, but I would be amiss if I didn't ask if I could steal a kiss from you tonight?"

I'd never kissed a boy, and I didn't even know how. What I did know was that I wanted Ernest to kiss me. I wanted to feel the warmth creep from his lips to mine, and I wanted to act on the spark that I had been feeling all night. I leaned into him slowly, until he placed his pillowy soft lips on mine, and we exchanged our first of a million sweet kisses. "Goodnight. I had a wonderful time tonight, and I will be eagerly looking forward to our next date together, darling."

"Goodnight Ernest! I had such an amazing time. I'm positive this was a night I'll be dreaming about for a while. Drive safe, and I can't wait to go out with you again!" Maybe I sounded a little too *enthusiastic, hopefully he didn't mistake that for desperation. Whatever he took it as, he laughed hard from his belly. His eyes twinkled as though they were full of stardust, and he cautiously watched me as I entered my house and turned in for the night.*

"So based off of that one date, you knew?"

"Ivy, I know it's hard to believe. My heart knew before my brain did, but my brain eventually caught up. Don't get me wrong, we had our bad days. But in every lifetime, I would take a bad day before I took a day without him." She smiled, longingly. I knew that comment was about his passing. I never know how to talk about or fully fathom death.

"You two really do sound like you were made for each other. Especially from day one. So what happened?"

"What do you mean what happened, honey?"

"I don't know. All of it. Everything."

"That's awfully broad…" Elsie looked into the distance and gave a chuckle before clearing her throat. "Things fell apart before they came together all the way for us."

About a year ago I graduated and then almost two years ago was when we officially started dating. I can't believe it. It feels like we have known each other for a lifetime's worth. It's crazy to think my teenage years are about at an end, and today is the day I move in with my husband.

Our honeymoon came to an end just about two weeks ago. We went on a road trip down all the way to Florida. We snaked over to Georgia on the way south, and on the way back we went through South Carolina. We stayed at a house on the gulf side of Florida and spent our time traveling to springs, relaxing at the ocean, exploring the everglades, and really doing whatever we wanted. No major agenda. Wake up and see where the day takes you and what adventures it brings. The nicest part of it all was finally being away from our families and together. Alone. With no obligations. It made me even more excited to be moving in together. It's like having a sleepover with your best friend everyday, but better.

I was never a city girl like Goose or Sally, but they seem to like it. When Goose came down for our wedding last month, all she did was rave about New York and how I needed to leave Ernest at home and visit her for a long weekend. As fun as it would be to go visit, I really didn't want to be anywhere without Ernest. I wouldn't say I'm codependent, but why spend time away from your favorite person on the planet if you don't need to? I am happy for her though. Our new home was about fifteen minutes away from downtown, which was perfect. If there was ever an emergency at Sweet Sandi's or Dan's Mechanic Shop (which was now officially Ernest's Mechanic Shop, but he felt too bad to change the name so soon) we could be there in almost no time. My parents lent us money for a down payment on the house, while Ernest's parents berated him for leaving. Mainly his dad, but his mom guilted him as well. I think she was just scared of Lars, but Ernest needed to escape that environment. Frankly, they all needed to. The kids are upset Ernest is leaving, but they haven't quite fully grasped or come to terms with how awful Lars is becoming. When I saw Charlotte last week, her eye was puffy and the color of a perfectly ripe plum. Ernest was supposed to be bringing it up soon, but I didn't want to push the matter too much.

The house was quaint and cozy—maybe not a forever house, but definitely a great stepping stone. A paved, narrow walkway led the way between a white picket fence right up to the front door. Pillowy, squared off hedges lined the backside of the fence to almost give our yard a privacy screen. Double fencing, if you will. Empty flower beds fell along the perimeter of the house just begging to be filled with colorful blossoms. Inside the house felt backwards, because the kitchen was the first room you stepped into. Practically the front half of the house was the kitchen/dining area which overlooked the back half of the house, which was a spacious living room. The separation between the two rooms was a large breakfast bar I could imagine drinking my coffee at and reading a good book. I actually really enjoyed the layout because cooking, baking, and sharing those creations with others was not only second nature, but also my love language. The only secluded area are the living quarters. To the right of the living room was the master bedroom and bathroom, then to the left of the living room was a half a small bedroom, and an even smaller bathroom. Both bedrooms are pretty cramped—probably couldn't fit a king bed in it. Fitting two people in the bathrooms would be pretty challenging, too. But we didn't mind at all. The closer together and cozier we could be, the better.

A sliding glass door separated the living room from the backyard. A set of rickety, old steps led down to a large blank canvas. Relatively flat land stretched out about half a square acre. A barricade of birch, poplar, and pine trees lined the backyard along the fence. Ernest and I didn't have an exact vision yet, but we knew we wanted some sort of lounging space as well as a fire pit out back.

I pulled up to the house and saw the guys were already there unloading some of the bigger items. Couch, furniture, bed, other odds and ends we couldn't fit in our cars. John and Dusty have been Ernest's friends since early childhood, and now also his coworkers.

They ended up introducing me to my bridesmaids—Alice and Cora, their wives. They were coming over after work to celebrate the new house with us. Alice is a nurse down at the hospital with Charlotte, and Cora is a seamstress.

"Well, aren't you a sight for sore eyes! You look so damn beautiful, Mrs. Carmine!" I slammed my car door shut and headed towards the bunch. Mrs. Carmine. I'll never get tired of hearing that. Still made me feel warm and gave me butterflies.

"Hi there, handsome!" I said with a twirl, almost losing my balance.

"Jeez guys, get a room!" Dusty joked with an eye roll, grabbing another box from the truck to bring inside.

"Better than that—you guys got a whole house to christen now! Not just a room." John added. Ernest smacked him playfully and John ran inside behind Dusty. I could see Ernest's face slowly shift to a light hue of red. The topic of sex was still quite new, and it made him uncomfortable to joke about. I thought it was sweet. Ernest is a gentleman through and through.

The night continued on with lots of moving, rearranging, unpacking, and hanging. Luckily for me, Ernest was open to my decorative dominance so everything turned out just how I wanted. We ended the night with some board games, some drinks, which turned into drinking games, and a lot of takeout pizza.

"Bye guys! Thank you so much again for your help, we owe you one!" I yelled out to John, Dusty, Cora, and Alice as they waved their way out and skipped down the driveway. Ernest shut the door and looked at me with beaming eyes.

"Which room do we christen first?" I shuddered as he took my hands in his.

"Let's start in the kitchen." I felt my face turn hot and the blood rise to my cheeks.

He pulled me swiftly into the kitchen and snatched me with hands on my jaws into a deep kiss. His warm lips sucked into mine and I felt home, safe. Hands traveled down to my waist and pulled me closer. I could feel my body getting hot with desire as he grinded into me. In one fast motion he picked me up and placed me on the kitchen island. Wet, trembling lips advanced to my jawline and then my neck where he latched. A gentle hand shifted the bottom of my dress from under me as he tenderly ran a hand up my body until he gently started grazing my nipple with his thumb. I leaned back involuntarily as he pinched. He pulled a strap from my shoulder, and dug his face into my chest, slowly working down in sweet, hot kisses until his hot breath hit my nipple and made me moan out accidentally. While he did so, a sneaky hand traveled up my thigh, giving me goosebumps. He teased me through my panties, rubbing me in gentle circles until I was spread so far open begging for entry that it hurt. His kiss became so strong I gasped, and as I did so he shoved my panties aside and pushed a strong finger inside of me. He started slowly pumping with a curled finger, and I couldn't help but gasp. His thumb was flicking me while doing so, and it was almost too much to handle. I leaned back against my elbows in defeat. He pulled his hand out and pushed me back firmly, but with care, all the way down. He threw my dress back with an animalistic need to get to my core. He kissed aggressively against my stomach, giving me slight bites where I had some extra to nibble. Ernest dragged his tongue along where my panty line was, then slowly pulled them off of me, exposing me to the cool air. He looked at me with stars in his eyes, then shot a hot breath over my center before diving in for a taste. He started licking slowly, with closed eyes, which *made me feel so hot. I spread my legs open more to give him as much access as I could, which I so desperately craved. He started sucking on that burning, bundle of nerves, and drove two fingers into me, which sent me into a moaning frenzy. The consistent pumping, hungry suction, and the flicks of his tongue made my need and desire to climax unbearable. I pushed myself into him to get him as deep as I could, and I heard him laugh. He came up for air and kissed me, tasting myself as he did so. He grabbed my face hard and bit my lip as he did. I fumbled with his pants until I could eventually get them down and feel his rock hard member graze my thigh. I scooted down on the island for easier entry, almost begging to feel him, and he obliged. This was still new for me, so the gentle push with just the tip made me squirm as it stretched me. I clung onto his neck as he started slowly pumping into me. I felt my body start to cover in beads of sweat as he started to thrust faster. I dug my nails into the skin on his back and his neck, which made him thrust faster. His thumb shot to my center, and he started rubbing me in tandem with every push in me he made. Light screams started breaking our kiss and making me feel a heat build up in my lower stomach. I told him to go harder, and to go faster. The pain I felt began turning into pleasure. Our moans almost started to sound like they were synchronized. The pressure building up in me from his shaft already made me feel like I was going to explode, let alone having his fingers glide so fast over me I could feel my legs starting to shake involuntarily. White hot, blinding heat built up inside me until I shot backwards uncontrollably in a screaming, shaking bout of ecstasy the same time as Ernest did. I felt myself tighten around his quaking member as something started oozing out of me. Ernest fell on top of me limp in exhaustion with deep breaths. I pulled his face to mine and kissed him deeply in between panting gasps for air.*

"So, which room next, Mrs. Carmine?"

A few weeks went by in sweet bliss. Meeting neighbors hopeful to have as friends, hosting dinner parties, staying up late drinking out back planning our whole future. Everything was building towards our positive future until we got the phone call. Late, a Thursday afternoon we got a call from North Carolina Central Hospital. They informed us that Ernest's mom Charlotte was admitted to the emergency room, then the intensive care unit following a brutal assault. The assault was so horrible that Charlotte was left in a coma, attached to all sorts of machines that were keeping her alive and breathing. The first couple days, we put our jobs on hold to spend almost all day with her, Danny, and Sissy. While on the other hand, Ernest's dad Lars was missing in action. Quite conveniently for his sake. That confirmed our suspicions that Lars was, in fact, the culprit to this horrid attack. I can't confirm Ernest's opinion—because I didn't want to strike a nerve—but I knew this was going to happen at some point. His rage and his drinking and all of his issues were building up and you could clearly see him seething. It didn't take much to make him boil and spill over the top. Danny and Sissy started staying with us in our small house, and I became a stay at home mom, in a sense. After Charlotte's condition didn't improve, and we took off work for a week to spend waiting for her miraculous recovery, which didn't happen, Ernest resumed his normal hours. We weren't well off, but we had enough money to be flexible with work and afford to feed the four of us. I wanted the kids to have a stable home life with us where they didn't feel so alone, so I cut back my hours a bit. Sissy was in kindergarten and Danny was was in fourth grade, so I adjusted my work hours around them. I went into the bakery after the kids got on the bus, and I was home an hour before the kids got home. Ernest usually got home at five. My mother Sandi was relatively quiet in voicing her opinions, but you could tell she missed me being at the bakery all the time.

Next thing you know, you blink your eyes and there's a dusty blanket of snow laying gently on the frozen Earth. Christmas Eve.

While everyone was excited, there was a silent, hanging, melancholic aura surrounding all of us. We didn't talk about it or acknowledge it, but it lived in all of us, just a little bit. Charlotte and Lars. This was my first time taking care of kids for Christmas. Of course Ernest had before, but I felt the pressure was on me. It took the kids forever to tire themselves out and eventually pass out waiting for Santa. We thought it would never happen. As much as I loved being a maternal figure and having the responsibility of womanhood, I still craved one on one time to be dumb and have spontaneous fun with my new husband, and I know he wanted it too. As soon as kids out, we cracked open some wine, got to wrapping, and made sure the evidence was around, proving Santa ate his cookies and the Reindeer had their carrots. Don't forget the letters, of course. Bikes, books, games, trinkets, and toys were wrapped and bowed perfectly and placed all around the tree. Once the hard work was done, Ernest and I drank more wine than we probably should've, played cards, romanticized our future together, and spent the rest of the night laughing and we fell asleep cozily under a blanket of love in each other's arms.

Christmas Day was beautiful. A thick fog of pillowy snow was blowing in from the north. It was going to be us, my parents, Goose, Sally, John, Dusty, Alice and Cora. I had been preparing for this forever. A whole honey baked ham, green bean casserole, mashed potatoes, homemade sourdough, roasted vegetables from our garden, mac & cheese, then cupcakes and cookies. Not hating on tradition but we were NOT a jello mold family. Family started filtering in one by one, helping themselves to spiked eggnog and Christmas cranberry sangria. Ernest and I were wondering if Lars would crash, and he didn't. Not even a word. We were holding our breath for a Christmas miracle in hopes that Charlotte would wake up, but we didn't get that lucky. What we certainly weren't expecting was for Goose and Sally not to show. They seemed more than excited when we brought it up to them and they guaranteed their arrival with a promise of dip,

cheeseball, pigs in a blanket, and some sort of bark they had made.
We gave their place a ring with no answer, so we carried on trying to
make the best of the situation.

"Dinner time!" I chimed out through the kitchen, not that I needed
to yell loudly. Ernest was wearing one of my floral aprons and
chasing the kids around with pot warmers on his hands. Sissy was
laughing harder than I've heard in a long time, calling him the chef
monster.

"Coming, honey!" Ernest yelled back. "You guys be good! Don't
make the chef monster come back out!" He scurried back in the
kitchen to help me move pots and Pyrex dishes to the table.

"You're such a good brother to them, Ernest. I know we haven't
talked about it much, and I'm sorry about that. I know this isn't easy
for them but I know this isn't easy on you either." I sliced a small end
of the crusty sourdough and popped it in my mouth with a loud
crunch.

"I know, love. I know this is a big change for you, as well. You
married into my fucked up family and took my siblings in basically as
kids of your own. But this was basically my life beforehand. Raising
my siblings while my dad was crashing and burning, and while my
mom was always gone at work. The only difference now is my dad is
fucked up away from us somewhere, and my mom is...away from him.
In a coma." A lengthened breath of silence made the kitchen feel
smaller. "I love you. As long as I have you, everything else will work
out and we can handle it as a team." Ernest smirked at me with
glistening eyes. Maybe from welled up tears, maybe from the
reflections of the snow flurries outside.

"I love you, my dashing husband." I drew him into a deep kiss. I
could feel him smiling. "Now. Make you and your apron useful and

set the table." I smacked his butt as he gathered up silverware. We got everything organized on the table and the rest of our merry little crew filtered in.

"So…has anybody heard from Goose yet? Has she returned your call?" My mother questioned.

"I called her right before we sat down." My father sliced the ham for us. I hated doing that. Same with turkeys. His tone made me think she didn't answer. Again. "I got the voicemail." Silence filled the room again.

"You know, maybe they got stuck in traffic or stopped at a bar. Or maybe they stopped on the way somewhere cool, like a road trip. Or maybe they got tired and stopped for a nap." I started to ponder more possibilities. "Hell, maybe the weather is even holding them up. Those two are always getting into trouble and doing things spontaneously. Like moving to New York!" Everyone gave a chuckle. They were both so unpredictable.

"We'll call again after dinner. Let's talk about happy things!" Ernest was trying to shift the energy. "Who has something exciting to say!?"

"Well…" Alice cleared her throat and took Dusty's hand in hers. He looked at her dreamily. You could almost see little hearts circling around their heads. "You wanna tell them, babe? Or should I?"

"We're pregnant!" They shouted in unison.

"No fuckin' way!" John shouted as he threw his napkin down and slapped the table in enthusiasm. "Congratulations guys! That's incredible news!" Rounds of cheers of happiness circled the table.

"Well." Cora began while swallowing a big gulp of mac and cheese. "Good thing, because I was afraid our little bean would grow up alone!" She belted out with a toothy grin.

"You've gotta be kidding me! You didn't tell me!" Alice piped in excitedly.

"You didn't tell me!" Cora giggled out. "We're pregnant together!" The girls jumped up excitedly and ran to each other in hugs. Dinner was as merry as it could be, given the external situations.

We gathered around the tree, and picked our desserts to snack on while the kids tore through the wrapping paper. Seeing joy on their face I don't know if I've ever seen them express. It almost brought Ernest to tears seeing his siblings this happy. Part of me wondered if we would have kids, but part of me didn't care. This was good enough.

"That is so much to unload…you should write a book. So what happened to Goose!?" I questioned Elsie. She smiled in a way all of her wrinkles pulled upright. It wasn't a happy smile though. I think it was…sorrowful.

"That's a story for next time, dear. Even more to unload. Why don't you stop by in a few days? I'll show you the best cookie recipe you could imagine and we'll revisit then. This old girl needs some sleep. Get home safe, honey." Elsie took our dishes and began inside. I would've loved to see her back in the day.

"Sounds like a plan to me! Bye, Elsie!" I hopped onto the small, graveled path to my car. The whole ride home all I could think about was Elsie's life. I had so many questions. Would I find a love like that? Would my life grow to a point that is that interesting?

ZZ was waiting at my doorstep. Laying down absorbing the moonlight and starshine. "Hiya, baby!" I greeted loudly with a slam of the car door. He rose to attention with an arched back and a loud meow. I must've interrupted his cat nap. I unlocked the door and ZZ pushed me aside hopping to the spot where I normally put his food. I topped off his small bowl and gave him some milk too. Can I even call him a stray?

Since the parents were coming tomorrow I needed to tidy up. I poured myself a glass of cab and started organizing knick knacks and wiping down all my counters and tables. The floors just needed a small hit with the swiffer and that was about it.

I showered off the weight of the day and got cozy. I tied back my black hair in a French braid so my hair would be wavy in the morning. I was excited to hear about my parents little road tripping adventure. They were on their way back home to Tennessee, and were taking a pit stop at my house. I wondered how ZZ would feel about new faces around his stomping ground. I glanced in the bedroom and saw he had nestled into the bed and was peering at me through his sleep filled eyes, tail gently flicking. I cozied up next to him and drifted into a deep sleep before I could even reflect on my day.

Chapter Four

I woke up around 8:30 by a phone call from my mother Gail, informing me her and my father Lane would be over at my house around 11:30. I rolled out of bed and got myself ready for the day. I figured I should make some lunch for them as well. I let ZZ out the front door and locked it behind me in preparation to go to the grocery store. ZZ ran into the woods to hunt critters and absorb the sunlight like a damn plant as I entered my car.

I was thinking something nice and cozy for lunch—maybe some good sandwiches and sides? Browsing the deli led me to picking up some fresh, shaved meat and cheese, along with some tomatoes, pickles, lettuce, avocado, and onion. Then some potatoes too for some yummy homemade fries. And of course wine, because wine not.

Getting home I realized I needed to start on some bread. I whipped up some simple, no-knead focaccia that Elsie had taught me how to bake. I figured by the time they got to the house it would be baking in the oven, and I was correct!

Knocks at the door preceded an excessive scream of hellos. I opened up the front door and my mother launched herself into a hug. My dad kind of waited until she unlatched before he gave me a simple squeeze with a back pat.

They hadn't seen my house other than pictures, and I was more than excited to give them a tour. It was short, but a tour nonetheless. I started to assemble the sandwiches as they settled in and started talking about their vacation.

"Honey, you need to travel. Your father and I have had the best time ever!" My mother accentuated with a giggle. "We have enough saved up so we decided we are going to travel overseas next. I've always wanted to go to Egypt, Thailand, Italy, Greece, and so many other places, and we decided to do it now before we get old." She was beaming with a smile. "We leave in a month!"

"A month!? For real!?" I popped slices of focaccia in the oven with meat and cheese to toast and locked at her in awe.

"Yeah, honey. We couldn't be more excited. What's the point of life if you don't get to live it?" As basic as that thought was, it sat with me. She was right. Sometimes you need to grab life by the balls and see where it takes you, right? Nothing is ever promised. "I'm a little jealous, not gonna lie…but what an exciting adventure for you guys— you deserve it. That's going to be so amazing. How long are you going to stay there?"

"I would like to go for maybe three months…I'm not too sure. We bought a one way ticket, so we're pretty flexible." My dad giggled at her reply. Like, actually giggled.

"Listen, she's the boss. I just do what she tells me." He kept on laughing as he cracked open a bottle of sauvignon blanc. I sliced the veggies and salted the tomatoes to prepare for the rest of the sandwich to cook. I cracked a laugh. It was nice to see my dad retired and living life.

"I expect pictures…you won't be missing much here!"

"How's everything going, honey?"

"The shop is going well…steady income. I have a good group of friends. Plus an elderly lady who lives right up the street nearby me named Elsie has become my best friend. She teaches me amazing recipes. Including this fabulous focaccia recipe!" I pulled the partial sandwiches out of the oven and added all the fixings. We sat at my table, and shared fun stories that have happened recently. Really, more them than me. But I loved it.

Soon enough, they needed to hit the road. I was sad, but also happy for them and their upcoming adventures. I decided I would run the rest of my errands tomorrow after work, stop by Elsie's the following day after work, and figure out the rest of the days after. The rest of my night got drowned away with a good book and the rest of the wine we cracked open.

It was a sunny day out. I got an iced macadamia nut latte from Hazel and wondered what the day would bring. Mondays are normally really quiet. However, today it was slammed. I had people coming in from basics like house plants they want, tooth aches, tummy troubles, and clear skin all the way to immunity diseases, weight loss, hair growth, and love potions. I am not the one who thinks you should mess around with love potions, so I don't. Nor would I know where to start. However, I have some really interesting grimoires I picked up the last time I traveled to New Orleans and Salem. Lord knows where to begin with them, though. I really should read up on them more, but I don't. Maybe I'll do that tonight…

Soon enough it was closing time at the shop. The day felt like it had just flown by because of how busy it actually was. I met up with Missy at The Witches Brew. She had narrowed down her venues, flower selections, meal options, cake ideas, and everything possible for her wedding and wanted to run them by someone. She was pretty much sold on the idea of peonies with different greenery intertwined within for the bridesmaids, which I told her I would provide. For her bouquet, she actually was really open, she just knew she didn't want any "basic" roses or anything that traditional. Bright colors with a lot of varying shapes and sizes was her request. Missy had the dinners planned out too, including options for vegans and those who are gluten free. She just had to decide whether she wanted to do tilapia or salmon. Deciding between inside and outdoor venues was a difficult selection as well. Who knows how the weather would be? How do you even know what to select when the date is far away and unknown? I suggested she select a place with a primarily outdoor venue with inside options in case of rain. Lastly, cake. That was the hardest. Without trying them you couldn't really give the best insight or advice, you know? If any cake is done professionally, it should all be good. At least in my book.

We had a few drinks for the night before I had to head home to let my loving, feral cat inside for the night.

The next day work was pretty slow. I sold about $400 before I decided it was time to leave and go see Elsie. I arrived at her house with her already sitting outside on the porch.

"Honey, I'm so glad I get to see you! I was thinking for cookies we could make either brown butter chocolate chip walnut cookies or blueberry pancake cookies. Do you have a preference?" Elsie asked with a smile.

"They both sound amazing! I'm intrigued by the brown butter, though. So let's do those!" I replied. She led me inside and I watched her pull out all of the ingredients from the pantry with expertise. She showed me how to brown a stick of butter, and she mixed a perfect dough, explaining how to do so on the way. Then it was time to bake the cookies. And we know what that means. Story time.

I awoke around 4:00am with Ernest sitting up on the edge of bed, his breathing appeared ragged.

"Honey? Are you okay?" He let out a deep sigh.

"I just got a call from the hospital. They aren't sure how it happened, but my mom got unplugged, I guess. From all the machinery keeping her alive you know…" His voice trailed off.

"Oh…is she okay?" I shuddered at my own reply, because I knew the answer. Dumb question of me to ask.

"She's gone Elsie…" I blinked before my eyes welled up with tears. I was never close to Charlotte, but seeing Ernest in pain and knowing how it would affect Danny and Sissy stabbed me so deeply. He turned around a tad so I could see the profile of his face. "Is it fucked up I'm not even that sad? I mean, I am, or I was…but I just feel like the first day we got the phone call about her going into a coma and needing all those machines, I knew we lost her. People don't bounce back from that. At least in my mind they don't. And if they do, they aren't the same. The only difference now is that I know she's finally resting and hopefully at peace." It's March now, and Charlotte in the hospital hasn't been as heavy on our minds. We've adjusted to having the kids at the house now, and we go see her Sunday mornings. It's like our own fucked up kind of church.

"Ernest, I'm so sorry. I don't really know what to say, this is just so tragic. I really hope this was fate's way of pulling the plug and

letting her go into a better world." I had no idea what to say to comfort someone in this situation. He was quiet for a while.

"I think my dad was somehow able to sneak in and pull the plug. I don't know how or if that's even a possibility, but that's what my gut is telling me. How else would it happen? Who else would?"

"I...I don't know, love."

"Babe. I know we have been playing fake family. Well, er, not fake family. But you've been playing fake mom in a sense to my siblings these past few months. You've been doing such an insane amount for the kids. We haven't really talked about it, but I'm sure you've thought about it as much as I have. I know we aren't really on the baby train like John, Dusty, Alice, and Cora are, but it looks like it's going to be my responsibility to raise my siblings. Obviously, I want you to be my partner and help me with this and do this crazy thing called life with me, which is why I married you," he smirked. "However, I feel like it's rude to not ask. You didn't sign up for this task, and I want to give you an out. If you don't want to do this, I will let you go..." Ernest's eyes glazed over.

"Honey bear...I would never choose a life without you in it. Every challenge life throws you, is my challenge too. We are a team. For better and for worse, you know?" I smiled and inched towards him. I pulled him to my chest and back into bed to hold him as he came to terms with this sudden shift he would have to deal with. I pushed a kiss into the top of his head and wrapped my arms around him. I pulled the blankets over him as well and stroked his back, chest, stomach, and thighs until his breathing evened out and I could tell he had fallen asleep.

The next morning breakfast was...uncomfortable. Ernest smoked a cigarette at the table while I dished everyone up pancakes, eggs, and bacon. Ernest doesn't even smoke, for the record. I poured up some orange juice for the littles, and coffee for us. I finally took my seat next to Ernest and coughed, to hopefully bring Ernest back from wherever he mentally was. He cleared his throat. "Danny, Sissy...I have something to say, and I really don't know how to. Mom..." he let out a deep sigh. "Mom went to heaven last night. God wanted one of his angels home and she was the next in line to go. You guys will be staying with Elsie and I. We love you very much, and if you have any questions or if you are confused, we are here for you." He mustered out a smile. The kids were quiet. Part of me thinks they weren't crazily affected by this news either considering she went comatose months ago. The rest of breakfast, Ernest and I tried to keep light and not in the same vein as dead mother.

In other news, Goose and Sally were still missing. Cops had no leads, no nothing. I called them every week for a while, and now every other week to see if there was any new information. I also made sure to keep pretty constant contact with my parents to chit chat and hopefully distract them from the potential horrors of the what ifs that could come with their missing daughter. I've exhausted myself and worried myself all the way to the edge with the possibilities of what happened. At this point, I don't know what I hope for or what I wish. All I know is I won't be able to heal or accept anything, or live my damn life if I spend every second of my life obsessing over the worst case scenarios. I'm just trying to keep my cool until I have any facts at all to work with. I just try to take one day at a time, and now I know that's something we will all need to do now, us a family.

Ominously gloomy, yet fluffy clouds overcrowded the sky. Full of water and ready to burst like water balloons at a kids birthday party. The deep rumbling of far away thunder still seemed to shake the ground and the leaves of the trees around us. Crumbles of dirt shifted *with the reverberation of the thunder, and debris tumbled into the grave where Charlotte would soon lay. Slowly, fat and over engorged raindrops gently began trickling from the sky. Not enough for an umbrella, or even a rain jacket, but it was enough to bring you back to reality and stop your brain from drifting into a distant place.*

Black clothes clung against my body, hugging me tightly when the wind blew from the breath of the oncoming storm. Black didn't suit me. It didn't fit my new family either. I'm not sure who deemed black the color of funerals, but they certainly would have made a better choice.

It felt fake. Almost like a play, just going through the motions as Charlotte was laid to rest. I gripped the kids shoulders tightly, and Ernest held me. Almost silent cries were hidden by the whistling of the wind and the sound of Charlotte's coffin being submerged into the Earth. I wondered if we would be doing this for Goose and Sally, next. Part of me almost wished we would be, so that way I wouldn't have to wonder anymore.

Weeks following the funeral, things seemed to be on the come up. Everyone's morale started to increase, Ernest and the kids started to smile and laugh again. We really did become a tight knit family. Work was going great for both of us, and the highlight of my day was when I got to see Danny and Sissy after school. This particular Friday evening, it was dinner party time. Alice, Cora, John, and Dusty were coming over for some appetizers and some time by the fire. Cocktails for the boys and I, mocktails for Alice and Cora. I was planning on making potato skins, mini quiches, spinach artichoke dip, and a pasta salad. I figured for drinks I'd make some sangria, and fake sangria with grape juice for Alice and Cora. How cool is it that they're pregnant at the same time? That's gotta be so cool. On some level I'm jealous, I think. I don't know why. But I am.

Hors d'oeuvres were a blast, as always. I'm so glad Ernest has such kind, caring, strong, men in his life. As silly as that sounds, he was never been around men like that, and it's nice that he draws like minded people towards him. I wonder if he shares deep, emotional feelings with them that he doesn't share with me. Part of me hopes he does. We're so open with each other, but I find it so strange he has barely spoken to me about his mother or Lars.

The fire crackled loudly and shot sparks out towards us. Smoke billowed in a heavy cascade up to the stars, and made their brightness blurred and cloudy. Danny and Sissy roasted marshmallows for all of us as dessert. They loved making s'mores and we loved eating them. Perfect match. Well, perfect when the kids didn't burn the marshmallows.

"So neither of you guys know what gender you're having!?" I asked with thrill in my voice.

"Nope!" They chuckled out in unison.

"How do you plan anything? What color are you painting the room, or how are you buying toys or clothes?" Ernest leaned forward as he questioned them.

"I'm going neutral...probably green, yellow, brown, orange...I don't know. I just figured surprises are fun, and this is the biggest and most important surprise in the world, so why not keep it one?" Alice nodded in agreement with Cora's reply. I can understand why they'd want the surprise.

"I don't know, guys...Dusty thinks I'm crazy when I tell him but I think we're both having girls!" Both the girls giggled and the guys side-eyed each other.

"Baby, crazy isn't the word…I just don't understand why you both are so certain!" John and Dusty clanked their sangria together in agreement.

"Call it mother's intuition I guess…" Cora's southern accent seemed to have a little more twang than usual. "We just both feel it! Y'all will see when it's time. Just wait." She grabbed Alice's hand tightly. In some way I felt…left out. I don't want to be pregnant with a child, but I have been starting to feel like a third wheel in the friendship. I know, it's not that way in real life. But in my head it is.

The rest of the night was…light. Airy. We shared many laughs under the stars, and let the moonlight guide our dances beneath her. Barefoot spins in the lawn with careless prances around the fire filled the evening. The delicate singing of the wind, the twinkling of the stars, and the intense light of the fire filled the space between all of us with more life than ever. This was the happiest we had all been in so long.

"You can't leave me hanging!" I bit into a cookie, chasing it with a glass of milk. "Were they right? Were they girls?"

Elsie smiled, almost longingly. "Alice and Dusty had a boy. Cora and John had a girl. They were wonderful kids. We had such a beautiful life filled with so many great people. It really brings me back talking about the past, and I'm so grateful I can share these memories with you." The wrinkles around her eyes deepened as her smile widened. The silence between us grew as she fell back into deep reflection. We finished up our cookies on that front porch I've come to love. The breeze tussled my hair and the sweet scent of wildflowers just about overpowered the smell of freshly baked cookies. The warm colors that illuminated the horizon rained down in sparkling gold while the coolness of the sun setting and the twinkling of the overhead stars produced a much chillier feeling.

"This is your time to make memories that you'll share with people one day, Ivy." Elsie broke the silence and collected our dishes from the table. "I never hear you talk about any guys, barely any friends, really anything. Just work, and your cat for the most part. You don't need to keep this old lady company, you know. My feelings won't be hurt. I'll understand." She giggled out that last part and shuffled inside.

"Elsie don't say that! You are my friend! I think I'm just in a place where I'm more career driven, and everything else is background noise. Just trying to find my place before I get settled down I suppose." I followed her in and helped her load up the dishwasher before she gave me a Tupperware full of cookies to take home.

"Okay, honey. Just making sure you don't feel like my caretaker or anything like that. Not saying I don't want you here, but there's no obligation. When's the next time you're coming over?"

"Friday?"

"Sounds great. What should we make?"

"Muffins?"

"What kind?"

"I don't know, Elsie! You're the baking goddess!"

"Okay, we could do…carrot cake muffins, since the carrots in the garden look good…same with the zucchini. We could do zucchini bread muffins. Blueberry muffins."

"Elsie those all sound so good. I wish we could have them all! I can't decide which, you just pick the day of and surprise me."

"Okay. Sounds good. Please be safe driving home, and I'll see you soon." She pulled me into one of her warm, cozy, old lady hugs and waved me along my way.

"Love you!"

"Love you, too!"

Friday morning rolled around and it was a beautiful, sunny day. ZZ snuggled with me all night long, all the customers at work were chipper, I sold a lot of product, I got a delicious white chocolate pistachio latte from next door for free, work flew by quick, and I got a new shipment of inventory unloaded and organized today. What more could you ask for?

Closing time came fast, which meant muffin baking time was right around the corner. After I locked up, I grabbed another round of coffees from next door, decaf for Elsie. Coffee goes great with muffins. Plus Hazel assured me vanilla & rose hip lattes pair well with any baked good.

The drive to our road is so beautiful. Mostly twisty turns lined with trees or through grassy hills. Every leaf and blade of grass was coated in thick golden sunshine, like dripping honey. Today just seemed extra bright, and I was so excited to be spending the rest of it with Elsie. I have been dying to hear the rest of her story. I am really thankful for her. If I didn't have her, I wouldn't have anyone. I mean, of course I have my friends. And I love them, for the most part. But the friendships are very one sided, if you know what I mean. I think we are all at very different stages in our lives and they have a lot of shit to be focused on in their own lives, let alone my little life. I'm still searching for a meaning, I suppose. That's what's nice about Elsie. Her life has been packed to the brim with meaning, and I get to be taught baking secrets from someone who cares about me. Plus, I get awesome life lessons and stories. I wonder if life would have still brought us together if situations were different.

I pulled up through the overgrown jungle of wildflowers, swaying in the wind, caressing my car. No doubt leaving a trail of pollen graffiti. I wonder which muffins she decided we would make today. I left my windows open, hopping out of the car door. No wanderers around here, plus that beautiful breeze would hopefully leave my car aired out and chilly.

"Hi, Elsie! I'm so excited for our muffins and story time today!" I hollered out as I sauntered up the steps, rapping on the door. No answer. Maybe she was sleeping or didn't hear me. Or was busy doing something else. I knocked again. Nothing. "Elsie, it's Ivy! Open up!" I knocked louder this time. Still to no avail. Maybe she wasn't home? But she's always home?

I don't think she'd mind if I let myself in. She has a hard time hearing sometimes. I gingerly grasped the handle and pushed—the door creaked open. Weird, it's unlocked. "Elsie? I'm coming inside, it's Ivy."

I poked my head into the dining room—no Elsie. Should I be nervous? I'm getting nervous. The hallway seemed to elongate before my very eyes, as I took careful, gentle steps down it, that way I wouldn't startle her. I blinked and squeezed my eyes hard, as if to blink away the distance from me to the rest of the house, but it seemed to almost make the hallway grow more.

Things were eerily quiet. Something didn't feel right. My pulse seemed to throb painfully throughout my veins with every beat of my racing heart. My lip trembled with every call of her name, and my voice became weaker and weaker. I ran my fingers against the old wallpaper on the wall, feeling its coarseness and grit with the change of the colorful patterns. I was tracing a maze between the photos on the wall, the never ending wall, bracing myself with every stroke I made.

I rounded the corner into the kitchen, and—

And.

Before I saw, the smell of pungent iron singed my nostrils, making me recoil with instinct I hadn't known before. Heat from the smell alone made me cringe and pierce my very soul with an unknown kind of fear. Smeared pools of crimson lined the floor of the beautiful, sanctity of the kitchen I once knew. Elsie…splayed out on the floor. More pale than anything I've ever seen before. No color left in her body, because all of what made her glow was spattered and puddled upon the floor. A violent, involuntary heave came up from my stomach as I vomited all over this scene I had come across. Hands so shaky, hands I hadn't seen before, reached out to her to check for a pulse that I knew wasn't there. I struggled to get my phone out of my pocket and dial 911 as I struggled to attempt what I thought CPR was. To the tune of Stayin' Alive.

"911, what is your emergency?"

"My neighbor is…dead," my voice quivered. "My address is right after hers on the right, going north. I'm 216 Jade Street, I think she's 212, but I'm really not sure. It's the dirt driveway with a lot of wildflowers lining it. She has a bright mailbox. Her name is…was…Elsie Carmine." I didn't even recognize the way my voice sounded. Especially between the pants I was making trying to revive her.

"I've dispatched EMS and officers your way. Stay on the line with me. What is your name? Where are you?" Lukewarm blood oozed out on my hands, not as warm as I thought it should be. I wondered how long she had been here. "Hello?"

"My name is Ivy, I'm trying to do CPR…I don't know if it's working." I barely mustered out.

"Stay with me Elsie. You won't be alone for long."

It seemed like a very long time. It seemed like multiple lifetimes, actually. EMS took over until she was declared officially dead. That made me vomit again. Officers had to help walk me away, because my knees were so weak I couldn't stand. This was a dream, right? This couldn't be real. Officers taped everything off and took my statement, which I gave to them so numb I can't even remember what I got out in between weeps. Officers drove me home, and made sure I got inside okay. My hands fumbled with my keys, such an easy yet grueling task, but it seemed so complex. The rest of the night was on autopilot, as if to preserve the human part of me from suffering anymore.

I thought sleep would help, but it didn't. The dreams started the first night after her death. I dreamed of an old, decrepit, run down theater. Hadn't been inhabited in years, it looked like. I walked through, fear in every inch of me. Backstage was musty and dust filled costumes hung along the walls. Old puppets and dolls lined shelves that were so dirty and broken from who knows what, that you couldn't even tell what some of them were supposed to represent. Mold had overtaken floorboards that creaked with every step I made. Once beautiful maroon curtains were now mildew consumed and stained brown. Little holes decorated them from hungry moths, like organic lace. They hung, half falling, along the stage. As I approached center stage, the old lights came on. So bright and blinding I needed to shield my eyes. Particles of dust, pollen, and who knows what else danced in the wake of them. As soon as my eyes adjusted to the spotlight, wooden slats of the floor broke beneath me and I fell. Consumed like a white rabbit down a hole. A prisoner of what may lie beneath. As soon as I hit the bottom, I woke up in sweaty, gasping breaths. The dream continued every time I fell asleep. Needless to say, the shop stayed closed the next few days.

A letter in the mail came informing me I was Elsie's next of kin. For everything. That means it's my job to clean out her house. Her house, that has become my safe place. My happy place. Where I go to feel loved. Or, where I went. Now it's mine.

I went on a run that morning. Tuesday? Wednesday? Thursday? I don't know. That same nightmare was waking me everyday once I finally drifted into a peaceful sleep, which in turn, made all of my days blur together. The only change was this run. I needed to start dealing with Elsie's…my…house. Plus, I needed to get my car from there.

I guess her death was ruled as an accident. It didn't make sense to me considering how fucked up her body looked. Apparently, she died from head trauma. It was assumed she died of a slip and fall. I'm no detective but there was a lot of blood. It looked…unnatural. Almost completely violent.

I was going into today, or trying to, with a fresh head. Clear mind. Not reminiscent of anything. Just pack it all up. Get a storage unit if I need to—just pack it all up.

Bathroom, dining room, and living room were easy. That I could store…or sell. Kitchen, most of it at least, I could move into mine. Especially the gadgets and cook books.

Elsie's bedroom was mostly empty. A lot of keepsakes. I couldn't pardon with any of those, I would keep those in totes. Maybe some in my house, too. Was that morbid? I don't know. So many pictures revealed faces I had heard so much about. I felt like I knew a bunch of these people. Ernest, Sissy, Danny, Cora, Alice, Dusty, John, Sandy, Michael, Goose, Sally, Charlotte, and even Lars. I couldn't let them be forgotten. Not like this. I packed them up in a keep tote.

Finally, a couple days later I got to the spare bedroom. The old master bedroom upstairs. It was chock full of knick knacks, that I assumed were keepsakes that I didn't know the meaning of. A thin blanket of dust covered most things…except one thing, specifically. A drawer full of old letters and cards yellowed from time past. That made something stand out. Brighter than everything else. And, oddly enough, an envelope had my name on it. A shiver ran up and down my spine that made me shudder visibly.

I sat on the carpeted floor as I plucked out the envelope with Ivy handwritten on it. My hands quivered as my thumb slid through the seal locking the contents in place. I pulled out a handwritten letter, in cursive, with quite a few thousand dollars in old cash wrapped inside of it. I didn't know what to expect. I slid the money in my purse and unfolded the letter.

"Ivy,

If you're reading this, unfortunately it means I'm gone. I have enjoyed my time with you more than you know. Sharing my baking secrets is one thing, but sharing my life with you is something words can't fully comprehend.

I knew this day would come, and I knew it would be hard on you to hear. I just hope you didn't have to witness anything too graphic.

Nobody ever figured out what happened to Goose, Ivy. I have dedicated my life to figuring it out. I fear I will meet her same fate. I believe she was murdered and I think her killer will come after me one day. If you're reading this, my thoughts will more than likely be confirmed.

All expenses should be covered, and in my will I have specified to be cremated. Once I am, you remember that theater I had my first date at with Ernest? I want you to spread my ashes there. Inside there. That will make my soul finally be at peace. It's condemned now, so it shouldn't be an issue. I just want to lay in the place I found love for the first time with the love of my life.

Thank you for everything.

With love,

Elsie Carmine."

What do I do? Do I call the cops? No…they didn't rule it a murder. How did she know? Finding a letter like this is the last thing I suspected. It felt surreal.

I packed the letter into my purse strapped to me, and packed up the rest of the room. Once I got home…the planning would start. I would make Elsie's last request happen. And once I did, I would look into what happened to Goose.

Chapter Five

North Carolina. Luckily enough for me, there weren't a lot of very old, condemned, theaters around. From what Elsie has told me about the area, it actually was pretty easy to find. It looked like it had gotten shut down almost forty years ago. I posted a notice on social media and the doors at my shop, stating that I would be shut down for a few days to take care of matters regarding a death in the family. I even left out a lot of food and water outside for ZZ. I'm sure a lot of other animals will be attracted as well, but at least I will know I'll have taken care of my stray inside outside house cat. I packed up a small suitcase and tossed it in my car. Oddly enough, ZZ wasn't in sight.

The drive was oddly peaceful. I skipped through some audio books, music, and podcasts along the way and everything seemed to slowly fade away and murmur out into nothing. The scenery, and my thoughts, took over every time until I forgot what I was even listening to. What happened to Elsie, Goose, and Sally?

I got to the theater at night. Well, just before sunset. I figured I would just find a hotel or motel and settle in there for a few days after the deed was done, and start my research then. I think a mini vacation, despite the reason, was deserved and could do me zoom good. After all, my main mission here shouldn't take that long, right?

The rubble, probably not driven on for years probably, crinkled underneath my tires as I rolled to a slow halt in front of the theater. If you could even call it that. It easily looked like it hadn't been tended to in a decade. The personification Elsie gave to this place was wild to think about visualizing how it looked now. Would she even want to be laid to rest here knowing how horrible and creepy it looked?

Thick, dark emerald ivy was slowing crawling up the height of the theater. It looked like an organic cushion, padding the theater from nature's own brutality. Or maybe the wild was starting to engulf it, break it down. Consume it back into the Earth, like it was never there to begin with. Wild vines speckled and dotted with colorful varieties of flowers danced and twirled around the columns, window sills, and framework. Maybe even holding the damn place together like rope or glue. Once a beautiful, fanciful, elegant theater that used to bring joy to families, couples, and friends every day. Now, nothing. Forgotten. A place left behind, lost in time.

I grabbed her urn and stepped out of my car, shutting and locking the door behind me, gently. Afraid to wake the stillness of the forest, like I didn't belong. An uninvited guest. Why did this feel so…familiar? I haven't been here before, so why did it feel like I had? Major deja vu.

I approached the dooming steps that looked more than eerie in the cast of the sunset. Every step creaked with a scary sort of welcome, or maybe a go away. The ticket booth had shattered windows. I was assuming from asshole kids, not from the elements.

The doors were padlocked at one point, but someone had clipped the lock and chain long before I had been there. Graffiti sporadically illustrated the once regal and inviting walls and doors with words and phrases that mostly looked uninviting.

Even standing outside I could smell the age. Old mothballs, wood rot, mildew, must, wet dirt, and old books. I grasped the old brass door handle of one of the doors and pulled. It was a lot heavier than I thought it would be. As the door groaned open, I secured Elsie against me and turned the flashlight on my phone on. Not much natural light shone inside other than two small windows. I didn't have much time before the sun fully set either.

Even covered in a blanket of dust and cobwebs, this place was incredible. Elsie did such a wonderful job describing it. She described it perfectly, like she was in here yesterday. I tried to put myself in her shoes, back in the past, here on a first date. Just damn incredible.

I couldn't help but cough when I walked in. I must have inhaled a straight shot of dust. The cream and ivory colors inside have turned a light gray brown. Reds and greens that Elsie spoke about were so dark they were almost black. I traced a finger along the intricacies of what I assumed was the snack counter as I strolled by. Where I touched left a noticeably naked trail. I flicked the dirt off my finger and gazed around. Old posters, once bright and hopeful, hung all around the walls. I wonder why this place closed?

Elsie and I made our way towards the second large set of French doors leading into the auditorium. As we approached I could see those handles were in fact, still locked. The lock and chain corroded and dusty. This lock must've been here for years. I set down the urn on a nearby table and surveyed the area for something the right size and weight to smash the lock.

A stone candelabra stood tall near one of the couches on an end table. I figured that should do the trick so I snatched it up and walked back to the lock. I was excited to go into a place, untouched for years.

It took a few a few sharp hits in the right spot to loosen up, but it eventually gave in. I swung the doors open on either side of me. Wow…breathtaking. I'll admit, I haven't been in any theaters before, but this one was incredible, even in its old, broken down age. I grabbed Elsie and we made our way inside. I wasn't rushing, I wanted to take my time. Find the right place to leave Elsie. I wish I knew what seat she sat at when she came here. I wonder how many times she had been here. I would have assumed more than the one time since she wanted her ashes to be spread here, right?

While I was here, I figured I might as well explore. It took a couple minutes to trek down the aisle all the way to the right side to an old employee's only hallway, to then continue to make my way backstage.

Wait…how did I know how to get backstage? Weird. Deja vu again. It's like that dream I've been having.

I'll tell you what. The cobwebs, darkness, dust, spiders, centipedes, abandoness, and creepy crawlies were one thing. But entering that pitch black employee hallway ignited a different kind of spook inside me. I clutched the urn closer to me, like it would protect me, in a sense. It must've been a couple hundred feet of just plain midnight. Nothing on the walls. Just battered wooden floors that let out sighs with every step I walked down them.

That door on the other side couldn't come fast enough. I wasn't sure what exactly I would find on the other side, but it had to be better than in here. My pulse started to thrum and I felt pressure in my eyes, fingers, and toes. My breath seemed to intensify, I almost wanted to run.

Don't panic don't panic don't panic. Just a hallway.

Were the walls on either side of me closing in? Where had the space gone? It was like the hallway was getting longer and skinner.

Cold beads of sweat ran from my brow. My breath became shaky.

I tried to hide it.

Why? Nobody was watching?

It kind of felt like someone was, though. Like I wasn't alone. In this stretch of blankness.

I turned around, just to make sure I wasn't followed.

Nope, nobody was there. But I swear the shadows whirled and spun in an unnatural light, mocking my fear.

I turned back to the desired end of the hallway, gripped Elsie and ran for it. The cool doorknob couldn't join my hand fast enough. Once it did I just about knocked the damn door down. Ran right through it.

I was out of the hallway, I could breathe. How silly of me to get scared by a little hallway? Maybe I'd just hop off the stage on my way out of here instead of facing that damn hallway.

As I peered around, chills jolted up and down my spine, leaving me frozen with fear. The dream I was having. It was identical…literally identical. To this theater. What does this mean?

Old costumes were hung up on movable clothing racks on wheels. Holes filled them, but boy you could tell how beautiful they were in their prime. I set Elsie on the floor beside me. As I approached a rack closest to me and pulled the dress closer to inspect, it was obvious it was hand stitched, homemade. A name of Nicole embroidered on the tag. A sticky crust of debris clung to my fingertips as I let the dress fall back into its place on the rack. Moths fluttered out in a cluster, like blowing the fuzz off of a dandelion. Instinctively, I hopped away, swatting them away from me before I realized they were just moths. Mirrors, chairs, vanities, and couches appeared in rows until I couldn't see any further. Shelves asymmetrically lined up over the walls held dolls and puppets galore. Some perfectly intact, while some ripped apart, broken, cracked, smooshed, and smashed.

A sock puppet caught my eye. Black beady eyes, a little homemade hat, red yarn smile. I wonder who he belonged to back in the day, and why was he forgotten in this seemingly lost land.

A porcelain, lemon yellow duck puppet found my attention next. It had a little red beret on and a white and navy striped tee shirt like a mock sailor.

A Victorian looking little girl doll was sitting besides captain duck. Covered in pink and lace with an ivory little bonnet. A crack spread like veins or a web over her face and one of her feet looked like it crumbled. She looked too fragile to touch.

These gave such a personality to the theater, back here at least. I bet some were the staffs, and some were used in the shows. Must've been comforting to see when coming into work. Dolls that hadn't turned creepy yet, beautiful architecture, colorful, outrageous costumes, bold personalities. All coming together in one place. Must have been so lively.

I retreated back and scooped up Elsie. Exploring is fun, but I started to get an eerie sense of unbelonging. Maybe things in here wanted to be left alone, untouched. I made my way to the length of the curtain. My eyes climbed upwards, and I couldn't even see where the curtain stopped and ceiling began. An upwards abyss.

Elsie should be buried onstage. Onstage, offstage, center stage, wherever a star would be. She wanted to be buried here and she deserved to be spread in the best spot attainable here. I found my way to a break in the curtain, and spread them apart to make a small entrance for me and my old friend. I slowly, and now shakily, marched towards what I assumed was center stage. The stage felt hollow beneath me. I've never been on a stage before, but this didn't feel right. It was soft, like walking on a sandy beach by the water. Footprints left behind me. A cool thought until remembering you were walking on a hard wood stage that shouldn't do that. Creaks and grumbles got louder and louder until I could hear them reverberate throughout the auditorium, and in my very bones.

I stopped, and set Elsie down. This was a real goodbye. I wasn't sure exactly how these things worked. Did I save some in the urn for me to keep? Did I spread all of her remains in the same space so she stayed…together? Did I say a few words, like a funeral? I think it'd be nice if I did. She'd like that.

The top is the urn slipped off easily and I gently cupped my hand inside to scoop out some ashes.

"Elsie. You were the best friend I never asked for, never expected to have, and never would have given up for the world." I threw a handful of ashes. "The memories you have shared with me are something I value more than…most things." I sprinkled more all around. "You are such a beautiful soul, and you deserve more than what this world could have ever given you." I flung another large handful. "I vow to you…and I promise you, that I will do everything in my power to figure out what happened to you and your sister. I love and loved you, Elsie. I wish…" Another handful. "I wish for a way to start. How to start. A sign from the world to put me on the right path." Tears were welling up in my eyes and burning hot trails were left down my cheeks, oddly cooling my neck and leaving it wet. Soon, I couldn't stop crying. Uncontrollable sobs left me in deep, billowing, weeps. I needed to finish spreading these ashes and get the fuck out of here. The beautiful awe I started off in here has now turned dark, eerie, and mysterious. I threw out the rest of the ashes and bent down to pluck up the urn, and yet again, I had to stop in my tracks. The ashes thrown around me started to glisten—glow. What was there? What was that? There was no light?

Then the whole stage around me started to glow, just a bit. Looking forward, it looked like the spotlight in front of and above us was slowly turning on. Goosebumps formed all over my body, in places I've never even had goosebumps. How the fuck…why the fuck…was this on? What was happening?

My whole body started to paralyze in fear and I froze in the wake of terror. The spotlight illuminating us was one thing, but the color these ashes were turning was something my mind couldn't comprehend. Blues and yellows swirled into reds and blues that danced into purple and gold glitter. Thecoloros danced around me into a neon shade of ethereal green danced all around me, almost encompassing me into a bubble. My mind certainly wasn't seeing things the way they should be seen. Vermillion and lavender clouds started to form where the ashes lay, and a heat started to rise from the stage where Elsie touched. My tears fell along the ground beneath me, leaving a trail of steam in their wake. A whirlwind of heat, color, and emotion, rose from the ground like a sauna, releasing energies all around me. The floor moaned loudly, releasing screams it has held in for years.

Suddenly, the sunken and soggy wood around me caved, like loose fabric. The world around me pulled like an overstretched sweater until it ripped. The floor boards gave out until I slipped into a rickety, wobbly, spiderweb. What I would have assumed would be a straight shot down into a dark hole into oblivion, transformed into a neon spectrum full of different electric shades of rainbow. I fell into twists and turns of a kaleidoscopic tunnel that threw me around like a childhood slide.

The vivid, dazzling, overcast of colors slowly turned into an overcast of dark, unwelcoming, undesirable casts of midnight, blinding my vision around me. Whirring yells and yelps got louder and my vision went completely dark until there was nothing, and I fell into an involuntary sleep.

Chapter Six

My eyes opened, with a headache like no other. I thought red wine gave me a hangover, but this was out of this world.

I looked around, and I was obviously lost. But things looked lit up. The flooring—or ceiling above me didn't look broken. How did I get here? I stood up and put a hand to my head, hoping to relieve some of my pain, stumbling upon the ground beneath me. Like I was in a boat on the ocean.

I followed the dim light of lanterns to the right to a small set of stairs that I assumed would lead me to the regular stage. When did those lanterns get lit? How did they get lit? Where did they even come from?

Dizzily, I started to ascend to my feet. Once I was about half way up and finally got my footing, two little twin boys came barreling down it, seemingly playing with a paper or cardboard airplane.

The breath got taken out of me and I shot to the rails of the poorly put together wooden staircase. I was yet again frozen, by the unsuspecting company. I thought I was alone in here? I actually couldn't have been more sure of that.

Slowly, I continued upwards once my heart regained a semi regular beat. Oddly enough, it looked like more light was greeting me the closer I got to the top of the stairs—and I was right.

As soon as I got to the peak of the staircase, lights shone so brightly into my eyes that I had to shield them at first.

Girls ran past me, covered in spandex and tulle, giggling under the glimmering lights of the spotlights above us. I was inadvertently surrounded by costumed girls and boys scampering around with joy. Where did all these people come from? I thought this place was condemned?

I moved to the side skirts, behind the scenes of where all the movement was. Once—the dust covered, broken vanities with dolls and old costumes and trinkets galore that I'd become familiar with, were now coated with the light of golden hope and opportunity. Shimmering with the glistening importance of show time. Nothing covered in debris and dust and darkness anymore.

Everything looked fresh and new. Lights were bright, floor wasn't creaky, staff was booming with exuberance. Nothing eaten by mold or moths. That stale, old book smell wasn't present anymore.

I slowly braced myself against the wall, taking everything in. All the chitter chatter, running though of lines, giggles while young ladies did their makeup. What the fuck happened?

It's a dream. I fell through the boards, hit my head, got knocked into an unconscious state, and it was now a dream. I'd wake up at any second.

I started pulling my hair, pinching myself, smacking my face, and nothing. I didn't wake up.

"Excuse me miss, are you okay? You're acting weird." A lady about my age asked me about, with uncertainty.

"Ye...yeah I am."

"Okay...you just look confused. And your outfit doesn't really fit in here." She looked me up and down. Not so judging...just honest. "I think you must be at the wrong theater."

"What?" I questioned with doe eyes.

"Your costume just looks like it was probably made for a different show than what we are performing."

I looked down at my dirty crop top and leggings. "Oh yeah...I bet you're right. Thanks."

I started walking away, towards that once narrow, dark, intimidating hallway. The cracked and worn out dolls I've seen before were now put together seamlessly and brighter in color. When I swung open the door, my feelings were entirely different. It was incredibly bright and covered in Polaroid pictures with kids racing each other up and down it. Seemed like a much faster journey through this time around. Coming out of the entrance, my jaw could've dropped. Men in suits, girls in beautiful, colorful dresses with fresh roller sets, finger waves, and pin-curls done looked like something out of a movie.

Lights illumined the mass amount of seats, even second story seats that I hadn't noticed before because of the darkness. Whites, golds, greens, and reds appeared their true shade, expressing exuberance and class throughout the theater.

Making my way back through the lobby was shocking as well. No dust, no cobwebs, no padlock I had to shatter on the door. I even searched the floors for any semblance of chain or lock and there was nothing. Not even a damn trace of dirt. The floors looked like they were just mopped. People flooded the lobby having drinks, snacks, socializing, and even smoking. What did I miss?

I dodged the crowd, pretty well for the most part. Like a fish swimming upstream. That was until I ran into a beautiful, melted chocolate haired young lady with piercing teal eyes with skim painted with freckles, holding a small toddler. I must've woken up the child because she erupted with a cry.

"Oh my god, I'm so sorry I didn't mean to do that." She rested her against her shoulder, and began rocking her back and forth. She patted her back and giggled.

"No no, it's okay. It's an absolute frenzy in here, especially coming out when everyone is coming in."

"Okay, thank you. Again, I'm so sorry." I went to brush the interaction off and walk away, but she grabbed me by the arm.

"Look, you seem a little…frazzled. Can I buy you a drink? The play doesn't start for another half an hour." The nice lady offered with a toothy smile.

I mean, I must've hit my head or something. The place was condemned…right? I didn't imagine all that shit? This place was decrepit as fuck, right? Would a drink clear my head or make it worse? At this point, I wasn't sure. But I swear I fell through the stage and it was fine when I was coming out, so there's definitely a disconnect somewhere. Maybe chit chatting would help. "Sure, I'd love a drink."

"Okay, great." She started to head towards the bar. "My name is Cora, and this is my daughter, Bea, short for Beatrice. I'm here with my friend Alice and her baby boy Calvin. We both had our babies a little bit ago, around the same time, how cool is that?!"

This was definitely a fucking dream. Or maybe a nightmare.

We got a bottle of sauvignon blanc from the bar and chose a cozy little corner couch to sit in. My mind was still spinning. At this point, I couldn't be more convinced I was in a dream, passed out understage in a shut down dump somewhere inhaling asbestos and killing my brain cells while simultaneously having a wicked coma fever dream.

"I'm Ivy, by the way." I smiled, trying to hide my confusion, and my fear. If I assumed I was in a dream, things weren't as bad. Not as scary.

A bouncy, pale blonde girl with chocolate eyes and her giggling baby boy that smelled of fresh baby powder joined us.

"We must have picked up a friend!" Blondie exclaimed.

"This is Ivy! She's stag tonight, I believe. Anyways, I asked her to have a drink with us!" Cora explained.

"Wonderful! I'm Alice, and this Calvin!" She bounced the baby on her hip until he giggled.

"Wow! What cuties you guys have!" I complimented while taking a hefty gulp of my wine, to hopefully subdue the terrifying thoughts and feelings brewing underneath.

"What are you doing here alone? Excited for the play?" Alice chirped excitedly.

"Oh, I was just exploring. I've heard this is the best theater around and wanted to check it out. My date cancelled, but figured I would still have fun by myself! And I made friends now! Would you look at that." It technically wasn't a lie. I was honest. Adjacent. Technically my date did cancel by dying and making me spread her ashes here. Plus, I have heard wonderful things about this theater.

"Bummer about your date, but I'm glad you at least stayed for a drink. And for yourself, of course! I couldn't imagine being a single woman at our age." Alice replied while looking behind her shoulders to scan the crowd. At our age. What a weird thing to say.

"Oh, no kidding!" I answered with a chuckle interrupted by another mega gulp of wine that I could feel slowly begin to numb my fear. "Are you guys like best friends or something?" I feared I knew the answer already.

"Yes, we are! And our husbands are too. It works out nice because we get to have outings like this and our husbands get to pick us up after!" They chuckled and clinked their glasses together.

"Wow…that's really sweet."

"Where are you from? Are you local?" Cora questioned.

"Yes…I am. I guess. Local enough. I live a few hours away but my best friend lived here, so I'm here now too."

"Lived here?" Cora inquisited with a raised brow.

"Yeah…she really liked it, so I thought I would give it a try." How can I even lie my way out of this one? "It was so nice to meet you ladies…but the show is about to start." People began filtering into the theater. "I hope to see you both in the future!" I gave them awkward side hugs and we said our goodbyes as I staggered out through the front door. I wasn't staggering because of the wine, to be clear, but more so just shock. Hopefully they didn't think my going outside before the show was odd.

Every parked car was an old, vintage car. Mine was nowhere in sight.

I went up rows of cars in case I parked somewhere I didn't remember, and still to no avail. My car was nowhere. I felt pressure build up beneath my skin and begin to boil. What the fuck was happening.

Shaking rigor spread throughout my body until I got uncontrollable jitters. My breath began to ring heavy and my heart started racing at an unrecognizable pace. My vision seemed to get clouded with white sparkles and I sprinted into the forest that surrounded us. I ran and ran, essentially towards nothing. Moss and overgrown weeds crowded the ground beneath me, but my pounding feet crushed everything in my line of fire. I dodged boulders and fallen trees as I began getting further consumed into the thicket and congested land full of trees. I ran until I couldn't feel my legs anymore, and I tripped over myself.

The landing struck me hard, like a wall of bricks. I squished the damp earth and fluffy overgrowth between my fingers and felt the realness of the situation, as well as the squelched liquid from the plants coat my skin. Dew spread throughout my clothes and saturated my skin. The smell of dirt and nature felt so real. This wasn't a dream. It couldn't be. I would have woken up by now.

Something hot dripped slowly and ran into my eyelashes. I gingerly tapped it with my fingers, and brought them down to my line of sight. Red, hot, sticky blood. Like Elsie's blood. Dripping down into my eyes.

My pounding heart was the only thing I could focus on until my vision started becoming fuzzy, phasing out into sprinkles of black and white—then nothing.

I awoke to blinding sunlight that made me squint, and chirping birds that sounded as though they were right next to me. I pushed myself up from my palms, and braced myself on my knees.

As I looked around, I could see I was unfortunately still in a forest. Am I really here? Am I hallucinating this? A coma dream would be more pleasant than this, I hope.

I looked down at my hands and saw dried, crusty blood on them. Maybe I was concussed from falling on a rock I saw nearby, and that's what I was experiencing.

I was shaky standing up on my two legs, but I know I also haven't eaten in a while. I began walking. I wasn't sure what direction, but I know anywhere would be better than staying put here.

I felt as though I walked miles passing streams and giant hills, but still to no avail of civilization.

Eventually, I heard the roaring of cars. I could feel my skin starting to burn pretty bad at this point, so I made a run towards where I heard the noise coming from.

I tumbled down a hill and ended up on the side of a two lane road, on the side of a hill. I was never a believer in hitch hiking, but my beliefs, and maybe my sanity, were being tested now.

I began walking on the side of the road, and raised my thumb at everyone who passed by. I felt like it was going to be a lost cause. After all, who picked up hitch hikers?

Took a few tries, but finally someone passed by that slowed down to a halt. I ran to the little red truck that slowed down and pushed open the passenger side door for me.

"Pardon me miss, but you don't look too good." I buckled up my seatbelt as he began driving. I'm gonna get murdered. I feel it.

"I don't feel too great." I murmured.

"Where are you going?" The stranger asked.

"Uh…I don't know. Whatever main city is closest."

"Luckily for you, we aren't too far out from one. What happened?"

"I was at the theater…and I must've hit my head leaving and gotten lost in the woods. Things are a little foggy."

"Oh, man. Should you go to the hospital?"

"I'm not too sure…I think I'm fine. Just a little confused." I looked around in the truck and found a newspaper on the floor by my feet. Perfect. I snatched it up, and my mouth went dry and I felt my jaw open in shock as I scanned the first page. This isn't accurate. A paper from August 1st 1966?

"Anything good on this morning's paper? I haven't had a chance to look." I shuddered at his words.

"This is this morning's paper?"

"Yes ma'am. Just picked it up."

"Oh."

"I'm Ernest, by the way." I slowly faced him speechless.

"Ernest…" I repeated blankly.

"Yes ma'am. Ernest Carmine."

My jaw dropped and my eyes continued to see things my brain couldn't believe. Just like Elsie described. I saw a grocer, a linen store, a couple clothing stores, a diner, a gas station, a hotel, a laundromat, a toy store, a mechanic, a school, and even Sweet Sandi's Bakery—I felt my heart skip a beat, just as Ernest slowly began pulling into a parking spot.

"Listen, my wife works at Sweet Sandi's Bakery. I'm not sure how long you're staying in town, but her mom recently retired and she desperately needs help. It's just her now. I'd be happy to introduce you."

"Oh, wow Ernest. That would be great. Thank you so much for the offer."

I stumbled out of the truck door and made my way alongside Ernest into the bakery. "You just wait right here, and I'll be right back." I took a seat and Ernest waltzed right into the back portion of the bakery. Elsie described everything so crazily perfect. I wondered how she remembered it so spot on. I still halfway felt like this was a hallucination.

I could hear faint chitter chatter, but nothing distinct or clear. A couple minutes later, Ernest strolled out. "My wife is coming out in one second. It was so nice to meet you, Ivy." He extended a hand and shook mine firmly with a warm handshake.

As soon as I saw her, I felt goosebumps rise up fiercely on my skin. Pale skin, ocean blue eyes, strawberry blonde hair, a permanent plump smile, rosy cheeks. She was in a bright, pleated, red skirt and a red and white polka dot collared top that tucked into her skirt. I gasped.

"Hi! I'm…I'm Ivy. Nice to meet you! I apologize for my appearance." I stuttered out, I could feel sweat forming lightly on the back of my neck. I extended my hand out to her.

Elsie gave me a warm, welcoming smile, that I had come to know and love. "It's so nice to meet you. Ernest told me about how he found you…are you okay? How long are you in town for?"

"I think I'm fine. I just think I need some food and water, maybe some rest. I'll be in town for a while, I think. Looking for a new start. Your husband mentioned you might need some help around here?"

"I'd love that! Do you know anything about baking?" She inquired.

"I know a little…I actually learned a lot from someone really important to me, and she also taught me to fall in love with baking, as well." I explained.

"Wonderful! Why don't you go and rest up and take care of yourself and come back here tomorrow around 9:00 in the morning?"

"That sounds amazing! Thank you so much for this opportunity, you won't be disappointed."

"Awesome! I'll see you tomorrow!" She bounced off back to the kitchen, leaving a light dusting of flour behind her.

I walked out the front door into the comfortable, late summer sun. Now what? My growling stomach answered me before my brain could think. I headed to where I saw the diner.

My heart dropped as I remembered the year we were in. I pulled my purse to my side and dug for my wallet. I certainly can't spend money past 1966 here. Huh. On further inspection, it looks like all of the cash Elsie left me was pre 1966. Weird…but helpful. If it wasn't, I would certainly be in some trouble.

I walked inside of Mel's Diner and it was the cutest thing I've seen. Exactly what I would've thought for a vintage diner. Black and white checkered floors, red vinyl booths, chrome and teal accents. I loved it. I wonder if this is where Ernest and Elsie went on their first date for milkshakes.

I walked up to the counter and scanned the menu. "Hi there!" The boasting cashier greeted me.

"Hi! I'll please have a double cheese burger, and fries. Oh, and the largest water you have."

"That will be $1.50." I gave her two dollars and told her to keep the change as I slid gingerly into a booth. My aching head, feet, and entire body really started to sink in. Watching out the window felt like a movie as the people sauntering by wore all these bright wild outfits and intricate hairdos.

Shortly, the cashier dropped my food off to me and man, I've never smelled anything or tasted anything that good. I practically inhaled it all. I wonder if maybe the lack of GMOs in this time period made things taste this much better or what. Even the water was the best I've had.

I peered down the street and saw a couple clothing stores. I suppose I did need some clothes…I guess I've found my next stop. I gathered my dirty napkins and silverware onto my plate, and pushed it towards the edge of the table.

I slipped out and patted my bloated stomach with satisfaction as I walked out and almost skipped to the boutique. As weird, scary, and unrealistic as this situation was…I felt happy. I felt free. Like I could reinvent myself and my life. I still wasn't fully convinced this wasn't some crazy coma dream.

I swung the door open and was greeted by an overly charismatic lady in a bright, swirly, neon colored dress. She asked me for my sizes and she told me to go ahead and take a seat by the dressing rooms.

She handed me hangers and hangers full of bright skirts, pants, dresses, and blouses. I gave this lady quite the fashion show and honestly, a lot of the clothes she picked out I never would've picked out for myself, and I loved them all. She also presented me with a small selection of makeup that she thought I would like, too. At this point I just figured she was trying to upsell me, and it was working.

"I'll take them all!" I chirped to my stylist.

"Woah, really?" She asked, a little shocked.

"Yeah, of course!"

"Well…Excellent!" She rang me up.

"$80!" I handed her the money, said my thanks, and went right next door to the laundromat to wash everything. While I waited for my clothing to wash and dry, I pondered my next steps. I suppose the hotel I spotted on my way into town would be my next best bet. I folded up my clothing neatly, and placed them in stacks back into the bag. Then I made my way to the hotel.

A young guy at the reception area who couldn't have been more than 18 welcomed me in.

"Hi. I'm looking for a room to rent. For a while, I suppose. Full amenities if possible."

I'm not sure what I was expecting for a 1966 hotel room but I was pleasantly surprised. Quaint, but very clean. Fresh wallpaper, full size bed, cheesy looking bathroom, itty bitty kitchen with a fitting mini fridge and small round wooden table with two chairs. Complete with a couple square foot balcony with a glass door.

I lined up my new makeup in the bathroom, and showered the remaining dirt and grime away until the water ran clear and my fingers were pruney. I'd never felt happier for a hot rinse or to be able to brush my teeth. Who knew time travel would make you so gross?

An ancient TV and radio that almost looked like children's toys sat atop a medium sized dresser. Mindlessly, I packed my new wardrobe inside. Air fresheners were stuffed in the back to attempt and cover the smell of must, but it really just created a gross mixture of old plywood and peppermint.

Was this actually real life? My real life? Setting up my new life in a hotel room where I'll be living…and as of tomorrow working for my former old new young best friend…in 1966. Where I'll be solving her sister's murder and her potential future murder. Talk about twisted.

My thoughts were suddenly disrupted by a subtle rapping noise coming from the balcony. I peered behind the curtain, and a cat…a black and white cat was sitting outside the door. Tail flickering with eagerness, head tilted. The coloring almost appeared like a tuxedo... a sharp dressed man. ZZ.

Sliding the door open couldn't have been a bigger invitation for him to come on in. He rubbed against my feet and shins with a loud purr, a greeting of remembrance and familiarity. He leapt onto the bed and made himself at home. I snuggled up against him and let his purrs lull me to sleep. Amongst all this craziness it was so nice to see a familiar face. Regardless the species.

A chime sang as I opened the door to not only my new job, but my first real day in my new world.

"Come on back!" Elsie peered her gleaming, flour dusted face through the swinging door leading to the kitchen as she waved me back. It felt so surreal seeing Elsie's stories she has told me come to life, painted so perfectly once by her words. "I got in early today to get the majority of the work done so we can use today for the basics!" She slid me a notepad scribbled with blue ink.

"Show up with a smile…Be ready to learn…Take constructive criticism…Take creative risks…Have flexible hours…Have fun, because if you have fun, it isn't work.…Give everything your all…Clean up at the end of the day, and throughout the day keep your work area tidy. Well, as tidy as you can…disregard the flour on my face." That last part made me giggle. "Is this my…"

"Think of it as your job description. Or your responsibilities. I'm not really sure what to call it. I've never had to hire someone, or yet alone work with someone other than my mom before. I've been racking my brain all morning trying to come up with a physical list of things. In reality, I just need you to be my second pair of hands. Oh, and I'm thinking $1.75 an hour. It's a little more than minimum wage, is that okay?"

"Oh yeah, totally okay. I'm really excited! Thanks for giving me a chance. Especially to a stranger."

"As silly as this sounds, when Ernest told me what happened I almost felt like it was meant to be. Like he was supposed to run into you so you could work with me. Like fate brought us together." She laughed half heartedly, almost in embarrassment as she wiped the sweat from her brow. "Sorry, that was weird."

I laughed and shook my head. "No no, not at all. I think you're right." Little does she know HOW right she is. "I live…lived in Georgia. I wanted to come here to start over, learn new things. Really live my life on my own accord, I suppose. My really good friend told me this was a great place to live so I took her advice, and here I am!"

"Well, welcome to your first day!" She clapped. "Our mornings start off with checking the calendar we have here hanging on the wall." She gestured to a floral filled, larger than usual sized calendar, tattooed with writing all over it. "This is how we keep track of what special orders are due each day. We normally always have a few. We're the only bakery around, so we stay pretty high in demand. Then every Sunday, I create the menu for the week. We bake fresh everyday, and we have a couple cookies of the week, muffins, breads, cupcakes, whole cakes, stuff like that. Not always everything everyday, but you get the gist. I make an outline of plans and wing it everyday. Sometimes rush orders come in and you need to adjust. Just think on your feet."

"Okay, so that makes sense…but since you said you came in early and did everything today, what are we going to do?"

"You have to learn the basics!" Elsie chirped.

Until three that day, she spent the day explaining all sorts of recipes. She educated me on why brown sugar can be better than regular sugar, how to tell when dough is proofed correctly, what you can substitute eggs or buttermilk with if you run out, what flavors compliment with which, why salt is important in baking, all sorts of things. I took pages of messy, but diligent notes so I could study them and become the best damn assistant baker I could be. She showed me how to check customers out when they pay, which I was quite familiar with…just in a more modern sense. We then wrapped up the day by cleaning the dishes and going over what we would be making tomorrow. Lemon poppyseed cookies, jalapeño cheddar sourdough, blueberry muffins, and chocolate hazelnut cupcakes with peanut butter frosting. We also have a couple special orders tomorrow for some kids' birthday parties. Strawberry cupcakes with vanilla frosting for a little girl named Sherrie, and a blue vanilla cake with dinosaurs for Teddy's first birthday.

"Listen, I had a lot of fun with you today. Forgive me if I'm overstepping, but Ernest and I thought it would be fun for you to come over for dinner. We figured since you don't have anyone here…you could come over and meet some of our friends." Well, I figured I already had met the friends she was referring to…so how uncomfortable would it be? I mean in order to solve the murders, I would have to infiltrate the family at some point.

"That would be so much fun! Is 7:00 okay, so I can go to the hotel and clean up and get ready first?"

"Absolutely! Now, I'll write down the instructions to get to our house from here." I forgot googling my way there wasn't an answer. There was also something else I forgot…I don't have a car. At least it's only 3:00 now, and I have thousands of dollars of cash at the hotel sitting around for me to spend. Now just where do I find a car.

I still feel like I don't look like I belong. I showered and put on a pastel green dress with some flats, but was lost on my makeup. And my hair. I don't look like I belong in the 60s. I still looked put together, green really is my color after all. But I don't know how to do my hair and makeup like the ladies from this time. Maybe Elsie and her friends can teach me how and give me a makeover. Or I can go to a salon, I suppose. That would be a fun adventure in itself. But now, my adventure was to find a car.

Thumbing through a decently new telephone book led me to a place that I thought to be relatively close. Marvelous Automotives. I tore out the page and stuffed that and a thick wad of cash into my small purse before heading out the door.

As strange as I felt doing this, there was also a comfort knowing this was used to be a common way for people to get around. Once I got a few blocks down on Main Street, I popped my thumb up and threw a smile on my face. I was hoping my memory steered me correctly in remembering all the hitchhiking horror stories came out of the mid 70s and 80s, not the 60s. I could be wrong, but I don't have many options at this point. To my surprise, an older lady in a baby blue car, I wasn't sure the make or model, pulled over and waved me in with a gentle smile.

"Hi, honey! Where are you off to?" The older lady greeted me.

"Hi! Thank you for stopping." I brought my purse to the front of me and pulled out the folded up, torn page. "I'd like to go here, if it isn't a bother or too far."

"Absolutely, we pass it on my way home. This is going to sound so silly but I've always wanted to pick up a hitchhiker and it just scares my husband to death. You just looked too nice to drive by and ignore." While I was sure, or at least hoping, she had good intentions—she still gave me the vibe of the old lady in Hansel and Gretal. "But you going here leads me to believe you'll be the one picking up hitchhikers now!" Her joke made her laugh comfortably, and I joined in. The rest of the car ride was full of pleasant small talk. Her name was Ginger, and her husband was Mark. They had three kids together all around my age that lived close to her. Picture perfect happy family.

I waved goodbye to Ginger once we reached my destination, and I started browsing cars in the lot. Colors from this time were so much cooler, at least in my opinion.

Big surprise, the first car that caught my eye was a beautiful emerald color. As I made my way to it, I was cut off by an overly eager salesman with slick hair and a sharp suit.

"Sure looks like you have your eye on something!" He chirped with a smile that was way too big. It almost made him look like a cartoon. I don't think anyone is that happy normally.

"Yeah…that green car over there looks pretty interesting." I slowed my pace down as I walked around him so he could follow.

"Actually, that color is technically called tropic turquoise…but I would agree it looks more green." Man, do I love a know it all. Doesn't everyone.

As I got closer I could tell it was a Chevy Impala, brand spanking new. Well, actually I read it on the car. Close enough. It was so beautiful, nonetheless.

"Can I take it for a test drive?"

"Sure, I bet your husband would love it. Is he around anywhere?" He spun his head around as if to check. Was he hitting on me or did women not buy cars without their husband present? I couldn't tell.

"Nope, just me. I'm car shopping. So can I or what?" I was hoping to keep this interaction as short and sweet as possible, after all I had places to be.

"Oh, uh, sure thing. Let me go get the keys." He scampered away, taking large strides. He was a pretty tall man.

I peered inside and saw it was a manual, thank god I knew how to drive them. Very thankful at this moment that my dad taught me how before he let me drive an automatic. The price on the car was way cheaper than I thought too, $2,799. I'm not sure what I expected, but it was definitely less than what I had anticipated.

Mr. Chipper tossed me the keys and called shotgun ironically as he slid into the passenger seat. You could tell he's been in this industry a while, or at least in the sales industry for a long time.

As I cruised around the block, I was pitched all the goodies of this car along with the new designs and innovations this new model had. I drowned him out with my inner monologue and the hot new tunes the radio was spewing to me. As scary as my situation was, there were so many new things to me. New old things, to learn.

I shifted the car into park and brought myself back to the present, where the salesman was still incessantly trying to make his sales quota.

"I'll take it. Do I have to go in for paperwork?"

"Wow! Good for you! You might have a husband in store for you now, since you don't already!" I was so sick of this man.

"What if I want a wife?" He went silent, and it seemed his tan faded and his skin paled. "I'm actually quite attracted to women."

"Uh, let's go inside and figure out financing." It seemed he couldn't get out of my new ride fast enough.

I met him in front of the car, fumbling through my purse. I met his gaze and slapped $2,800 in his palm.

"Just show me where to sign. I have no interest going inside. "

Driving to Elsie's was actually a piece of, well, cake. Ironically. A few cars were parked out front, which confirmed my idea that Alice, Cora, John, and Dusty were here. It would be interesting to explain how I met them already. Unfortunately for me, I can't just say fate, because that's what it is. And I have to pretend like I don't know they all know each other.

Knocking on the door only led to more commotion inside, which could be heard outside. A little girl opened the door, who must've been around 8. Give or take a few years. That must've been Sissy.

"Are you Elsie's new friend?" A small, inquisitive voice pondered.

"I am! My name is Ivy. What's your name?"

"Sissy. I have a brother Danny. Want to come meet him?"

"Sure! I'd love to!" Creaking the screen door open led Elsie to bounce to the door and greet me with an overly excited hug.

"I'm so glad you came! I see you met Sissy already. That's Ernest's sister. Her brother Danny is running around out back. I have some more people you need to meet too! Our best friends." She bounced into the kitchen and pointed out everyone along with their kids and spouses.

"Oh my God!" Cora almost choked on her wine. "We met at the theater! Remember? Alice, remember?!" Elsie and the boys looked confused, as I tried to do at first as well.

"Wow! You're right! So sorry I didn't recognize you at first!" I gave them both big hugs and tried to brush past the small talk of that night and how I happened to get acquainted with Elsie and Ernest.

"Sheesh. I said this earlier to Ivy, but this just keeps feeling like fate more and more! Like the universe pulling us together!" I nodded in agreement, but for what it's worth I'm getting tired of hearing that, and thinking it.

The rest of the night just felt so easy. So peaceful. We sat down for a big family meal, shared laughs and drinks. Played with the kids until they all got worn out and crashed hard, even the babies. We ended the night by the fire pit outside under the brightest stars I've ever seen. I'd like to think my mental clarity, fresh start, and new outlook on life has something to do with that but in reality I'd have to guess it's the lack of pollution back in this time period. The boys downed some Budweisers, and all the ladies shared a few bottles of wine. Slowly, the couples dipped out. Alice and Dusty left first, and then Cora and John followed their lead. Shortly after that, Ernest went to bed and left Elsie and I outside. Strangely enough, I didn't feel like I was overstaying my welcome. I felt like I was perfectly at home, hanging out with an old friend or even a sister. Something in this crazy world made sure our spirits would dance and mesh together, in any lifetime, I suppose. She opened up to me about everything. Ernest's parents, siblings, and their drama. Elsie's parents, the bakery, everything. I felt up to date on everything.

"My sister and her friend went missing a few years ago in New York. We don't really talk about it anymore. Just like we don't talk about Ernest's dad probably pulling Charlotte's plug and then going on the run. I think…I think they got murdered. I haven't said that out loud before. I think someone killed them and the cops gave up and it won't be solved. And more than anything in my life, I want to know what happened. I fear that's something I'll never get to find out." Elsie sniffled and took another huge gulp of her wine, trying to hide the inevitable tears.

"This might sound crazy. But what if we try and solve it?" I dodged eye contact and Elsie barked out a laugh so ferociously it startled me. She clapped her hand over her mouth, to keep quiet just a little bit, and not wake everyone inside. Or the neighbors for that matter. "No, I'm serious. We could go to New York and we could go and try and figure out what happened to them."

"Ernest isn't a controlling man. But in one thousand years he would never let me go. First off, he'd think I'm crazy as hell and secondly, he'd be so afraid something would happen to me just like Goose and Sally. I don't even know what I'd do with Danny and Sissy."

"Easy fix. You tell Ernest we're going there to study some of the fancier bakeries, new techniques, and tools, that New York has to offer. Research for business purposes. I had a friend who passed away before I came here, which kind of sparked my new start. Anyways, she left me a lot of money. I can fund our trip no problem, and Ernest can stay at home for a week or so. He's been working like a dog, like you said, so he might not mind cutting back his hours a tad for a mini vacation. He's the owner so he can make that call. Plus he can work while the kids are in school and just come home early. I'm sure Dusty and John can close down shop for him at the end of the day too. They seem trustworthy and reliable. I bet your mom wouldn't mind coming out of retirement for a week to run the bakery, too. It will give her some meaningful purpose. She probably would actually love it. It all works out perfectly, see?"

"Ivy, that's crazy. Where would we even start? No…not even that. I could never ever ask you to do that for me. For my family. And from someone I practically just met."

"You aren't asking me. I'm offering. You keep saying this feels like fate, so maybe this is the reason fate wanted us to meet. To meet someone crazy enough to help you find out what happened to your sister and her friend. All I'm saying is to think about it. Sleep on it for a bit, and let me know. Offer will still stand. On that note, I think I'm now sober enough to drive home. We have an early day tomorrow, so I'm going to head out. Thanks for everything, Elsie. I had a great night." We hugged goodbye and said our goodnights before an extra quiet drive back to the hotel let my mind run rampant with where to begin.

Chapter Seven

The warm jingling of the doorbell was almost as welcoming as the smell of hot, fresh, sourdough bread spilling out of the kitchen. Elsie was pulling a batch of the crusty and perfectly proofed jalapeño cheddar loaves out of the oven and tore into one of the cooler loaves with her bare hands.

"Quality control, right? Plus we need breakfast too!" She handed be a fluffy chunk of bread to me, and I dug right in.

"What a great way to start the morning! This is absolutely delicious. Totally gonna fly off the shelf."

"Okay, this is what I'm thinking for the day. I will handle the two special orders and the customers up front. You will make the cookies, muffins, and cupcakes. When you're done with that, you'll start prepping stuff for the rest of the work day. Deal?"

"Absolutely. Deal." We shook on it jokingly.

The day really flew before I knew it, and I was impressed with how quickly I caught on. If I had to give credit to something, I'd have to say it's Elsie's magical time traveling pixie dust, or something like that. Around three we wrapped up and polished off the rest of the dishes before closing down shop for the night.

"Want to grab a milkshake with me before I go home?" Elsie held the door for me as she exited, then looked back, pondering my answer. I tried to stifle back a chuckle, but failed.

"You work in a place called Sweet Sandi's. You are surrounded by sugar constantly. All of your recipes make batches the size of a baker's dozen, that way you can, ahem, quality control. Now, the first second off work you want to get a milkshake? Crazy."

"What am I supposed to do, ask you to get a water with me somewhere? Now that's crazy. Very lame too, may I add."

"Fair point. In that case, yes I'm in. Mel's Diner?"

"Look at you, getting to know the town already."

We strolled inside the bustling diner, filled with students just getting out of school for the day and placed our order up front. Elsie ordered a chocolate malt and I decided on a banana milkshake.

We scooted into a booth in the back away from the rowdy teens. I felt like I was living in that diner scene from Grease. It was incredibly difficult to monitor what I said to Elsie so I didn't slip up and mention something from anytime after 1966.

"I've been wanting to say something all day. I thought about what you said yesterday. Honestly, it's just absolutely absurd. We have no clue what we're doing, and it's preposterous to even think about lying to Ernest. Let alone, leaving him with the kids to go on some literal wild goose chase. It's the craziest, most insane idea someone brought up to me in a serious matter before." Elsie shook her head with hand gestures just as dramatic as the words that poured out of her mouth.

"Listen, Elsie, I'm sorry. I—"

"And I want to do it more than anything. You didn't let me finish. I want us to go to New York and figure out what happened to Goose and Sally." My jaw literally fell open with shock, and Elsie took a giant slurp of her milkshake.

"Oh—wow. I wasn't expecting that. That fast. Or at all."

"It was so crazy, I thought it just might work. Absolute worst case scenario—we try and we don't get anywhere. We spend the rest of the time there enjoying good food, looking at The Statue of Liberty, oohing and ahhing at tall buildings, studying bakeries, and just having a vacation. Best case scenario, we do the damn thing. So, are you still in now that I am or what?"

"Of course I am. Where do we start first?"

"I guess we start by me going home and whipping out this…educational New York City bakery tour idea to Ernest and then go from there."

The rest of the night went smoothly. We went our separate ways, and I navigated my way all around town looking for a grocery store. The cheapest grocery trip I've ever had, by the way. I didn't get anything too crazy, just some odds and ends to keep in the hotel. Mostly non perishables and bathroom supplies. I didn't want to get too much fresh produce or meat, considering my hopeful, upcoming road trip.

The next day at work I was expecting Elsie to tell me all about her little chat with Ernest, but she didn't. We talked about everything else, just not that. I worked on forming the cookie and bread dough we didn't use yesterday, but made and stored for later today and tomorrow. I also whipped up French vanilla cupcakes with a plum frosting. Once I finished up those, I helped Elsie with the special orders. We had three for the day. All two tier cakes. A spice cake with cream cheese frosting, an orange cake with white chocolate frosting, and an earl gray angel food cake with a whipped cream frosting. I manned up front the whole day, too. I was beginning to feel like quite the little baker. As satisfied as I was in that aspect, I was curious why Elsie was pretending our conversation yesterday didn't happen. Or at least didn't acknowledge it. We closed down shop at four and I strolled back to my new home base. It was so beautiful outside today, I couldn't help but walk in this morning.

The air on my skin felt different. The wind blowing my hair, and the sun kissing my skin. It was like everything was more vibrant. I couldn't help but think I have a purpose now. Of course, in the future…or my present time, I had my apothecary, and that's wonderful and all. But nothing was holding me there, I felt like I was just floating. Existing. Now I have a new outlook, a new mission, a new appreciation of life. Plus, little ZZ somehow was also a time traveler, too. That was one of the many otherworldly mysteries I couldn't even begin to decipher. And there he was waiting for me, stretched out in front of my door, like my own little trip wire. There wasn't a way I could sneak into my hotel room without waking him up to follow me, not that I would want that. My fuzzy friends' company is the thing keeping me grounded at this point, in a way. A tangible thing I can hold on to from the future that reminded me it was all real, it all happened, and everything is fine.

Luckily for ZZ, I accounted for him during my grocery shopping yesterday. So when I made myself a tuna salad sandwich for dinner, ZZ got a tin of tuna, too. We cozied into bed and I snuggled with him like he was my old teddy bear. I'll tell ya, that's the most restful night's sleep I have ever gotten.

The rest of the week ran smoothly, routine. Still no mention of the New York trip. I brainstormed and thought all about it, though.

Sunday was my first day off, so I spent the morning and afternoon exploring my new little town. I went into all the local stores, drove down all the quaint streets, I even packed myself a little bag full of first aid supplies, lunch, and water to take on a light hike with me. I wouldn't call it a mountain by any means, but it was more like a glorified, densely forested, trek up a hill. You could see the trails underneath the canvas of golden sunlight, but they certainly weren't broken in enough to see during the night. After a few miles, the crashing of a waterfall roared loudly enough to drown out the singing of the leaves rustling and the birds chirping, so I followed that noise. I settled down on a rock alongside the outskirts, and slipped off my boots and socks so I could dip my feet into cool water. Lunch never tasted so good. After fueling up, the hike back to the car seemed so drawn out, but not in a bad way. Maybe I was just savoring it more. The day was still early, but hiking was really kicking my ass. While I liked nature and things from nature, outdoorsy was never a word used to describe me.

Showering off the grime and finally standing still after that long hike, it made my legs feel like jello. It was a struggle to towel off and robe up before collapsing into bed, with my trusty steed ZZ of course. Slowly, the whirl of the fan and white noise from outside lulled me into a cozy, late afternoon nap. That was until pounding at the door woke me up. I wasn't even sure how long I slept. I could feel my blood start rushing and pounding through my veins. Who could it be? I leapt out of bed and quietly lunged at the peephole. Oh god, it was Elsie. I bet my quick afternoon nap turned into sleeping through the whole night, and part of my shift too! I fumbled with the locks furiously and swung the door open in panic of the lecture—or firing, that I was about to get.

"Elsie, before you say anything, I'm so so sorry. I took a hike on my day off, which isn't even like me in the first place. It totally wiped me out and I laid down to take a nap and it must've drawn out into my shift. I'm so sorry you had to come looking for me. This is so embarrassing. Please give me a second chance, don't fire me yet." Elsie stood in the doorway like a deer in headlights, before letting out a giant laugh.

"Okay, calm down." She barely mustered out without laughing. "It is still Sunday, and it's 6:00 pm. So take a breather and invite me inside your hotel room. With your…cat?"

"Oh yeah, come in. Sorry. Wow, I feel so much better. This is ZZ, my little buddy." He let out a mew of agreement. She took a seat on my bed next to ZZ and scratched his belly, which he was more than happy to oblige.

"Okay, I haven't been avoiding talking about our plan. Well, I have, but with Ernest, not you. I wanted to wait until we had a day off together to really sell it to him, so I did today." My eyebrows raised and I waved her on, hoping she'd continue faster. "I'm shocked I'm saying this, but he was supportive. Like really supportive, and excited. And I told him we're leaving tomorrow."

"I'm sorry, say that last part one more time. I don't think I heard you right."

"I told him that we're leaving…tomorrow. My mom was even thrilled I asked her to help at the bakery. I think it gave her a sense of purpose…or feeling needed. We are officially a go to solve this thing!" She pulled out a bottle of wine wedged in her bag and started jumping. "Oh, and I'm spending the night. We need an early start tomorrow. Well, we don't need one but I want to get a jump on things. My anxiety and thoughts have been keeping me awake anyways."

"That's a lot to digest…but yeah I'm in, obviously! Now let's crack open that bottle and celebrate!"

Chapter Eight

The next morning, I put a hefty amount of cat food and water outside to give ZZ some back stock while I was on my little getaway. I gave him a smooch and shooed him outside. Elsie and I decided on essentials only, so she didn't bring that much. Clothes, a small amount of makeup, and travel sized bathroom supplies. So I packed the same into a bag I picked up on my first day here, along with my purse, cash, a notebook, and a pen. We decided to drive my car, so we packed up the backseat, and she started off at the wheel. By the time we were ready to hit the road, the sun just finished rising up and began casting beautiful, golden rays all around us. We stopped by Sweet Sandi's to grab a cup of coffee and a muffin or two for the road. Plus, Elsie wanted me to meet Sandi. I wanted to meet her, too. Sandi was very sweet, but you could tell losing Goose made her a little empty. She would smile, but it felt hollow. She was missing a piece of her. Sandi wished us well and safe travels, and said she couldn't wait to hear about our time in New York City. We thanked her again, and she waved us on our way.

After savoring our cups of coffee and chowing down on some delicious muffins, I decided it was time to make a plan.

"So, you talk and I'll write. I want to know everything you know about Goose and Sally since they went to New York. Even if you think details are irrelevant and don't matter, I still want to know them. Start from the beginning."

"Alright. Goose is three years older than me, so she's 26. She's bold, warm, adventurous, flirtatious, creative, and a risk taker. She makes friends with everyone, and she loves attention from everyone. I don't want to use the word promiscuous to describe her, but Goose always had multiple boyfriends lined up for her."

"Goose is her real name?"

"Yeah, believe it or not. Goose Elizabeth Buford."

"Huh, I always thought it was a nickname."

"Always?"

"Always since you told me. Anyways, go on."

"Her and Sally went to New York City to pursue fashion and fashion design. They both got internships at a company called Silhouette Society. They opened up a few years before Goose and Sally moved there. They really loved their wild kind of style and design. They design clothes far too risqué for casual street wear or outings. Very much so fashion forward, runway, magazine, stuff like that. Avant garde, crazy outfits. Their whole deal is showing a silhouette. That could mean skin tight clothes, exposing a lot of skin, or exaggerating shapes of the body with crazy shoulder pads or wings or additions like that. That certainly isn't very common or acceptable in most places, and that's why Goose and Sally were drawn to them. They believed Silhouette Society was like peering through a doorway to the future of fashion design. Do I agree? Certainly not, but I wasn't going to tell that to them. Really cool to look at, but not practical by any means. They would draw out designs, help sew, pitch ideas, get people ready for the runway, assist their bosses, stuff like that. Of course they could be exaggerating, but Goose said she was the front runner of all the interns, and Sally was right behind her. There were a lot of interns, like thirty or something, but in their specific group there were only six of them. So four others they worked directly with. I know both of them were juggling multiple men, but only two were mentioned by name. Goose's favorite suitor was Vince, and Sally's was Max. They're brothers or cousins or friends or something. They knew each other before Sally and Goose came around. The girls shared a small apartment, and normally I wouldn't be able to remember the address, but it was really easy. It's above a pizza restaurant called Doughy Joey's, not too far from her work in the city. There was a dive bar close to where they lived too, where the girls frequented. I don't know the name of it, but it was walking distance from their apartment. That's really everything I can think of." I took shorthand notes hastily, trying to scribble all of the information she was spewing out down before I got lost in the tale. In the back of the notebook, I also jotted down some facts about Elsie, and future Elsie, to see if I can find a link between why both of them were potentially murdered by the same person. Of course, Elsie isn't one hundred percent sure Goose and Sally were killed. I think she still held out a small amount of unspoken hope. However, deep down I'm positive she knew as well as I knew if we did figure out what happened to them, it probably wasn't good. Fatal, really.

"Okay. Here's what I think we should do. Let's go by Doughy Joey's first, speak to them, check out the apartment, find a place to stay nearby, get settled in and go from there. Maybe we'll have time to visit their work today, too. Or maybe the pizza shop employees can give us another lead we can check out."

"That's exactly what I was thinking…and maybe we'll pass a bakery on the way, too."

"You have the biggest sweet tooth out of any person to have ever existed. I'm sure of it. You are like the female version of Willy Wonka."

"Who's Willy Wonka?"

"Gene Wilder? Johnny Depp?"

"Ivy, I'm so lost…"

"Oh, sorry. I meant a book. Charlie and the Chocolate Factory."

"Oh the book! Yes, I've heard of that book, but I haven't read it, so I don't think I get the references that well." God, I'm so dumb. That book just came out a few years ago and hasn't even been made into a movie yet.

"You should read it. It's gonna be a big deal one day in the future, I guarantee it. How long did you tell Ernest we were going to be gone?"

"I didn't tell him an exact number, I said a week or two and he was totally fine with it. He just wants me to try and call him once a day to keep him in the loop."

"Perfect. He seems a lot more relaxed about this than I thought he would."

"Yeah, me too. But hey, I'll take it. Regardless of what happens, I'm just glad you decided to go on this crazy adventure with me."

We switched a little less than halfway there, and the drive was much smoother than I expected it to be. I didn't realize I couldn't really navigate using a map, which Elsie made sure to roast me about. Needless to say, Elsie was a better navigator and I was a better driver.

The streets were pretty packed in New York City, but we took our time and gawked at all the skyscrapers and colorful signs and billboards plastering the streets. Coming here now makes me wish I saw the city in my previous time period, So, I could compare it. Alas, this was my first time in New York. Still, no Twin Towers. I guess the World Trade Center wasn't built yet. Maybe I'll never see them.

Something I've been beginning to think of more and more is how my time traveling excursion will affect things to happen in the future. Or, if they will. But the butterfly effect has to have been thought of for a reason, right? I wonder if anyone else has time traveled and what ripples they caused? I suppose stressing out about it won't do me any good because I'm already here, so it's best to just push it to the back of my mind and not distract me from the reason I came here in the first place.

We pulled up across the street from Doughy Joey's and I could feel Elsie's aura and demeanor change. I wouldn't say she was getting nervous, but it all started to feel very real to her, I think. We were about to go into one of Goose's last known locations.

The breeze chilled us getting out of the car, but I think the majority of my goosebumps came from the anticipation I was feeling. As we approached the front of the door, the smell of pizza grease wafted all around us, making both of our stomachs growl.

"We should get pizza, right? It'll give us a good excuse to chat with people while we're here." Not that I needed to convince Elsie, because she was practically drooling.

A jingling doorbell alerted the staff that new customers have entered the building, and some looked up with a smile and gave us a brief hello. We confidently made our way up to the counter and ordered two slices of pepperoni pizza, and took our seats at the bar.

"How are you two ladies doing today?" An older waitress filling up a coffee machine with tap water asked.

"Oh, we're doing great! Very excited to try your pizza, we've heard some great things about you guys! Just stopping in before we look for a place to stay, we came to the big city on vacation." I decided to take the lead. The waitress adjusted her crooked name tag, which read Donna.

"In my opinion, I think we are the best pizza joint around. My brother owns the place, and I've been waitressing and helping him manage for years. We're the oldest pizza place around here, too." She scooped generous heaps of coffee into a filter.

"That's great for you guys. Say, since you've been here for so long do you know Goose and Sally? I believe they rent the apartment above your restaurant. Goose is my friends sister." I gesture to Elsie, and the waitress froze and pursed her lips. Thick, viscous looking coffee began dripping out into the old, stained coffee pot. She let out a deep sigh and shook her head.

"They moved in summer of 1961, which I'm sure you know. They were both lovely girls. A little crazy, but so much fun and so outgoing. We loved them like family. Not afraid to be bolder than most ladies. Normally after work on Fridays, they would go to a place adequately named The Dive Bar right down the road. Once they were done they would come roaring in here after they drank like fish with friends, guys, random people they met, and coworkers. They all would order loads of pizza, and even try to buy us some, as well. Everyone loved them and boy, they sure made me laugh. On busy days, they would bring us good coffee, not this crap we make. Sometimes they even brought us dinner they had leftovers of, or even just takeout." A younger fellow slid our slices across the bar along with some napkins and gave us a nod. We wasted no time digging in. "Anyways, one day they were here, and the next they were gone. We were expecting their Friday shenanigans like usual and nobody came in that night. About a week went by and we hadn't heard from them. I know work was getting crazy for those two, so we didn't read too much into it, until they missed payment when the rent was due. We weren't mad or nothing, but they were never a minute late paying. We went up to the apartment just to check on them, and they weren't there. The door wasn't even locked and the place was a mess. I wasn't sure if they were just messy girls or someone could've broken in, but it gave me a bad feeling in my gut. I went ahead and called the cops, then that was basically the end of it. A few months went by and we didn't hear anything. My brother Joey and I cleaned up the place and packed it into boxes. Nobody lives up there now. We've been meaning to clean it out and remodel, but the business has been booming so we haven't had any time to do so. I wonder everyday where those two went, or what happened to them. What I always found odd was that their car sat out front for months, and one day it was gone. Probably to impound. Their flavors of the month, Vince and Max came by to see them because they hadn't heard from the girls either. Their coworkers even came. It's like they just vanished into thin air." The corners of Donna's mouth pointed downward, and her eyes began to look heavy as she examined Elsie's disappointed face. "I'm sorry, I'm sure that's not what you guys wanted to hear. But listen, why don't I give you guys the key to the apartment? You can go through the boxes we packed up and you can stay there for the length of your vacation." Donna fumbled with the cash drawer until it opened and she pulled out a key, then tossed it our direction.

"Donna, that would be so wonderful. Thank you so much, and thank Joey too. We should only be here for a week or two." Elsie's eyes glistened with gratitude, and maybe a hint of sadness. I pulled some cash out of my purse and handed it to Donna. By the look of shock on her face, I figured a couple hundred would be enough to cover rent and then some. I snatched the key off the table and we said our goodbyes. We unloaded the car and followed Donna's directions to the apartment. Alley to the left of the building, and then the second door on the left.

The door opened with a cloud of dust poofing out and causing us to cough in unison. This place definitely did need a good remodel. Creaky stairs were splintered with primarily flaked off paint leading up to the apartment. I think the paint was once white, but now was coated with enough dirt and dust to appear a light gray or blue.

The staircase opened up into one, medium sized room. You could tell it was used as a living room and dining room. The room was mostly void of furniture, excluding a couch and small table. There was one bathroom to the right of the staircase and two small bedrooms on either side of the main room. A quaint kitchen was tucked in the back left corner. A large window lined the back wall across from the staircase. Near that window, we saw the boxes. We counted thirteen of them. Goose and Sally's whole New York life fit into just thirteen boxes.

We placed our belongings in each of the rooms, and met in the middle to divvy up how we were going to start sifting through their belongings. Nine boxes were full of things like clothes, blankets, decorations, stuff like that. Nothing too juicy. The other four were chock full of drawings, designs, sewing patterns, sewing equipment, material, pictures, and more personal memorabilia. Sally's drawings seemed to be more on a retro gothic side. I see what the company valued in her. I've never seen anything like it. Imagine Victorian gothic, with odd peekaboos of color and a lot of asymmetry. Goose's drawings seemed to be very bold, with no real blacks or whites. Vibrant, bold, loud designs and fabrics. A lot of accentuation on body figure. She outlined things in marker where she wanted the fabric to accentuate the body. Besides upcoming fashion knowledge, after hours of going through everything, unpacking, and repacking, we essentially got nowhere. No new clues on where to go next. It was getting pretty late, so we decided to make a plan for tomorrow.

"Where do you think we should go first tomorrow?" Elsie inquired.

"I say Police, Silhouette Society, then figure it out from there."

"I think we need to find Vince and Max, too."

"Agreed. I'm sure we will get some leads on where to look for them tomorrow. Overall, not a bad start."

We got food again at Joey's downstairs for dinner, and ate on the floor of the apartment brainstorming more theories. Shortly after that, we got ready for bed and went our separate ways. It was hard to believe this was my real life now, and I wasn't playing some crazy role in a movie.

Chapter Nine

The morning came swiftly and we were both woken up by the sound of car horns, angry drivers yelling, and chitter chatter along the street. Since today we were going to Silhouette Society, we decided to wear some bolder outfits. Elsie selected a form fitting, knee length leopard print dress she paired with red heels, a cherry purse, and crimson lips. I, on the other hand, wore my crop top from the future along with a houndstooth skirt, moss colored heels, and a forrest green purse. Elsie helped me do my hair more "fashionably" as she put it. She was not a fan of the high, messy bun which happened to be my go to.

Looking at a map Elsie had gotten before we left for the trip, we sketched out our route for the day and solidified our plans. So around nine, we were out the door and in the car.

"Do you want to take the lead at the police station?" I slithered out of our parking spot and peered over to the passenger seat to get a glance at Elsie.

"Yeah, I think I will. And then you take the lead at Silhouette Society." Elsie contemplated before telling me.

"And then the bakery after? Or before?" Elsie pulled out her neatly folded map again, and examined it.

"Well, we pass the bakery first, so let's go there initially. We can even grab a box of pastries for the police station, too. I bet they'd like that. Unless they think it's bribery. I need some liquid courage anyways." Her answer made me chuckle.

"It certainly isn't bribery, just a nice gesture. What do you mean liquid courage? I don't think bars are open yet."

"I meant coffee. Liquid caffeine courage. To get me amped up." We both laughed as we continued up the street that was packed like sardines in a tin. Eventually, we spotted Twisted Teacup on the right, and we were lucky enough to find parking out front.

The outside of the building was nothing spectacular. Just rows and rows of shops lining both sides of the street, nothing unique about any of them except the names on their windows.

However, inside was incredible. And it was packed. Imagine a fancy garden tea party inside of an expensive dollhouse. That's what it looked like. Bakers were loading all sorts of fresh tea cakes, croissants, biscuits, and scones into shelves on the back wall as we filed in, and took our spot in line.

"I've always wanted to make croissants, but I never have." Elsie muttered. I wasn't sure if she meant to say it out loud.

"Well, perfect. There's your bakery research to report back to Ernest for the day. When you get to the front of the line, tell them you run a bakery in a small town in North Carolina and you are here doing research." Just like that, we were at the front of the line.

We got two dozen assorted tea cakes for the cops, two lattes, two plain croissants, and two hazelnut Irish cream biscuits dipped in chocolate ganache. While they were preparing our order, one of the bakers actually invited Elsie to go in the back with him when he heard her plea to the cashier. She gleefully went out of sight with him to the back, and I just stayed posted up waiting for our order.

Good thing she popped back out when she did because I was having one hell of a time trying to carry everything myself. My saving grace was that if I dropped everything, nobody would record it and put it online. She was smiling from ear to ear as she came up and scooped the lattes off the counter for me. She scampered ahead and held the door open for me behind her.

"Well? I'm waiting!" I pushed as we got situated in the car. I divided up our treats and she gleefully pulled a scrap of paper out of her purse and placed it on the dash.

"They just gave you their croissant recipe?"

"Yup, they were happy to spread the knowledge. They thought it was so cool I owned a bakery so young and was traveling around to grow my ideas and recipe bank."

"That will have to be the first thing we make when we get back, then." We both gulped down our lattes and inhaled our breakfast before we continued on our route to the police station.

Precinct 12 looked almost like it was put together with legos. Bright red bricks formed a perfectly neat cube with symmetrical windows over the facade. Not too much commotion outside, but inside was where the action was. Phones were incessantly ringing, papers were rustling from one desk to another, harsh clanking of typewriter keys, it was almost beautiful. Precinct 12 symphony.

"Can we help you?" An old man perched front and center at his desk grunted our way. His desk blocked off the majority of the rest of the precinct. He was like the riddling troll guarding a bridge—you may not enter.

"Yeah, good morning." Elsie fluffed up her hair and approached him, closing the gap between them. "I'm here to follow up on a missing persons report from a few years ago. I wanted to see if there was any progress made." She then placed the box of goodies on his desk and popped it open for him. "We brought you guys some goodies to sweeten up your day, too." She flashed a toothy smile at him. If I didn't know better, I would think she's flirting. The guardian troll was flustered, probably taken aback by her beauty and forwardness.

"Absolutely, uh, okay." He fumbled around grabbing a clean sheet of paper and a pen. "Can I get your name, the missing persons name, as well as your relation?"

"Elsie Carmine is my name. Goose Buford and Sally Mell went missing in 1963 after moving here in 1961. I am Goose's sister, and Sally was her roommate and best friend." Troll took notes avidly as Elsie spoke, then stood up briskly.

"Ladies, take a seat." He gestured to the benches lining the hallway along the entrance. "Someone will be with you shortly."

We did as he said, and I could almost feel the atoms around Elsie vibrating with anticipation. She was rapidly bouncing her knee and fidgeting around with her hair and clothes.

"Liquid courage getting to you?" I smiled, attempting to make light of the situation. She giggled.

"I guess so. It gets the job done though." She shrugged it off with a smile.

The guardian troll returned back to his desk followed by the single most attractive man I have ever seen. He stood tall, well over six feet. I'm assuming six foot four. I could tell he was heavily muscled, even with a full uniform on. Slick, jet black hair along with a thick cookie duster mustache and heavily tanned skin made his eyes appear like pools of melted amber. He confidently paced over to us, and I literally think my heart stopped beating for a second.

"Miss Carmine?" Elsie nodded. "My name is Detective De Luca. If you follow me back to the conference room I'd be happy to talk to you about your sister." He turned around and gestured that she follow him. Every word he said melted together with a thick, New York accent.

Elsie popped up, and paused before taking a step. "Wait, can my friend Ivy come with me? For moral support, you know. It just can be…so hard to talk about." She batted her thick eyelashes at him, and Detective De Luca just peered at me, and gestured for me to come with them as well.

We followed him through a maze of desks into a barren back room labeled Conference 1. Shuttered blinds hung from the windows, hiding nothing from the outside except a long oak table lined with chairs, and a coffee pot half full of burnt coffee with a stack of paper cups beside it. Detective De Luca pulled two chairs out for us to sit in, and he circled around and sat across from them. We joined him at the table, and he placed a folder in front of him and flopped it open. I must've been too busy checking him out to notice he even had a folder when he came and got us in the lobby.

"I'd like to start off by saying, I'm very sorry that we haven't found Goose and Sally yet." He cleared his throat. "Detective Bates initially handled their case underneath Sergeant Blackwell. Those were the main two people overlooking their case and they reported to Lieutenant Penn, who in turn reports to Captain Sullivan, who finally reports to Chief Cutler. Bates retired in 1964, and that was officially when the case went cold. Not because people gave up, but he and Blackwell worked on that case and exercised every idea they could think of until they hit a dead end. Since then, we have been at a standstill. With that being said, unfortunately, crime has been on a rise recently and I have been assigned the task of going through all the cold cases since 1960 until now to make us look better. The hope there is to give people the answers they need. People need heroes in the world, and unfortunately a lot of people are beginning to see us all as villains. I cannot speak of active cases with civilians, but since this case is cold, I am able to talk about this relatively freely, with some boundaries, with you both. Keeping that in mind, I have solved all cold cases that I was assigned, except one that I am in the process of wrapping up, until the date of their disappearances. That means Goose and Sally's cases will officially be reopened within the next couple days. It's pretty impeccable timing you two showed up when you did, because once it's reopened, our lips are sealed." I furiously scribbled down notes in our investigative journal, trying to write neatly enough to understand later, but also keep up my pace with him. Our sexy detective really was a fast talker.

"So what can you tell us?" Elsie questioned him. Unfortunately for us, he told us everything we already knew. We did gain the last names of Vince and Max—Vince Rossi and Max Amato. We discovered that the car they shared, a Chrysler Newport, was never recovered or seen again as far as the police knew of. That would make sense if they went missing on the drive to Elsie's for Christmas. However, according to Donna their car sat outside of Doughy Joey's for months and she assumed the cops took it to impound, but Detective De Luca said they never got it. Which in turn means…they never even got on the road to come home for Christmas. We shared that information with him, and we concluded that they probably never left New York. That confirms what we suspected, there was foul play. It didn't come as a surprise, but it still felt more real now. More official. Elsie took that surprisingly well, all things considered. Other than that, no new information. He assured Elsie once fresh eyes took a look over it, AKA his eyes, they would get some new lead or information.

"Ladies, I would like to say something to you both. I get the sense you didn't drive all the way here just to ask about the case when you could've called. Especially when you both are from out of state. I hope I am wrong, but I sincerely hope you stay away from this investigation and let us do our job. We cooperated with you today in hopes of easing your mind, not feeding it fuel. Wanting information is one thing, and doing something with it is another. I fear this is dangerous water to tread in, especially for two solo women in New York City. Please, stay out of our way." Detective De Luca stood up from his chair and opened the door to the conference room, and we followed his lead up into the front door.

"Thank you ladies for stopping in today. Please…be safe. Take care." He closed the door behind us, and we both looked at each other.

"Police never got the car." I stated.

"The car sat outside of Doughy Joey's for months." Elsie followed up.

"Detective De Luca was super hot, right?"

"So hot." We both laughed.

"I wonder who has the car now." We both pondered before making our way into the car to head to Silhouette Society.

I was surprised how similar and indistinguishable all of the buildings looked around here. Silhouette Society was no exception. Tall, bland, symmetrical, lots of windows. However, if you looked closely into the windows, you saw a different story. A colossal amount of fabric, all in varying textures and colors, strung about on racks and layered in shelves. Each waiting to get chosen for a unique design. Bustling employees rushing about holding folders of rustling papers. Some probably full of fashion we would come to see in the 70s and 80s.

We strolled into the front, French doors. We both were dressed the part, and we walked with an air of confidence to really sell ourselves. Every employee we saw was dressed in the most unique and bold of fashions. If I saw them in my time, I would still feel the same. A receptionist with a full face of makeup on and a Mohawk made of messy buns looked up from her task, which seemed to be a crossword puzzle. Her steel, rather intimidating face melted into something much more warm and welcoming.

"Hello pretty ladies!" She boasted. "I'm Amy, and welcome to Silhouette Society, where the future is our fashion! How can I help you?" She stood up, and towered over us. She was an incredibly tall lady, and her chunky high heels just added to that category. She wore a tight, shin length plaid skirt with a long slit, that she complimented with an oversized Rolling Stones shirt and gold jewelry.

"Hi!" I made sure to match her enthusiasm. "I'm Ivy, this is my friend Elsie. Her sister used to work here with her roommate. We were hoping to speak to some of her old colleagues. Maybe you can point us in the right direction?"

"I'd love to! I've worked here for a very long time so that's something I'll be able to do. What are their names?" Amy inquisited.

"They were interns. Goose and Sally." Elsie spoke up. You could see Amy's face tighten a bit.

"Oh…yes. I remember them. Follow me right this way."

We followed behind her skating footsteps, each one of hers equating to two of ours. She cut through a couple rooms full of people so concentrated on cutting and sewing that they didn't even notice us. It was entrancing to see people so caught up in their work that nothing else seemed to matter.

She led us up two flights of stairs to a smaller room with just four people in it lightly chatting and sketching in notebooks. They looked at us, confused. Like they didn't get many visitors. Amy cleared her throat.

"Ivy, Elsie, these are the four people that interned with Goose and Sally. Alex, Brittany, Paul, and Savannah. Guys, this is Goose's sister Elsie and her friend Ivy. They were hoping to talk to you."

All four of them looked caught off guard, and a bit bewildered. Amy waved us goodbye and left, shutting the door behind her.

"We aren't interns anymore. We are still basically the bottom of the totem pole here, but a rung above interns. If Goose and Sally were here still, they'd be our bosses, I'm pretty sure. Especially Goose." Alex began. Her blunt, black bob brushing her jaw lightly as she spoke. Savannah shut her sketch pad and leaned back in her chair.

"The six of us worked directly together, and there were four other groups of interns with six people as well. Goose and Sally were the best out of all thirty of us. Everyone loved them and saw their raw talent for this business, and this career in general." Savannah added.

"It wasn't the six of us that worked together." Brittany corrected "Christian was here before Paul. Paul replaced Christian, guys. Remember?"

"Okay, I did work with Goose and Sally, though. Just a couple weeks. To my understanding, Christian was originally in their group, he got fired, I replaced him." Paul filled us in.

"Why was Christian fired?" I interjected. Everyone looked at each other.

"We never knew for sure. Goose and Sally were the closest with him out of all of us. About a month before he got fired, they distanced themselves from him. We all would hang out, but after time Christian seemed like the odd one out. He purposely brought drama into our group just to entertain himself. It doesn't help that when we went out either, he dabbled in snow, if you know what I mean. Mix that with excess alcohol…and you see where I'm going. He was just a mess. I'm imagining his horrible personality or addictive habits got him fired. Then Paul started a few days after Christian got fired, and a couple weeks after, Goose and Sally stopped showing up." Alex chirped up again, and shook her head.

"I really liked their boyfriends…they actually first came to us when the girls went missing. We assumed they were on their holiday, until Vince and Max showed up here looking for them. They went to see their girlfriends off, couldn't find them, but saw their car, so then they came here assuming the girls walked here to work to say bye or something. The next few nights we scouted all of their favorite places.

Nobody, including us, saw a trace of them. It's like they just fell off the face of the Earth." Brittany shared, flipping her long, golden locks over her shoulder.

"What places did they go to?" I looked around the room, wondering who would talk first.

"The Dive Bar and Holy Water are the only places I knew they frequented besides Doughy Joey's." Savannah looked around the room for confirmation, and everyone nodded alone.

"Do you know where we can find Christian?" Elsie prodded. I'm not sure if the room needed a second to ponder where he could be, or if they were trying to decide if they should tell us.

"Um, I'm not sure if he still lives there…" Alex began, "But there's a kind of run down, pale, Easter egg yellow apartment building called Marvel Ridge. It's on your way back to Doughy Joey's. It's actually not too far from Holy Water."

"Thank you guys, really. We were just trying to get some answers. Or a little clarity." I announced.

"You're welcome…I can't really think of anything else pertinent. Can you guys?" Brittany raised an eyebrow with her question. Everyone shook their head no.

"If you guys need any help with anything, or have more questions, please stop by. We're always here during the week." Alex tagged on.

"For what it's worth…I don't know what happened to Goose or Sally—but I think of them every damn day. They were like sisters to me. I think I can say the same for Alex and Brittany, too. I'm sorry you're left without closure." Savannah let out a deep sigh as she tied her cayenne hair back in a bun and reopened her sketchbook, signaling it was time to return to work.

We said our thanks before turning around and going back downstairs, through the chaos. We didn't talk about it, but somehow when I got behind the wheel, I knew I'd be driving to Christian's.

"Why do you think Goose and Sally stopped talking to Christian?" Elsie prodded.

"Hopefully he'll want to spill the tea." Elsie giggled.

"You have the oddest way of saying things sometimes. I wonder where you come up with this stuff." She giggled again.

"I'm just…original I guess. Anyways, if something bad happened between them, why would he open up to us about it?"

"Should we pretend to be someone else?" I pondered that question once she asked. Who could we be?

"What if we pretended to work for another fashion company. We're dressed the part. We can say we're looking to hire Goose or Sally or both and we are talking to former bosses and employees they worked with. Or, we are scouting him out and looking into his background."

"That's actually a really good idea. We could potentially do both."

"Is that something companies even do?" I didn't know about that in my time, let alone here in the 60s.

"I don't know…maybe if we don't, he won't either." I laughed. I hope that was true. Soon enough, we could see Marvel Ridge coming up. The only colored building on the block, stuck out like a sore thumb.

There was a parking spot right out front, which I took as a sign from the universe that we were meant to be there. Sure enough, outside the door there was a small registry that listed the tenants so we could buzz up to them. Elsie found Christian's name right off the bat, and hit a worn out red button in hopes he was home.

"Hello?" A static filled voice piped through to us.

"Hi, I'm Mrs. Carmine here with Ms. Ivy. We were hoping to chat with you about a potential future job for yourself in the fashion industry." Elsie turned to me and waved her hands like she was freaking out about lying out of her ass on the spot. There was a brief pause, before static poured through the intercom again.

"How do you know who I am? I haven't applied anywhere and I'm not looking for a job."

"Our company got word that you are on the rise in the fashion industry and our job is to scout out talent that could be beneficial to create the future of fashion with us, and not against us. We are down to the last few candidates and we are conducting interviews before we extend this incredible offer to one lucky individual." My jaw dropped at how professional and real Elsie's reply was.

"Come on in. Second floor, second door on the left."

The butterflies in my stomach began fluttering more and more with every step up we took to the second story. This could potentially give us a good lead, or at least an idea of one.

I rapped on the door, and a rather handsome guy answered. He almost looked too pretty to be real, if that makes sense. I extended my hand first, and gave him a firm shake.

"Come on in." He gestured for us to enter and make ourselves at home, so we plopped on the couch. Elsie began spewing false information about this job out of her ass in order to get him to trust us, and he did. He began opening up.

"We heard from your previous employers that you were fired at Silhouette Society. Do you care to share your side of the story?" He rolled his eyes at my question.

"Respectfully, since you both are in the fashion world as well, I'm sure you understand what it's like working with mostly women. A lot of estrogen to go around, which in turn leads to a lot of catty drama. They were threatened by me and my talent, and I don't blame them." Christian straightened his back, crossed his legs, and wiped his perfectly arched brow. Almost to show his confidence and posterity.

"Why do you say that? Do you care to elaborate?" Elsie prodded.

"Specifically, my designs. They were superior compared to everyone else's. I had the most potential and that made people jealous. The interns I worked alongside wanted me out of the way so they told the higher ups I was harassing them. Such bullshit." Christian lit a cigarette. "Now I'm working at Velvet Avenue. I do a lot of assistant work. I was promised a ladder to climb up, and I hope to be doing that soon. Been a little stagnant. Took a year off, did a lot of drugs. Then I did a year as an intern, now I'm assisting."

"How did you get a job there?"

"The only avant garde fashion companies around here are Silhouette Society and Velvet Avenue. That's the kind of fashion I feel most connected to and passionate about. Once I got booted by Silhouette Society, my only other option was to wait for an opening at Velvet Avenue. Once an opportunity arose, I cleaned myself up a bit, and got back to damn work."

"I see. We also are so very sorry for your loss. I heard some interns you worked with have gone…missing. Were you close?" He raised an eyebrow and took a long draw on his cigarette. My upper lip began to sweat. I hope he wasn't onto us.

"We were, but they were the main bitches that got me fired. They were fun to party with and all in the beginning. We'd all go to work, go out, get drunk, wingman each other to pick up our dates for the evening, go to sleep, repeat. I spent the night there all the time, too. Once they got more serious about work and got closer with the other interns, we distanced a solid amount. We stopped hanging out, I stopped crashing on their couch, then everything just went downhill."

We continued on with our false interview, both picking apart everything he said.

"Listen, I'm happy you guys found me. I'm very excited for this potential job. Let me go grab you some of my drawings to borrow. Like a portfolio." He hopped right up and skittered away. We stood up as well, ready to be on our way. When he returned, he forked over a thick manila envelope. "Just bring it back when you're done please." Gracefully, Christian unbolted the door for us to exit.

"We will. Thank you for your time, and we'll be in touch."

"I can't wait to go through this thing." Elsie flittered through the pages as we strolled over to the car.

"Me too. What did you make of him?" I questioned.

"I don't think he's guilty, if that's what you mean. I do think he lied. I don't think the interns were jealous of his talent. All the other interns today even said Goose and Sally were the best and that Christian was basically the weak link. I think he isn't telling the truth and I think something probably happened. There must've been a reason for the fallout."

"Agreed, something was off but I don't know what yet. Maybe we should check out Velvet Avenue too. We'll have to google that."

"Google?" Elsie had an air of confusion all around her as I unlocked the car. Shit, I forgot Google wasn't a thing yet.

"Ha—did I say google? I don't even know what that means…I meant to say research. We have to research Velvet Avenue." I slid into the car. I could hear her chuckling as she swung her side open.

"There you go again, talking your weird mumbo jumbo nonsense."

"It gives me pizazz!" I paired that with some jazz hands, which even made me snort. "I say we head to Holy Water, since it's right around here. We can get some lunch, a few drinks, look over Christian's portfolio, and investigate some more. Sound good?" She nodded in agreement. It was about two o' clock, traffic was pretty slow. The drive was only about five minutes. Everything was so close over here.

Holy Water was actually very cool. Not what I expected at all, by any means. Definitely not in the 60s, at least. Like the outside of most places around here, it wasn't special. But the inside was themed like a church. Stained glass everywhere, pew benches at the booths, crosses, religious paintings all strewn around, a mural across the whole back wall of The Last Supper. This is a place I would hang out at in my time. The crowd in here was definitely more rugged than us. This didn't look like a bar that belonged in the 60s, and I could tell Elsie was shocked, and maybe a little uncomfortable by the atmosphere we entered.

"Are you okay?" I peered at her tensed jaw. As far as I knew she wasn't incredibly religious, but maybe I was wrong?

"Oh, absolutely. I've just…never been in a place like this. I didn't even know places like this existed. It's so…cool!" The smile on her face grew enormous. I wasn't sure the reaction I expected, but it wasn't that.

We plopped down at the bar and a less than eager looking bartender came over. He slid two coasters in front of us, and gave us a funny look, as if he was wondering if we were lost. He was average height, with a girthy build. He had a very neat goatee and a freshly shaved head. Must've been around fifty. His large belly jiggled as he laughed, which made his leather vest tighten.

"I'll tell ya what. I'm gonna guess your career—and if I'm wrong I'll buy your first round of drinks."

"Alright, bet." I extended a hand like an olive branch to shake, and he met me there.

"Fashion industry." He barked confidently.

"False." He frowned. "Bakers." I smiled keenly at Elsie, then at him.

"Well, no shit. I swear we only get riff raffs in here, and people who work in the fashion industry. Weird mix of people we get." He scoffed. "I'm Bill, and it looks like I'm buying your first round. What'll it be, ladies?"

"I'll have a sex on the beach, please." He looked at me like I just spoke another language.

"I'm flattered, but I'm married ma'am. That's awfully bold of you to say."

"No!" I quickly shook my head. "The drink sex on the beach. You haven't had one before?" Shit, I bet it wasn't invented yet. "One and a half ounces of vodka, half an ounce of peach schnapps, fill the glass up with ice, and top it with orange juice and cranberry juice."

"Oh, yum! Make that two please!" Elsie chimed in.

"Three, actually." A rather tough, intimidating looking gentleman with slicked back hair, and a worn out leather jacket at the end of the bar chimed in. He stubbed out his cigarette in the ashtray, then proceeded to light another.

"You want one of those frou frou drinks too? That's unlike you." Bill retorted back to the mystery bar regular.

"You should make yourself one too, if you're allowed. I'll even buy it for you. That's how confident I am that you'll like it." I straightened up my back and flipped my hair behind my shoulder. "Unless you're afraid of liking a frou frou drink." Bill laughed heartily, and lined up four glasses for us. As he began, Elsie leaned over to me and whispered.

"You know, I've never been out to a bar before."

"What!?" I suppose I shouldn't be so shocked for a young, married woman in the 1960s who is also practically a mother to her husband's siblings. "Well let's make this a fun experience for you then!" I squeezed her hand.

Bill finished up our drinks, and he even garnished them with a cherry and an orange.

"Come on over here, Vee. Let's all cheers to new customers and new cocktails." Bill waved a supposed Vee over. He stubbed another cigarette, snatched up his ashtray, then popped a squat next to me. He gave us a nod as a hello, but it was clear this solemn fella didn't want company today.

"Cheers!" Elsie squealed, and we all cheersed in unison. "Wow, Ivy, that's delicious! I could drink ten of these!"

"I hate to say it kid, but it is damn good. I'll have to add this to our specials board. I've never had anything like it around here. You were right." Bill took a noisy, satisfactory slurp.

"Oh yeah, this hits the spot. All the sugar masking the alcohol will probably get me fucked up quick, too." Vee chugged half his glass.

"Shut up, you mope. Don't bring these two ladies down in that dark place with you." Bill trodded away to help other customers at the bar, and Vee let out a long sigh and rubbed his temples.

"Is everything okay?" I asked the stranger.

"Did I say you could talk to me, lady? Leave me alone." He gulped up the rest of his drink, slapped money on the bar, and stalked out the front door.

"Wow, unfriendly fella. I never understand why some people become so cold and bitter." Elsie twirled her straw around her glass and sucked up the rest of it. Bill eyed her empty glass.

"Another?"

"Yes, please." Bill got to work making her cocktail.

"To give you guys some clarity—Vee there, lost his girlfriend a few years back. He's never been the same since. He's turned into a shell of a man."

"Oh man, what happened?" Elsie looked so empathetic for the man.

"They actually never found out. His girlfriend and her friend went missing. Practically gone out of thin air." Bill slid the drink to Elsie, and we both eyed each other. In that very second it's like we both came to the realization that Vee was probably short for Vince.

"Gosh, that's so terrible." Elsie shook her head in sorrow, playing her role well. "Did you ever meet his girlfriend and her friend?"

"Yup, they were nice ladies. Vee and his bud Max came in here to sit at the bar and bullshit after work almost everyday for a couple years. One day, two stunning ladies dressed very uniquely came in here for the first time on dates with two other gentlemen. Vee and Max were starstruck by these two girls. Every other day or so, the two ladies returned. Normally with coworkers or friends or something, but a lot of the time they left with guys they met here. Not to get into others business or sound like an ass, but I thought they were escorts for a bit. In time I learned they weren't, but they were very licentious. Nothing wrong with that. Except one night, the girls left with two fellas who didn't seem like their normal type…the friends they came in with tried to get them not to leave with those guys either. I didn't know who those guys were, but they didn't give me a good feeling. Anyways, the next week the girls didn't come in and I got worried, especially because I saw their friends in here. When they showed up next, they were covered in bruises. One had a nasty black eye and the other was in a sling. I'm not sure what happened, but it ain't hard to guess those guys they left with beat em to all hell. When Vee and Max saw, they finally approached the girls to ask if they were okay. From that moment onwards they were always with the girls. I can't help but wonder if those guys that beat em have something to do with them missing—but I have no clue who they are. I only saw them that once. Anyways, once they went missing Vee and Max had some sort of fallout. Max hangs out at The Dive Bar now and Vee claimed here as his territory. He used to be so friendly and optimistic, but now he's like a different person. He lost his job, too." Elsie was ready for drink three, now. Bill got to work.

"Woah, that's all so terrible. Why didn't those two guys give you a good feeling?" Bill sighed as he handed her another drink.

"It's hard to say, and I don't want to misspeak. I don't know anything for sure. Just the way they spoke, how they carried themselves, and the whispers I hear around here…I got the feeling they might be running with the wrong crowd. Mafia or mob looking guys." Elsie's eyes got wide, and I tried to keep my composure. That was a shock.

"Well, gee. I hope that turns out to be false, for the girls sake. What a scary thought. Do you know why Max and Vee had a falling out?" I questioned, trying not to make it obvious I was trying to be investigative.

"It was about the girls, I know that. I'm not sure what it was specifically." Bill popped open a beer for a customer and handed it off to them. "I really hope the girls are okay. I doubt they are, after this long. But I do think about them a lot." He began polishing glasses behind the bar.

"Elsie. That's crazy. I think we have a new lead!" I tried not to sound too excited, but I was.

"I wonder why she never told me about getting beat up? Or why her coworkers didn't." She stated a little solemnly, and a tad slurred.

"She was probably too embarrassed to tell you. Or didn't want to worry you. She probably lied to her coworkers about what happened too, so they didn't worry." She just stared ahead a little blankly and made patterns in the condensation on her glass.

"Can we get a shot?" Elsie blurted.

"I'm okay, I'm gonna drive us. You go ahead though." I nudged her and she smiled. Soon enough a small shot glass was in front of her filled with an amber liquid. Adding whiskey can't be a good mix. As soon as she threw it back, she took off towards the bathroom to throw it up. Bill and I couldn't help but laugh a little.

"I'll cash out."

The ride to Doughy Joey's wasn't far, but I was going fast. I wanted to hurry up and get her home before she puked in the car. She needed to let loose a little and have this experience, I think. Maybe all women in the 60s need to, if they haven't already. It really is crazy how fast people settled down in this time. I knew I was going pretty fast, but I must've gotten lost in my thoughts because cherries and berries popped up in my rear view mirror. Fuck. I could literally see Doughy Joey's from here.

I pulled over to the side of the road, and saw the officer do the same. I looked over at Elsie and she was slumped over and passed out.

I think she even had some dried puke on her face. This does NOT look good.

I unrolled my window, which was much harder to do with shaky hands and sweaty palms.

"Ma'am, license and registration." In that moment, I realized I have no license, and I don't even know how I have a registration. Do I have one? My hands shakily went towards the glove box. "Oh. You two ladies." As soon as I looked up, I knew who it was even underneath the thick sunglasses and the hat. Detective De Luca.

"Oh, detective. Hello."

"What's going on here? Is your friend—Elsie—okay?"

"Yeah, I'm sorry sir. I actually don't think I have an ID on me. I know I was speeding. Elsie had a little too much to drink and I was trying to get her home before she threw up all over the car. She's married and doesn't let loose so I thought it would be fun to let her get kind of wild. I'm DD, I'm totally fine to drive. That's why I'm driving." Elsie coughed up a bit of vomit and my voice began shaking. "But now I don't think I have an ID on me and I was just trying to be a good friend which is ending up getting us more in trouble and—"

"I, uh, that's enough. I get it. Don't make a habit out of this. And carry your damn ID on you." De Luca let out a deep sigh and adjusted his hat. I could see a light mist of sweat shimmer on his suntanned face. He leaned down to me and placed his forearms through the window. I could feel the warmth of his breath on my face, it sent chills down my spine. The good chills, like butterflies. He lowered his sunglasses. "If I can read correctly, that folder in between you guys says Christian's portfolio. Is that right, Ivy?" I loved the way he said my name.

"It…does."

"And if I'm not mistaken, there was a Christian who worked with Goose and Sally, right?"

"Hm…I can't say I know that." He laughed smugly, and I avoided eye contact.

"It would be a shame if you were interfering with police business. I might have to reprimand you."

"Well, I'm not interfering, so there's nothing to worry about."

"You're a bad liar, Ivy. Don't make me keep an eye on you. Get her home and clean her up." He pulled away, and his musk whirled around me like pixie dust. He tapped my car door and strolled back to his lit up cop car.

I pulled out in front of him, and just went forward another hundred and fifty yards or so. I parked a little crooked right outside of our temporary homestead. Elsie was coming to a little, so I just had to assist her up the stairs instead of flat out carry her. I led her to the bathroom and she plopped by the toilet. She puked another time, and then just giggled.

"Ivy, I know I'm a sloppy mess and I feel like I need to apologize but I had so much fun. I probably never would've done that if you didn't take me and let me loose. I love being married, but I hate having to be prim and proper and have my shit together all the time. I want to have all the experiences life has to offer, and I don't want to feel bad about it. I was forced to grow up extra fast and it just feels nice to not have an agenda. We're practically detectives now, too." She wiped her face and stood to her feet. "I've never been this drunk before." We both laughed as she wobbled. "You know what I want, more than anything?"

"What?"

"Cheesy, greasy, fattening pizza. Right from downstairs."

"I'll go get us some. I think the carbs could do you good, too." I left the bathroom and I heard the shower click on. It was so funny to see her in this light. Lost and found, confused and sure, old and young.

Pizza was ready fast, and Elsie was waiting on the couch, wrapped up like a burrito with a giant cup of water next to her. I've never seen someone's eyes light up the way hers did when I walked through the door. Well, more so when the pizza came through the door. We scarfed it down so fast we didn't even have time to talk. Shortly after that, Elsie fell into a sleep that made her snores ring throughout the apartment.

Left on my own now, I decided now is as good as a time as ever to look through Christian's portfolio. I sat on my bed and spread everything across it. A big, gaudy "Christian" was written in neat script at the bottom of each design. The first few drawings were wild dresses with cut outs, asymmetric sides, different fabrics, slits, wild necklines, and bold patterns sprinkled throughout. He used bold black and white lines to trace bodily curves of the women. Very impractical, very runway, all quite beautiful in their own distinct way. He used colored pencils with very precise shading. He really was talented, I think. I don't know much about fashion, let alone 1966 avant garde fashion, but I thought it was cool. The next few designs were essentially lingerie. I'm not sure if it was supposed to be, but all very strappy with bows and exposed skin. Hat designs followed next, Kentucky derby style with lots of flowers and ribbons. Some had enormous brims, some had veils, some even had beads hanging around the brim. The remainder of the folder had a little bit of a different style of drawings. They were still very bold, obviously. This seemed to be their thing. These ones had no real blacks or whites, just vibrant designs and contrasting fabrics that wouldn't normally go together. There was a lot of accentuation on body figure, and they were outlined in marker, where the body should be accentuated. Why am I having deja vu? Wait a second…

I quickly went over to the boxes that were left in this flat. I quietly began to rifle through the boxes so I wouldn't wake up Elsie. Clothes, fabrics, decor, mail, knick knacks, and everything all over again until I found Goose's drawings. I pulled the stack of them out, and hastily tiptoed back into my room and began rifling through them.

The last bunch of Christian's designs seemed to mirror Goose's. Other than his unmistakable signature, the colors, style, marker accentuation, fabrics, patterns, and fake little model all matched. It even looked like the last batch of Christian's designs were on a different paper. Not the color, but texture. They seemed to be on a heavier, better quality paper, just like the designs from Goose's stack.

I examined one of her drawings closer. It was odd she didn't sign her designs. I flipped her papers over, and no signature on the back either. Looking a little closer, there was a small smudge inside of her designs, by the bottom of each outfit. What was it? I had to put the paper practically in front of my face to see, and even then turn it upside down. And sure as shit, that was her signature. Miniscule, but there. I started to examine Christian's drawings…and to my surprise, the last bunch of his had that small signature inside each design, but the bottom of each outfit. Miniature and upside down, almost indistinguishable. My jaw dropped. Christian was stealing Goose's designs.

I wish I could wake up Elsie, but I knew it was best to let her sleep it off. I couldn't wait to tell her this. It sucks of course, but that's one hell of a development.

I pulled out our investigative journal and decided I needed to put together all the information we have along with all of the questions we need answered. I glanced at the clock and saw it was only 7:30. I was pretty wired and feeling kind of antsy, and sitting around here was just boring me. Probably against my better judgment, but I decided that it was time to check out The Dive Bar. I wrote a letter for Elsie telling her I ran out and not to worry, and placed it very lightly on her. I snuck down the stairs and gingerly opened and shut the door behind me, careful not to wake her. Not because I was trying to be sneaky, but I knew she needed as much sleep as she could get to not be violently hungover tomorrow.

Everything was so close around here. It was kind of cool to not have to go so far out of your bubble to go places. Even right now in the 60s. I was obviously shocked at Holy Water being the way it was in this time period, and once I pulled up to The Dive Bar I felt the same way. It reminded me of dive bars from my time, but with sharper dressed men now and practically no single women.

The outside was lit up by trashy neon signs, with an entrance out front and one in a narrow alley to the right. Well, I'm assuming that's an emergency exit or something. Everything looked kind of dirty, too. Trash was scattered about and cigarette smoke seemed to linger around the building like a fog. A flickering streetlight really set the mood, too.

I wasn't nervous to go in, but I did have a feeling that all eyes would be on me. As soon as I opened the door, I was correct.

Confidently, I strolled up to the bar, took a seat, and slapped my notebook on the bar.

"Hey there, haven't seen you around before. Where's your husband?" A younger guy behind the bar raised an eyebrow with his question. While I figured he wasn't being as smug and sassy as I took it, it was still annoying.

"Is that how you greet everyone who comes into the bar?"

"No, just solo women I haven't seen before."

"You remember every woman who comes into the bar?"

"Absolutely not, but I couldn't forget your pretty face, doll." While I wanted to reply something a little spicy, I generally try to not piss off people who touch my food and drinks.

"Gin and tonic please, with a lemon." I gave him a halfhearted smile, and opened up the notebook, giving him the signal the conversation was over. I began scribbling.

Chrysler Newport sat outside Doughy's Joey's then vanished. Police never recovered it. Where is the car?

Detective Bates and his superior Sergeant Blackwell handled the case initially. Bates retired in 1964 and the case went cold. Detective De Luca under Sergeant Blackwell is reopening cold cases. Why didn't they continue the search right after Bates retired? Why didn't they look for the car?

Goose and Sally distanced themselves from Christian a month before he got fired. Paul replaced Christian right away, then a couple weeks later the girls went missing. It's safe to assume the reason the girls distanced themselves is because Christian was stealing Goose's designs, and that's probably why he got fired. Christian made it a point to say he thinks his peers were threatened by him and his superior designs, which was a flat out lie. Why did he lie? How did he get a job at Velvet Avenue?

Vince, otherwise known as Vee, had a falling out with Max supposedly over the girls. What exactly happened?

The girls left with two sketchy, mafia, or mob looking guys from Holy Water. They were beaten badly, and the guys weren't seen again. The way Bill made it seem, it doesn't sound like rough sex injuries. Who were these guys? Why did they beat up the girls?

I let out a deep sigh, and just reread everything over and over. We gained a lot of information for one day, but that just opened up a door to more unanswered questions. Another thing I felt was odd, is that two women with zero investigative skills, putting aside knowledge I've gained from crime television shows, came into town for one day. No real knowledge on anything. But one day "investigating" gave us more knowledge than the cops gained in a whole year. How does that make sense? Were they even trying? I added that to my notebook.

I squeezed the juicy slice of lemon into my drink, and slurped some down. Maybe I was in my head about it, but I felt like food tasted different back in this time, more pure. Fresher in a sense. Maybe it's less GMOs or something.

I kept scribbling down ideas and theories that could carry some weight or potential. I flipped to the back of the notebook and started to write down some ideas of why our unsub could have targeted Elsie. Revenge on the family of Goose? Maybe they thought she knew something? Pure anger? Family drama? Maybe Lars was somehow involved? We still don't know where he's at. Soon enough, that drink was gone. And so were the next two after that. So easy to just suck them down while working. Detective work took a lot of brain power.

"Can I buy you another?" A husky voice behind me to my right startled me, and I jumped around to see who it was. Beefy, broad shoulders were the first thing I noticed. Then slicked back, shoulder length, chocolate brown hair that curled behind his ears. He had light stubble speckled on his cheeks and jaw. Aqua eyes shone under his thick arched brows and fluffy eyelashes. What was up with so many dreamy people back in the day? Men and women, really.

"Sure, I'd love one." I finished the rest of my drink and played with the straw in my mouth as I smiled. Maybe it was the drinks talking, but this was exciting.

A large, meaty hand pulled out the chair next to me and he took a seat. For being in a dive bar, he was incredibly overdressed. I kind of felt like everyone was overdressed, everywhere. I loved it though.

This man was enormous, even just sitting next to me. I think he had a light accent too, that I couldn't place because it was so faint. Italian, maybe?

"I'm Enzo. Nice to meet you, ma'am." He smirked and waved to the bartender to give us another round.

"I'm Ivy." I smiled. My gin and tonic was replenished, and a glass of what I'm assuming was whiskey, was slid to Enzo over ice.

"What's a pretty girl like you doing out all alone in a bar?"

"Everyone seems to be so shocked by that." I suppose for the time it was less common. "I just came for a nightcap to help me sleep easier, I suppose. To write for a bit, too. What about you?"

"Oh, what's a pretty girl like me doing out all alone?" His joke made me giggle. "This is kind of my local watering hole. I like to finish my nights off here. I'm here with some buddies now." He pointed over to a table of fellas that all looked similar. Similar hairstyles, outfits, and clean cut facial hair.

"Did they dare you to come talk to me?"

"What? No dares here, I swear. How old do you think we are?"

"Hey, I just had to ask." He laughed.

"What are you writing about?"

"Oh, nothing crazy. Just journaling. What do you do for work?"

"I work for my family's business. We buy and sell antiques and art."

"Oh, man. You've got to see some pretty incredible things come through that door. What's been your favorite?"

"There's been some ancient pottery it killed me to get rid of. Surprisingly in pretty good shape, too. There were also some incredible paintings by Caravaggio and Renoir that were in our hands for a moment, but not for long by any means. We were practically the middle man for a sale between two parties."

"I can't even imagine looking at something like that in person when just searching it on the internet looks stunning. It's gotta be ethereal."

"Searching it on the…internet?" Damn it. I have to stop doing that.

"Oh, it's a book. An art book."

"I'll have to see if I can find a copy of the internet. I bet my dad would love it." Enzo's going to shit a brick when the internet gets invented.

"I have to run to the bathroom. Can you order me another drink while I'm gone?"

"Wow, a lady telling me what to do. Absolutely." He smiled.

I didn't realize how drunk I was until I looked in the mirror. Eh, that's okay. I traveled through time, I deserve a damn drink! My logic made me laugh so hard I snorted.

After I used the bathroom I touched up my hair in the mirror and made sure my outfit looked good. I stumbled a bit as I situated myself before strolling back out of the bathroom to resume my conversation with my new…friend. He said this was his local watering hole, so maybe he knows who Goose and Sally are. I may not be in the best frame of mind to bring it up to him, but I may never see him again so it's worth a shot.

As I walked back to my chair, I couldn't help but notice a bothered look on Enzo's face. He let out a deep sigh.

"Don't react when I tell you this." His start made chills run up and down my spine, and I froze as soon as I plopped into my chair. "I snooped in your notebook. Not to be nosy, but more to make conversation with you easier. You don't know what you're messing with. You need to stay out of this, and leave this bar. Don't come back either. Don't ask questions. Leave, now." I was so dumbfounded by what he said, I couldn't form a reaction. I glanced over at his table of friends and half of them were gone. Enzo threw cash on the bar, slammed his drink and left. Didn't say bye to me, or them. Goosebumps spread rapidly on my skin like a wild fire, and I knew I must be stumbling in the right direction with something. What does he know? What did he mean I don't know what I'm messing with?

"Can I have my tab, please?" I spoke quietly to the bartender, hoping to blend in. I was almost embarrassed that someone might've heard that interaction.

"Enzo picked it up." He replied with a less than genuine smile, and sauntered over to the far sink to wash glasses.

I took another small sip of my drink, and decided it was best to not finish it and just get out of here. Mentally, I feel a little scared. That was a grim warning. As I stood up, I began to physically feel a little sick too. I wasn't sure if I was going to throw up or not, but that wasn't something I was going to risk. The only thing I knew for sure, was that I was in trouble and I don't think I should've come out alone tonight.

I tried to not draw attention to myself and walk as steady as possible to the back alley entrance. I figured I could try to gain some composure there away from prying eyes.

Cool air hit my face, and I felt a brief wave of relief. But something wasn't right. The dim lights outside were starting to blur and I felt as though things were moving a bit slowly. I suppose I drank a lot, but I've had more than this before and been fine.

I leaned my forehead against the damp, grimy, brick wall and tried to shove a finger down my throat to make myself gag.

Hot, sour vomit spewed out of my mouth and onto my shoes. My palms started to sweat so fiercely they began to slip from the brick wall as I tried to sturdy myself. I felt became weaker by the moment, and my heart started to beat thready and fast. Drinking this much has never made me feel this way before, and in general I don't think I've ever felt like this before. I think someone drugged me. Slipped something in my drink while I was in the bathroom.

Now, with my mind racing I tried to compose myself just enough to walk to the car. It seemed like an impossible task because it felt like I was walking the plank on a pirate ship in the harsh waters of the ocean. I stumbled between both sides of the alleyway, bouncing off either like a ping pong ball. I wasn't even sure I was going in the right direction.

"Help me!" I wailed out, but not loud enough. I barely recognized my own fucked up voice.

Warm hands grabbed my arms and slammed me against the brick so hard it knocked the breath out of me. I tried to fight back, but my body was practically jello at this point. The world was like a dark watercolor portrait, all splotchy and whirled together. The only thing I was coherent enough to notice, was that this was a man in front of me, and a man who shoved his hand over my mouth. I tried to fight, scream, whimper, but it was useless.

"Shut up, cunt. You came to the wrong place tonight. Bitches like you have no place in the real world, and need to learn to sit the fuck down, stay in your place, and shut up. Leave your stupid little investigation alone, or I'll make you regret it even more next time if I find out you didn't obey me."

A sharp burst of pain surged through my jaw, reverberating through my spine. Making my head spin even more than it already was. Another explosion of pain bloomed in my stomach, my nose, and then my eye. I began tasting blood, and my blurred watercolor world stained red.

I fell limp, unable to hold myself up. The weight of myself was now entirely being held up by him. Dank, pungent breath tainted with the smell of booze singed my nose. His calloused hands forcefully thrust my hips against the brick and he tore my skirt off, or pulled it down. I couldn't tell. My eyes were wet, with probable blood and tears. I heard the slight jingle of his belt come undone, and I tried to squirm, but I felt like prey becoming victim to a predator. I flailed disjointedly, just doing what I could to prevent the inevitable. I stopped fighting back, my muscles were frail and I felt as though struggling against my attacker would put my delicate body at more of a risk. He began to bite hard at my neck, and was calling me things I couldn't understand. Maybe because of the drugs, maybe it was a different language, maybe I was disassociating. I didn't have enough time to decipher what the causation was because suddenly, I heard a voice. Not my attacker's voice, but a new one. One full of anger, but not directed at me this time. One that swaddled me in a way that made me feel warm, and safe.

Before he was able to do the unthinkable to me, the pressure against me came to a halt, and it was like I caught my breath again. The cage of arms imprisoning me were torn away, and I fell to the moistened pavement. The chill of the Earth cooled down my overheated body, and leveled out my racing heart. Things stopped spinning as much and began to even out. The last thing I saw before slipping out of consciousness was someone with a thick cookie duster mustache beating the pulp out of someone who wasn't recognizable anymore.

The vivid beams of light made me squint. They bounced throughout the room like a way too intense laser show. I squeezed my eyes tight, and my head throbbed with every beat of my heart. I could feel a pulse reverberate through my whole body. I pulled the blanket over my face like a shield.

A blanket. Where was I? What the fuck happened?

I quickly pulled the blanket off my face and scanned the room. "Oh, hi." Elsie's smile was huge as I greeted her.

"You're awake! She's awake!" Who was she screaming to?

"Elsie, I'm sorry. I'm so sorry. You fell asleep early last night and I wanted to keep investigating and I did, I made some great discoveries and—"

"Hush, no apologies. I'm not mad. I mean I'm mad about…what happened to you. But not mad you went out without me. You're crazy and brave and strong and you don't need to apologize for that. I love you like a sister, and I'm sorry I had my own crazy time yesterday and wasn't there when you needed me most." I ran my hand against my face and over my body. I almost forgot. I ran to the bathroom and flung myself over the toilet, throwing up straight bile. Pulling myself over the toilet, I glanced in the mirror. I was beat to all hell.

"I don't know if I remember what happened? I mean, I think I do but not very great. I don't think I was that drunk. I'm just confused as to —"

"You were intoxicated, but not to the level where you couldn't function. That's not why you feel this way. Someone drugged you, slipped something in your drink." A male voice shocked me, and I tensed up. Detective De Luca rounded the corner of the bathroom and leaned on the door frame. He handed me a glass of water.

"I'm sorry…" My voice trailed off, and tears began to sting by already bloodshot eyes.

"Don't apologize. You didn't do anything wrong. I mean, I did tell you to stay out of the investigation, but other than that you didn't do anything wrong. That fucking low life piece of shit should be apologizing." He clenched his hands into fists, and I noticed how bloodied his knuckles were. "I apologize, I shouldn't speak that way in front of ladies. It just makes my damn blood boil that someone could do that to you, to anyone. You were taken advantage of. I took care of him."

"Took care of him?" I questioned.

"Yeah. When I showed up was around when you lost full consciousness. Luckily, you throwing up in that alley and not finishing your drugged drink made it so you didn't fully digest the drugs, which is why you didn't black out for a while. We arrested him, after I took a little justice of my own…"

"A little?!" Elsie guaffed. "You were covered in blood when you got here, and barely any of your own!"

"Yeah well he would've been a helluva lot worse off if he went further with her and Blackwell wasn't there to pull me off. I wanted to kill him." I saw his jaw clench.

"Then what…?" I asked, feeling so dirty, so ashamed.

"You came to. Paramedics checked you out. You were out of it, but they said the hospital wouldn't be able to do anything for you that they couldn't, except give you fluids. They patched you up and I told them I'd take you home and stay with you. I drove your car here, talked to Elsie. You both knocked out and I just watched over you." I didn't have a reply back.

"My notebook…" My voice trailed off.

"I grabbed it." De Luca added.

"Well, I know what would make me feel better. That would be a huge cup of coffee and some pastries!" Elsie tried to shift the mood. "I'm gonna go grab us all some breakfast at a bakery I want to check out! Is that fine with you, Ivy?"

"That actually sounds great." My stomach growled fiercely. "I think I need to eat." Elsie smiled at us and grabbed the keys off the kitchen table. Detective De Luca must've placed them there last night. "I'll be back soon!" She gave me a solemn smile, like she pitied me, and then pranced down the stairs. I hate this feeling I had growing inside me. Like guilt and embarrassment, but worse.

Silence grew deafening in the bathroom. "I'm going to shower now." He nodded and backed out of the room, shutting the door behind him. Leaving me alone. I flushed the toilet, and slowly rose to my feet.

Everything is fine. I'm alive, and everything is fine.

I turned the nozzle in the shower on, and slumped against the wall and waited to get in until the water was hot enough to send plumes of steam up. As soon as I stepped in, I tried to imagine all the beads of water running over my body washing away the nightmare of last night. I had dirt caked on my knees, and flakes of dry blood polka dotting my body in abstract patterns. I felt like I wasn't looking at myself. Dark bruises covered a lot of my body, and I just kept lathering up and scrubbing. Scrubbing to get the impurities off. If I couldn't see any physical proof of last night, it's almost like it didn't happen. I could pretend it didn't happen. But all these cuts and bruises…they won't come off. They need to heal. I need to look at them and remember. Until they do heal, I can't forget.

I was rubbing my skin raw, I could feel it. But maybe if I just scrubbed harder and harder I would feel cleaner. I would be cleaner.

Before I knew it, I was on the bottom of the tub. I felt numb, but I couldn't stop crying. Watching fresh blood run off of my ripped open cuts and bounce off my black and blue flesh was too much to comprehend. I was drugged, beat, and almost raped. And I felt guilty. How does that make sense? I pulled my knees up to my chest and draped my arms around them, pulling them close. Hugging myself.

"Hey, you okay in there?" Detective De Luca's accented voice rang throughout the bathroom and echoed in my head. He began pounding. "Ivy, if you don't answer I'm coming in." I couldn't answer. I was hyperventilating in between sobs. This simply could not be happening. You hear about this stuff happening to other people, and you can't imagine how they must feel. And then it happens to you, and you still can't imagine what or how to feel. "Alright, I'm coming in."

"Please don't look at me." My voice trembled as I said it. I heard him sigh. I sat up and pushed my back against the tub. I closed my eyes and relaxed my head on the wall behind me. I tried to imagine that the water was rain, and let the sound calm me a bit.

I heard him take a few steps closer, and sit on the ground outside the tub, on the opposite side of where I was sitting. "I know it doesn't make it better, but not only did I beat him senseless, but he's in jail. He will eventually be tried and sentenced and he won't hurt you or anyone anymore."

I tried to compose myself. Knowing someone else was there helped me regulate my breathing a little. Enough so that I could get words out, at least. "I just don't get it." I sniffled. "Enzo seemed so nice last night. I don't know why he would do this to me. I guess you never really know what people are thinking, or what they're capable of." It took him a minute of careful consideration to answer.

"Enzo?" He sounded confused.

"My attacker…"

"Enzo wasn't your attacker." I repeated his words in my head a few times to really understand them. I flung the shower curtain open enough to make eye contact, but not let him see anything other than my face. His eyes grew wide before they darted away. He dramatically covered his eyes.

"What?" I questioned, a little too loudly.

"He didn't attack you. Gianni Moretti attacked you. Him and his whole family are fucking scum bag pieces of shit."

"Like mafia or mob pieces of shit?" I asked a little too excitedly. I wasn't sure if he was thrown off by a woman swearing or my deduction.

"Yes…How'd you know?"

"Oh my god. Oh my god. Oh my god. Hand me a towel and get out of the bathroom. When Elsie gets back I think we might have a lead in the case."

"You aren't a detective, you know." He stood up and grabbed a towel off the hook, and tossed it to me.

"Oh, I think I could give you a run for your money right about now, detective."

"Declan." He smiled at me and left the bathroom.

Chapter Ten

Funny how a break in the case seemed to change my mood drastically. I quickly toweled off and threw on a casual dress I packed, and by the time I did Elsie had returned from the bakery. We all sat down around the dining table. I caught Declan up with everything Elsie and I knew, and what we did before I spilled the beans on new developments.

"Elsie, when you fell asleep yesterday I went through the portfolio Christian gave us. He was stealing Goose's designs and using them as his own." Her eyes widened.

"I bet that's why he got fired!" Elsie smacked the table, and it made Declan jump.

"Exactly." I took a gulp of coffee. "So I wanted to get out yesterday and collect all of my thoughts, and write them down. I was so awake, that I thought it wouldn't hurt to go out and check out The Dive Bar. Anyways, a guy approached me. Enzo. The one I thought attacked me, but I guess didn't. Well things were going great. I mean, not romantically great, but he was nice and friendly so we just had some drinks and were chit chatting. I went to the bathroom and when I came back the energy shifted entirely. I'm trying to remember what he said verbatim, but he told me he read our investigative journal looking

for some conversation starters because I told him it was just my
journal. He turned all dark and told me not to react to what he was
about to say. He said that I don't know what I'm messing with, I need
to stay out of it, and leave this bar. He told me not to come back, don't
ask questions, and to leave now. He left, I had a couple more sips of
my drink, and I guess he paid my tab while I was in the bathroom.
Then of course I started to feel like shit so I went to the alley."

"So he knows something." Declan said. "Can I read the journal?" I
slid it over to him.

"So…Bill from Holy Water brought up that Goose and Sally left
with those mafia looking guys one night, and were beat to shit after.
Are you thinking Gianni beat one of them?" Elsie pondered.

"I do. Or at least he knows something about it. If Enzo told me not
to react to what he was about to say, and told me to leave the bar, he
probably didn't want someone in there to know what I was up to. So
maybe he didn't want Gianni to hear."

"Was Gianni in there when that went down?" Declan asked.

"I actually don't remember what his face looks like. Maybe from
the drugs or darkness or whatever. I would need to see him again.
Maybe that would jog my memory. Enzo was there with a bunch of
his friends and I would recognize them. I'd probably recognize
anyone that was in the bar if I saw them again. Just not the alley."

"I can get you a picture of him, and we can show Bill a picture of
him too. Maybe we can figure out for sure if he was one of the guys
Goose and Sally left with." Declan brought up a great idea.

"We?" I asked.

"I figured now there's no way you guys would stay out of the investigation, so it's best we at least all do it together so I can keep an eye on you both. Especially you." Declan glanced at me, almost protectively.

"I think we should check out Velvet Avenue, too." Elsie tagged on.

"Alright. Let's go to the police station first, then Holy Water, then Velvet Avenue."

"We have a long day ahead of us!" Elsie chirped.

"We sure do." I added on. Declan wanted to go for a light jog, so he told us he was going back to The Dive Bar to pick up his squad car from last night, and then he would be back in a bit to pick us up.

As I was fixing myself up in my bedroom, Elsie peeped her head in.

"Hey…do you want to talk about last night?" She plopped next to me on the floor

"I'm okay, I think. It might not be the heaviest coping mechanism but I think moving on would be best. Suppress it, forget about it." My black eye in the reflection of the window said otherwise, but I digress.

"Okay. I don't want to push you. Just know I'm here for you. Anyways, I'll be out here when you're ready." She closed the door behind her, and I stared at my reflection. I didn't feel like that beat up thing looking back at me was me. I shook it off, and relaxed my tensed up body. After getting some caffeine in me, having some water, taking a steamy shower, and shoving some pastries down, I was starting to feel a lot better physically. Less sick.

Once I emerged, I saw Elsie all done up and Declan was in his police uniform. He must've showered while we got ready because he still had a thin, misty sheen of water on his face.

Elsie and I both slid in the back of his car, and looked at each other and laughed.

"I've never been in the back of a cop car." Elsie giggled out, and I nodded in agreement.

"It's weird having people I haven't arrested in the back of my car. I feel like I'm the chauffeur." Declan said with a smile.

"You kind of are." I laughed.

"Okay, when we get to the police station, you guys wait in the car and I'll run inside and grab some files. It'll only take a minute, and then we can go to the bar. Please understand, I know we are working together in a sense, but I'm going to take the lead. I want to keep you both safe from here on out. That's why I didn't want you both involved in the first place. You guys are now unofficially police consultants."

"So detectives." I prodded.

"Yeah, we're detectives." Elsie backed me up and I saw Declan crack a smile in his rear view mirror with an eye roll.

"Whatever title you want to call it."

Declan parked outside of Precinct 12 and reiterated to confirm with us to keep our asses in the car. Soon enough, he came back with a thick stack of papers shoved in a Manila envelope.

"We have plenty of reading to do." He waved the case file at us. "Ivy, I'm going to show you some pictures, okay? Let me know if you see Gianni." I nodded. Declan flashed a series of mugshots at me, and one struck a nerve. I pointed at that one.

"Yup, that's Gianni. My attacker. No doubt about it." I'm glad I didn't remember his face in the alley, just how it was at the table in the bar. Declan nodded, and I saw his jaw clench.

"Did you see any of the other guys too?" He flashed me pictures of the mugshots again.

"The first two and the second to last one were the other ones there. I couldn't be more positive." He nodded again.

"What does that mean?" Elsie chimed in.

"They are all part of one of the most notorious Italian mobs here in New York. The Moretti's and the people that associate with them make up a group we call The Black Lotus Syndicate. Enzo is part of them as well." Declan explained.

"Which begs the question—why did Enzo protect you and what did he protect you from?" Elsie brought two great questions to our attention.

"I guess we'll figure that out." I shrugged it off and made eye contact with Declan.

"We will, I promise you that." He shifted the car into gear and we made our way to Holy Water. "I want you both to stay in the car while I go inside and talk to Bill."

"No. Absolutely not." I protested. "I want to go talk to him. I built a repertoire with him yesterday."

"Plus we are detectives." Elsie backed my case.

"Unofficial consultants." Declan corrected. "Fine." I smiled, happy I got my way. He parked out front, and I asked him for the stack of mug shots he initially showed me.

Happy to see Bill behind the bar, he did not share my look of enthusiasm. He had a look of fear and disgust painted on his face.

"Lady, what happened to you?" He asked, like an old friend.

"You should see the other guy." I joked with a smile, trying not to cry.

"I have a weird question. You remember you said yesterday some mafia looking guys beat the shit out of Vee and Max's missing girlfriends?" My vulgar language made him laugh.

"Yeah, why?" I spread out the mugshots on the bar so they faced him. He looked at me with raised eyebrows.

"I'm not a snitch, I'm sorry." Bill turned around and rubbed his forehead, obviously weighing his morals. I slid a twenty on the bar, and he made a much faster decision. He pointed to Gianni, no surprise there. He also pointed to another guy. One who was at The Dive Bar last night with Gianni and Enzo.

"Thank you." I flashed him a big smile.

"Stay out of trouble, alright? You're a nice girl and these guys seem dangerous. I don't want you to end up missing too."

"I'll do my best." I waved goodbye and scampered out to the car. Obviously, this wasn't something to be happy about, but at least the case was moving along.

"It was Gianni." I confirmed a little too loudly as I swung the door to the squad car open. "Gianni and this guy." I showed Declan the picture. He huffed.

"Gianni's older brother, Alex. Of course it was his brother. Those two are inseparable." He informed us.

"I almost guarantee Enzo was trying to protect you last night." Elsie chimed in. "I bet one of the shitty brothers drugged Goose and Sally, too."

"I think we should talk to Enzo." I tagged a stop onto our list.

"No. You two aren't going near those guys. I'm drawing the line there. I'll drop you guys off at Velvet Avenue, and I'll go talk to Enzo."

"Well, where are you going to find him?" Elsie chirped.

"You realize I find people for a living, right?"

"Oh wow, are you a detective or something?" I mocked.

"You guys are unbelievable." He pulled away and started driving towards Velvet Avenue.

"You didn't say how you were going to find him." I reminded him.

"I'll go and say I have car trouble."

"What does that mean?" I retorted.

"When he's not working for his dad, he's working at a mechanic shop around here. The Black Lotus Syndicate operates it, but they play fairly well with the cops."

"How do you know that?" Declan paused for a second.

"We grew up together."

"All of you?" I asked.

"No, just Enzo and I. We both got into trouble growing up, but the difference was I wanted to stop the trouble and he wanted to continue. We grew apart, but he is a decent person. We've kept a civil relationship throughout the years and frankly, he's the only mechanic I trust with my car. It's about time I get an oil change anyways."

"It makes me wonder how we got so much information so fast." I spewed out.

"What do you mean?" Declan questioned.

"Well, Detective Bates and Sergeant Blackwell didn't seem to figure much out when they initially worked on the case. I just think it's funny how two girls who don't know how to investigate got this far this fast." I followed up.

"Hmmmm…" Was all he said.

"Ladies, can I trust you both to get a taxi when you are done here, and we can meet at your loft later?" He turned around and looked at us.

"Yes." We said simultaneously.

"It's odd how you both are so perfectly synched. It's a little creepy." He parked the car and shooed us out. "Get out of here before I change my mind." Declan smiled. I was the last out of the car, and I stopped when he called my name. I glanced back. "Can we talk later? Privately?"

"Uh, sure." I felt like I was about to get scolded.

"Okay." He smirked warmly at me.

Velvet Avenue was much different than we anticipated. Especially when we compared it to Silhouette Society. The interior was not busy and bustling—it was very relaxed, slow. People seemed to be chatting about their personal lives more than working. There weren't shelves and racks of fabric and material everywhere. It was very blank, very blah in there. There weren't that many decorations either. I felt like it was a bachelor pad. I kept a keen eye out for Christian, I didn't want him to catch on to us or see us. I didn't have much to worry about, because it seemed like nobody cared who came in or what anyone was doing.

Elsie and I took ourselves on our own little tour. Not one person was sewing or cutting fabric, they were just sketching, chatting, and unpacking boxes of clothing.

"Can we help you ladies?" An older woman walking down a center flight of stairs acknowledged. She had salt and pepper hair pinned up in a French twist, and wore a midnight blue dress that hugged her body tightly, down to her mid calves.

"Yes, actually. We are new to the area and we're hoping to get involved in the fashion scene and maybe start out our career. We heard you guys are the best around, and we were hoping to chat with someone about a potential job opportunity." Elsie lied effortlessly. Man, does she have a knack for that.

"Unfortunately, we aren't hiring right now. But thank you for your interest." She turned away and began to ascend up the stairs.

"Oh, I noticed you guys don't have many people sewing, sizing, or doing anything with fabric, really. Are you sure you don't need any help? I'm very fast and precise with measurements." I don't even know if that made sense, but I thought it sounded good. The lady turned back around and glared at us, before she laughed.

"No, no. We draw out designs, and send them overseas to be made. Our mother company, or headquarters is in Italy and it's actually cheaper to make everything over there and in one place. They send our designs back, which we sell. Again, thank you for your interest." She left us that time, and Elsie and I stared at each other, confused. Eventually, she was out of earshot and probably inside some office upstairs.

"I feel like there's no way it's cheaper to send designs away, get them made in Italy, of all places. Then ship them all the way back." I exclaimed.

"I couldn't agree more. I wonder who that lady was."

"That was Allegra, she runs this company. We hardly ever see her because she's normally camped out in her office, or in Italy. She has better things to do than supervise us." A rather plain dressed, younger girl unpacking boxes answered our rhetoric question.

"Do you like working here?" I asked.

"I thought it was going to be more hands-on when I first started. I feel like a cog in a machine, really. Unpack clothes, repack, sell, ship out."

"So essentially—this is like the middleman of the headquarters and the consumer?" Elsie worded that nicely.

"Essentially, I guess. I'm not sure why headquarters doesn't do it all there. The place is certainly big enough. Seems like a waste having this whole building here that essentially works as a distribution center." The young girl gathered up a mound of clothing in her arms, and walked away out of sight.

"Weird." Elsie and I both exclaimed at the same time.

We took a taxi back to home base, and stopped into Doughy Joey's to grab a hot slice for lunch. After that, we just decided to hang out and wait for Declan to return. I was very anxious to share our intel with him and hear how his day went.

We added into our new knowledge, which wasn't much, into our journal upstairs. I know Elsie was nursing a monstrous hangover, and I was nursing my whatever you want to call it.

Declan showed up around five, and I was actually surprised it took him that long.

"What gives? Did you forget about us?" I teased as soon as I heard him coming up the stairs. I heard him give an exhausted and exaggerated sigh.

"You guys know I still do have my duty to serve at my day job, right?" Elsie laughed. We explained to him what happened at Velvet Avenue, and he agreed it was odd they seemed to just work as a distribution center.

"You guys talked to the woman in charge of everything too? That's surprising."

"Yeah, we were shocked as well. She didn't seem like she really wanted to chat, though. She didn't even introduce herself. Someone else told us her name was Allegra."

"Allegra?" He asked rhetorically, and pulled out his wallet. He shuffled through some random things in there and pulled out a dirt, crumbled, old picture. "Is this her?" I tilted my head to see clearer. It was two little boys and a very elegantly dressed woman smoking a cigarette.

"She's older now, but definitely her." Elsie agreed too. "I could never forget those cheekbones."

"This picture is from my tenth birthday party. It was one of my favorite memories growing up, so I carry it around with me to remember how simple things can be if you're happy. It's me, Enzo, and his mom…Allegra."

"That can't be good. Wow, everything is all connected." Elsie replied.

"No. No it can't be. But it's starting to come full circle. Well, maybe a semi circle."

"You're right. More so, full circle." I looked at him, puzzled by his comment. Declan rubbed his forehead, obviously stressed out. "While I was getting my oil changed today, I walked around the lot. Behind the actual mechanic bays they have junk cars they use for parts to save a buck or two. I saw a Chrysler Newport back there that met the description of Goose and Sally's car. It had the same VIN and plate, too. I asked Enzo about it and he beat around the bush. I don't think he was involved in what could've happened, but I think he knows something. I asked him about yesterday, and Enzo said Gianni came to fuck with him while you were in the bathroom. He asked Enzo how it was going, and he saw what was written in the book, then he started to panic. He said he was going to slip you something to hopefully forget about you meeting Enzo and seeing them there. Enzo told you to leave right away because that way you didn't get drugged. I guess he knew the drugs were going to kick in soon if you did and he didn't want Gianni to do something stupid, like ended up doing. You barely drinking any of that drink and throwing up in the alley is probably why you remember things. He said he wouldn't have left you by yourself if he thought Gianni would do something that dumb. Anyways, I promised Enzo to keep his statements confidential if he was to tell me anything, and that I would essentially make him immune. He told me to pay Max Amato a visit."

"Did you?!" Elsie squealed.

"No, but I got his address. I was hoping to do that tonight. Elsie, I was hoping you would scan through some case files I brought home about The Black Lotus Syndicate, Velvet Avenue, and Silhouette Society to see if there's something there that I missed. Ivy and I could pay Max a visit and do some work outside of the apartment while you do that." The thought of alone time with Declan made my heart race.

"That actually sounds perfect. I am so spent…I would love nothing more than to read from the comfort of the couch." Elsie seemed relieved she wasn't asked to go back out again.

"Ivy, you ready to go hit the streets?"

"That's detective Ivy to you." I smiled, and his eyes lit up.

Chapter Eleven

Max lived on the first story in a run down apartment building in between a corner store and a Chinese restaurant. I was curious to see how Max was doing, given Vee's state. As we approached the door, Declan cleared his throat.

"Please, let me take the lead on this. If he's involved in this somehow, he could be dangerous."

"Okay, okay. Just please make sure you ask what happened between him and Vince." He nodded as he rapped on the door.

"Police, open up." His voice boasted throughout the street. There was no way if someone was inside they wouldn't hear.

A very clean cut gentleman opened the door with a smile. He looked almost like the polar opposite of Vee. Happy, clean, tidy, dressed nice. "How can I help you guys?"

"Yeah, I'm Detective De Luca with the New York Police Department with a private consultant. I was hoping to ask you a few questions regarding the disappearance of your girlfriend and her friend, Sally and Goose." Max's happy face seemed to dull out and plateau.

"Ah, yes. I had a feeling that's what this was going to be about. Come on in." He stepped aside so we could enter. His place had a very minimalistic, bachelor pad vibe. Not what I expected for 60s decor.

"Had a feeling?" I prodded and he gestured for the couch for us to take a seat.

"Yeah. I mean that's the only thing I could think of that the cops would want to talk to me about. Plus that other guy came by the day before yesterday to talk about their disappearance." My body stiffened.

"Oh, yes. Sorry for visiting you twice. There's a branch in the department that's going through cold cases trying to reopen them with fresh eyes and close them. Who was that again?" De Luca played it coolly.

"Yeah. It was Sergeant Blackwell." I peered at my partner, and he was nodding with Max's words.

"Can you tell me anything about the girls that we don't already know?" De Luca continued the interview.

"No. I mean, probably nothing. Everything was fine, they were getting ready to go back to Goose's family's house for Christmas. We never heard from them again. We even went to their job to talk to their coworkers since they all were so close. It's everything I've been saying for years." It was clear Max was a little annoyed needing to relive this over and over.

"We?"

"Yeah, Vince and I. That was Goose's boyfriend."

"And you two were friends right? Are you not now? What happened?"

"We handled their disappearance in different ways. Vince let it ruin him, and I didn't. Vince didn't like that I moved on so fast, but I couldn't dwell on it and let myself completely fall apart like he did. Being around him was a drag so we drifted apart." Odd, because I thought they had some sort of falling out. Maybe we were mistaken.

"Can I please use your restroom?" I interrupted their little chat.

"Yeah. Go down the hallway to your right. It's the last door on the left." I nodded and excused myself, before they resumed the interview.

I strolled down the hallway, and went into the last door on the right.

Oh, this must be the wrong door because this is a bedroom…or a library. Wait, what is this?

Newspapers plastered the walls along with photos, yarn connecting stuff, all sorts of shit. I peeped my head down the hallway and heard them still bantering, so I figured I had a couple minutes to snoop.

Chills ran up and down my spine, and made my hair stand on its end.

Everything on the wall was about Goose and Sally. Written theories, pictures, personal belongings, articles, clothing, it was like a collage of a madman.

A desk was stacked with loose paper of all sorts. There probably wasn't enough room for it on the walls. I quietly rifled through, but it was hard to retain all the information. A lot of it on the desk was just sketches, and nonsense I'm assuming Max had written. Maybe it just didn't make the cut for the walls.

Underneath all the papers, a red leatherback book poked out. I slowly and quietly slid it out under the mountain it lay beneath. A small golden clasp held it shut, and I popped it open. The first page, made my blood pulse coldly throughout my whole body. Sally's journal. I shoved it in my purse without thinking, or looking any further. I slipped out of the room, and crept into the bathroom, trying not to make too much noise. I flushed the toilet, and ran the sink, pretending to wash my hands.

I stared in the mirror, trying to compose myself and shake the adrenaline out of my body. Luckily for me, I suppose, since I was so beat you couldn't really tell what feelings my face was emoting.

I returned to my seat on the couch, and it seemed as though the interview was wrapping up. Little did they know, in my purse I have the cherry that goes right on top.

"Thank you for your cooperation and for your time. If we figure out anything new, we will be in touch." The men stood and shook hands, I gave Max a smile and nod, with a quiet thanks as he led us out to the front door.

Max closed the door behind us, and as soon as we got to the sidewalk I grabbed Declan by his elbow. Hard. I yanked him fast and forcefully to the side and shoved him into the alley on the side of Max's apartment. He took a deep breath about to protest, and I pressed my finger to his plush lips, giving him the indication to hush. He obliged.

"You'll never fucking believe what I saw." I whispered to him.

We snuck along the slimy bricks, and avoided trash and debris on the ground from the Chinese restaurant. While at first the air smelled like delicious Chinese restaurant fumes, once we got closer, the trash cans in the alley were overflowing with rotting food. It smelled so vile it was hard not to vomit. Flies swarmed all around us and buzzed so loudly I thought they were going to blow our cover. A window to Max's apartment was close to us, and I ducked beneath it to avoid being seen. I slowly slid my back up against the soiled and greasy bricks on the far side of the window. I tried so hard to regulate my breathing. I peered inside, and the room of horrors appeared to be empty and free of Max. I gestured to Declan to look in, and I saw his solid poker face shift. His chiseled jawline tensed up and his eyes slimmed in scrutiny as he took it all in. Once he had enough, I followed his lead out of the alley. Very cautiously, we kept our composure all the way until we were inside of the cop car.

"What the fuck was that? How did you see that?"

"I don't know. I went in the wrong door when I excused myself to go to the bathroom, but it was by accident I swear."

"Well, good thing you did. What did you see specifically?"

"Every single thing was about the girls. Alongside that, I got this!" I whipped the journal out. "It's Sally's journal. I wonder why he's keeping it?"

"I wonder why he's doing any of that. It doesn't paint him in a good light at all. We'll have to go in with a warrant. I wonder how much of what he said was bullshit."

"Me too. We'll have to comb through the journal tonight. I think we should pay Vince a visit and see what he says about him. He wasn't willing to talk to me, but maybe with a detective he'll feel better about cooperating." I tagged on.

"Lucky for us I know where he is."

Declan sped off, and despite of all this terror and how horrible these circumstances were, I couldn't think of a time where I'd felt this excited, this happy, and this full of purpose.

As much as I wanted to hear what Vince had to say, Declan wanted me to stay in the car while they chatted. Only because we already had a less than positive run in. I tried to convince him there was no way Vince would recognize me in this shape, but Declan didn't buy it. I certainly didn't want to risk it. Back to Holy Water we went. I patiently waited in the car, trying to peer into windows to see if I could catch any glimpses of them.

I yawned so harshly it strained my bruised, beaten face. Thick charcoal clouds rolled across the sky and brought a sheet of rain with them. That just added onto my recently onset fatigue. I let the dance of raindrops atop the roof of the car start to lull me into a state of complete relaxation. That was, until the driver door swung open.

"If you're gonna be a detective you can't fall asleep. How would you do a stakeout?" Declan teased and he joined me in the car.

"Well, that's a different circumstance. I'm simply not doing a stakeout right now." I smiled. "What'd you find out?"

"Vince claims the reason him and Max had a fallout is because Max went crazy. While it didn't crash his career, he got obsessed with it and let it consume him. Vince got crushed by it and spiraled, which is part of the reason they went separate ways. Max's obsession drove

Vee away because he couldn't handle hearing about it anymore. It was like Vince went through all five stages of grief and put them to rest in his head when the cops did. Max just seemed to be so obsessed with them both it freaked Vince out."

I shook the journal in my hand. "Well, it definitely tracks that Max is obsessed, with a screw loose."

"There's so many pieces and moving parts. I just don't know how Goose and Sally fit in yet. This has got to be one of the most intricate cold cases I have worked yet. I will say like you did, I am confused by how much new information we've gotten so quickly. Maybe Detective Bates was losing it before he retired, because it seems like the foundation and groundwork of this case wasn't done very well." He sighed. "I'm sorry. I feel like this case was initially overlooked and that's not fair to Elsie and her family. Well honestly not even that, it's not fair to Goose or Sally. The police should've done better. At least we're trying now. I am." It almost seemed like he had a bit of guilt rattling in his voice.

"I mean, I agree. It does seem like it was maybe pushed aside initially. That's not your fault, though. You're the one opening these unsolved cases back up and getting some answers for people and their families." He nodded in agreement. "I say we get back to the apartment and see If Elsie learned anything useful. Plus we can check out Sally's journal."

"Yeah, we can do that. Absolutely. Hear me out though, what if you and I go grab dinner first? We can bring Elsie home something, too." I contemplated. I didn't want Elsie to feel like an afterthought. "Listen, that was my very poor attempt at asking you on a date. That's why I wanted to talk to you alone earlier. I know the timing is less than ideal with everything going on, but I know you're from out of town and I'm afraid I'm going to miss the window of opportunity.

You are so unlike anyone I have ever met. I'm half convinced you're an alien or from a different timeline or something." We both laughed, but shit was he hitting the nail on the head there.

"I would love to go out with you. Anywhere but pizza, please."

"I know the perfect spot."

Sitting across from Declan at a dining table seemed to make things feel like they clicked in place even more. I loved my old life, but I really felt so alone there. Especially since my parents decided to travel the world and after Elsie passed. Plus, all of my friends moving on to different phases in their lives. Yeah, I had my store. Which I love, don't get me wrong. It just felt like I lacked a purpose. Here, I feel like my living is doing something. I have a point and purpose to be here.

Declan took me to a quaint diner. A lot of bright teal, pearly white, and chrome colors were scattered throughout the building. The booths were worn pleather, that were practically busting open at the seams. The particle board tables had laminant flaked off and peeled all around the edges and corners. The waitresses were dressed in skirts and collared shirts. They all looked very cheery, too. Like they were at home. The place was packed, and everyone seemed to be in a good spirited mood.

"This is the first restaurant I remember coming to as a kid. My parents, brother and I would come here every Friday night for dinner to celebrate a hard weeks worth of work. Or school, in our case. Even throughout high school we kept that tradition. We brought friends here all the time, too. This was the hot spot after football games, school events, prom, homecoming, everything. I wanted to take you here because this has been my happy place for years. Whenever I have a bad day at work, this is where I come. I know this isn't your happy place, but maybe it will rub off on you. I'm also aware we don't know each other very well. From what I do know about you, I'm hooked. Your humor, how you think, your drive, your optimism, how different you are, everything. Anyways, I'm rambling now. Think of this as the first window into my life."

Before I could get a word in, a cheery waitress who must still be in high school came over to take our orders. Two bacon cheeseburgers with fries, and two vanilla shakes.

"I appreciate the metaphorical olive branch you gave me." I giggled. I shared my story since I arrived in 1966, but for obvious reasons I didn't delve back deeper than that.

"What about growing up or your life before moving to North Carolina?" I pondered how to handle that.

"It's all very complicated."

"Or you're very mysterious."

"Maybe it's part of my charm."

"We can call it that if you want."

"I used to own a plant shop and apothecary in northern Georgia, almost Tennessee. I'd sell house plants and homemade holistic medicines, of sorts. Kinda suiting for my name, I suppose. My parents decided to travel the world, my best friend passed, I needed a fresh start. I'm an only child so it was pretty easy. Here I am."

"So an ex crazy plant lady turned baker super sleuth?"

"Yeah I'm actually getting business cards that say that exact thing right now. Very chic, I thought." Our waitress dropped off our food and we wasted no time digging in. I took a bite of my burger, and juice shot out, dribbling down my face and down my hands and wrists. We both couldn't help but laugh.

"I always appreciate a girl who doesn't mind getting her hands dirty!" His molten amber eyes seemed to sparkle when he smiled, or laughed. I couldn't help but check him out in his form fitting uniform. The way it hugged his broad shoulders and beefy pecs. "I almost hate to ask, but how long are you going to be staying in town for?"

"Elsie told her husband a week or two. At the rate we're going now, I assume a week, but we don't have an exact date for when we're leaving. I'm living out of a hotel for the time being, so it doesn't really matter to me. Elsie is a substitute mom so it matters to her, but I'm just taking things a day at a time. As silly as it sounds. Yesterday was a god awful experience, probably the worst moment of my life. But I feel so…alive. For a lack of better terms. I made it through something horrible and I'm alive, I'm okay, and I will be stronger because of it. While I'm not thankful for the experience, it's something I'll learn and grow from. I'm sure it hasn't fully hit me yet, but right now I'm grateful for life and the experiences out there waiting for me. And I'm grateful for you being there. And being here, right now. I'm open for everything."

Declan began chewing slower, until he gulped down his last bite. He glanced around the room, and leaned closer to me, across the table. "Ivy. The rage I felt inside of me was unmatched. The devil was in me, I almost killed him. And I wanted to. I would've." He declared shamelessly in a deep, rough voice that made me melt inside a little. "What he did to you is punishable by God. He will rot in fucking hell, whether or not I send him there. What he was going to do to you…makes my skin so hot I feel like it's burning." Declan's cheeks turned red. "I can't stop replaying it, and all the different scenarios that could've happened if I hadn't come. Or if I was allowed to fully let loose. It's like torture. The thought of his hands on you and ripping off your clothes…" He shook his head and leaned back into the booth. "I feel very protective of you. All of that to say, I will keep you safe, and that won't happen to you again. Gianni is going to go away for a while." He took a large gulp of his milkshake. "I'm glad you have a more positive outlook about it, but I'm waiting for my clarity on it."

The thought of his fierceness and power, made me feel hot. I squeezed my thighs together, and ran my hand through my hair. "I think we can overcome it together."

He shook his head. "I wasn't the victim. I don't need to overcome it. I just wish I was there to prevent it. I knew you were going to try and get involved, Ivy. "

"All things considered, as a positive I'm glad I got involved with you." I smirked, and he returned one.

We ordered a burger to go for Elsie, and the rest of the conversation before her food came was full of life. Smiles, laughs, and feelings I had never felt. I could sit here forever and talk to him, in fact I wanted to. I didn't want to lose this.

Declan paid the bill, and got the door for me on our way out. He brushed his hand against mine, as if almost asking for permission.

"Just take my damn hand, be a man! Don't beat around the bush. I'm not as fragile as you may think I am." I mocked him with a laugh, and he didn't protest. He gleefully grabbed my hand, and kissed it.

"As you wish, your highness." He winked with those beautiful amber eyes.

He opened the back door of the squad car for me so I could secure Elsie's dinner in the back. As I leaned down and slid the bag in, I felt a gentle pressure against my back, then a bulge harden and twitch against my ass. Gentle, but firm hands grabbed my hips and pulled me closer into him. He secured me against him with a hand on my hip, and let the other hand travel on my thigh. I pushed back against him a little, and straightened up my back a bit. Thankfully we were secluded where we parked and the open door was shielding the view of those inside of the diner.

"You want me to be a man?" He whispered and dragged his lips against my neck. Goosebumps rose over my body with his gruff question. "I can show you how much of a man I can be." He spun me around and cradled the back of my neck and rubbed it gently. He looked down at me with wide, tawny eyes and I could hear his breathing intensify. I could feel it hot on my face. It made me close my eyes and lean my head back.

His lips crashed into mine with a fierce kiss that was so passionate I melted into him. I felt my core getting hot, my panties getting more and more saturated by the second, and how ready my body was for him. How much my body was begging to be his.

His muscular arms wrapped around me like a cocoon. I felt swaddled, safe, secure. The only thing in the world that mattered, was us. I broke our kiss and made my way up to his ear, to chew on his earlobe. "I want to feel how much of a man you are." I whispered seductively.

Declan leaned down and swept me up, wrapping my legs around him. He pressed me against the squad car and I let out a moan when I felt his bulge graze my core. He began kissing my neck fiercely, and then he stopped, suddenly. He pulled his face away and let my legs fall to the ground. He turned my head to the side and gently brushed my neck. Studying me.

"What?"

Declan sighed. "The bite Gianni took is bleeding. The bruise he left on your neck here…it must be so sore." He stroked my face gently, and cradled it in his enormous hands before kissing my forehead. "This won't be how or where our first time is. But please believe how badly I want you." His voice trembled. I ran my hand over my bite mark, and I didn't realize how sore it was until after he said that. "Let's get back to Elsie and see what she dug up."

We pulled up to Doughy Joey's, and it was poppin' inside. Must be a busy night for them. Declan strode over to my side of the car, and opened the door for me. I draped my arm around his neck and pecked his cheek.

"I'm gonna go grab some sodas for us and I'll meet you upstairs?"

"Sounds perfect." I nodded and waltzed across to my humble abode. I unlocked the door and hopped up the stairs, two at a time.

"Hey Elsie, I'm back!" I chirped. Elsie was bundled up laying down on the couch with papers scattered about. "Real quick, before he comes up. Declan and I got dinner on the way back, and before you ask, yes we picked you up food, too. But we got dinner in, like, the sense of a date." Her eyes widened and she sat upright.

"A date?!"

"Yes, a date. I think I like him a lot. We kissed too." She squealed and clapped.

"He's so hot, Ivy. About time you had a win!" The door downstairs opened and slammed shut.

"I'm coming up! Elsie, I have some food for you!"

"Oh, and we have the tea." I added. Elsie rolled her eyes when she saw Declan's confused look.

"Slang for gossip. Ivy taught me that. Tell me what you guys figured out!"

Declan took lead, and explained everything. We showed her the notebook too, which we were all dying to read. Unfortunately for us, Elsie didn't turn up much in her research.

"There wasn't much on really anyone. The Black Lotus Syndicate seems to deal a lot with the illegal sale of art, guns, drugs, stuff like that. So Enzo wasn't being fully deceitful when he told you his father is in the art business. It's hard to tie them to illegal dealings directly because there is never enough proof or a paper trail to charge them with things or bust them in the act. I'm not quite sure how they are able to move so quietly around. Silhouette Society doesn't have anything super suspicious that stands out to me. They probably need tighter supervision or HR, but other than that there isn't much to note. Vince doesn't have a record, but Max does. A stalking charge from 1958. Christian ironically has gotten arrested for theft, and possession of drugs. A couple charges of possession, actually. There's a lot of information in here, but really nothing that seems super useful."

"Hmm…maybe the journal will give us more context. Things will have to connect at some point." Elsie nodded with my statement.

"Well, I'm actually super beat." Elsie yawned. "I should get to bed. Maybe you two want to read the journal and catch me up tomorrow? My eyes are shot."

"Uh, yeah. That's fine." I could feel myself blushing. I knew what she was doing.

"Night, guys. Oh, I meant to tell you, Ivy. Ernest and I have a phone call date tomorrow night. An alone, phone call date, if you catch my drift. I'd love it if you could make yourself scarce." She winked slyly as she slipped into her room, and shut the door.

"You told her." He nudged me.

"I simply have no clue what you're talking about."

"Uh, huh. Sure. You go ahead and start reading the journal. I'm going to take a shower and get out of my work uniform."

"Oh, do you have clothes?"

"Yeah, actually. I got some yesterday night when I stayed over." He went into the bathroom, and I took off to my room. I changed into something way more casual, but still cute. Not try hard, though. Going in with no expectations. I brushed out my hair so I looked slightly more presentable, and slipped into bed. I propped the pillows up and unclasped the little red journal. Its delicate pages could hold secrets, or the last words and thoughts, of Sally. It was hard to compartmentalize how personal and sentimental this item actually was.

I got about a third of the way through the journal before I heard the bathroom door open and close. I closed the journal slowly, and looked up at Declan. He ruffled his hair through his fingertips, shaking off some excess water droplets. He was in some navy boxer briefs and a yellow and navy NYPD shirt. What I failed to notice before, probably because he was always in uniform, was the beautiful ink artwork painted all over his body. Of course, 60s tattoos didn't necessarily match up against tattoos from my time…but they were still beautiful.

Ink wrapped around his whole left leg, like a pant leg to jeans. His bulging quads seemed to make the ink look taut. Both arms were full, too. His tattoos gracefully ran along the swollen muscles in his arms gracefully. I had a feeling what lay beneath his form fitting shirt also held more mysterious artwork. I must've been gawking for a bit because his mustached, pillowy lips pulled up into one corner into a snide smirk, that led to a laugh.

"What? Your mouth has been open so long, I think you might be drooling."

"Ha, you're funny. I just didn't notice before."

"Well, you've never seen me out of uniform before."

"I'm just surprised. I didn't think it was common in 1966 to have this many tattoos." Declan threw a confused look in my direction, and walked to the bedroom, leaning against the bed frame.

"Common in 1966? That's an odd way to phrase it."

"Oh, uh, yeah. I don't know. I guess I forgot how to talk for a minute. Anyways, nothing interesting so far. Sally did mention Christian's drug problem, but no new news yet." I sat up more in bed, and fluffed my pillows up behind my back against the wall.

"Are you gonna invite me in or should I just keep standing here for you to look at like a piece of meat?" Declan taunted.

"Hm. You're right. You might as well come in bed with me because I don't want to look at you anymore. Too ugly. Hurts my eyes." I shielded my eyes and opened up the journal again to continue reading. I heard footsteps approach with a laugh, then I felt a weight on the opposite side of the bed join me.

"You wanna share with the class?" He laid on top of the covers and leaned back against a stack of pillows. I continued to read aloud to him, and as I did so he very gently began playing with my hair. Him running his thick fingers through my silky hair, twirling it around with a gentle pull, felt like heaven.

I continued reading for about an hour with no avail. As we approached the end of the book, things began to pick up.

October 29th:

"Today at work, Goose and I rifled through Christian's sketches. We got absolute confirmation he's stealing Goose's drawings. We plan to bring it up to him tonight when we go out. He's been acting weird the last couple weeks so we knew something was up. We decided not to tell the other girls, but I think we should in case he's stealing their drawings, too. Goose doesn't want to stir the pot. I know the other girls would want to know, but I guess it makes sense not to cause drama yet. They didn't trust him for a reason and we were nieve enough to. Oh well, we'll see how it goes. He's always been fine with us, so I'm sure it'll blow over fast."

November 7th:

"We brought up the sketches to Christian last night, and he was fucked up when we did. More so than usual. We thought if we got him drinking it would act like a truth serum or make him less upset, but he was talking like a crazy person. He was saying how he only stole them

because they were so good and he wasn't intending to design them, just store them in his portfolio. He said he's been buying his drugs from someone who works at Velvet Avenue and they spoke of a big job opportunity at their company, but Christian's portfolio would need some help if he had any chance at getting it. I guess he hasn't been happy at Silhouette Society and has been thinking about leaving for a while, and once his drug dealer told him about this opportunity it sealed the deal in his mind. All he needed to do was stack up his portfolio. He was hoping he'd be dust in the wind before we even noticed he stole our ideas. It does beg a question, who is selling drugs that works at Velvet Avenue? Seems like a risky business move. I also don't know how Christian was told about this wonderful job opportunity when that place is always dead. There's no crafting, no art, no design. Just unloading from head quarters and distributing. I knew when Goose and I went there, it left a bad taste in my mouth. That place is supposed to be top of the line, and it's like a bland, crypt in there. Begs the question how they're number one in the avant garde fashion industry, and we're number two. Everyone talks about it at work. The amount we create, we put out, we sell, we design, we put on the runway, smashes what Velvet Avenue does and they are monetarily thriving. Yeah our stuff looks better, but they have the most expensive cloth, thread, and fabrics you can buy. I just don't know how they afford it. Anyways, we are going to talk to our boss when she gets back from vacation next week. Wish me luck, diary."

November 11th, 1966:

"Sorry I haven't written the last few days, diary. It's been hectic. And well...just quite awful. Goose and I met these incredibly attractive, rough looking fellas. Very tough, seemed intense, thought they would give us a wild night we wouldn't forget. Well, we were right, but not in the way I wanted. We met at Holy Water, then came back to our place. We were drinking pretty heavily, but Goose and I

started feeling funny. Weird funny, bad funny. I think they drugged us. The guys said not to say shit to anyone about Christian or who Christian was buying his drugs from. We told them we aren't really into drugs and we don't know who he buys them from, but they didn't believe us. They beat us and told us to keep our fucking mouths shut or they'd come back. I'm so scared."

November 16th, 1966:

"Christian got fired, which I don't feel too bad about. He had a job lined up already. Plus he was stealing so why should I feel bad? Anyways, because we were friends for a while he apologized to us profusely and begged that we don't tell our group about what actually happened. We agreed to keep the peace. He's kinda crazy, too, so he's not someone I want on my bad side. Sally and I are going out with our friends tonight, but just doing some late night dinner and Christmas shopping since we are going back home for Christmas. I'm so excited!"

November 23rd, 1966:

"We heard Christian is working at Velvet Avenue. You know what is crazy? We walked by Velvet Avenue today on our break to go get coffee...really, to spy and be nosy and see if we could see anything in those big glass windows they have. But listen, the best coffee shop in town is right across the street. Anyway, it scared us for a minute because guess who we saw? The guys who beat us. We saw them go into Velvet Avenue, and we saw them leave. What on Earth were they doing there? I wonder what connection they have to Velvet Avenue. We assumed we got roughed up because of all the shit with Christian, but what if it had to do with something at Velvet Avenue? Max and Vince don't like us diving in this deep and coming up with conspiracy theories, especially Max for whatever reason...I don't know. We met a very tall, handsome fella at the coffee shop who asked us to meet him

later at The Dive Bar. We haven't had a three way before, but I guess we'll figure out what we're going to do later..."

November 25th, 1966

"Okay, so no three way. Something much more interesting, if you'd believe it or not. The guy from the coffee shop? Yeah, well he wouldn't tell us his name. He said he was unintentionally eavesdropping on us at the coffee shop and he wanted to tell us in a less conspicuous place to stay out of the Velvet Avenue drama if we wanted to stay safe, because those guys will hurt us again if they see us snooping around. We asked why he cared or how he even knew, and he said it doesn't matter how he knows but he wants us to stay safe. Very odd. I don't know what to make out of it. But I know it makes me want to dig more."

November 29th, 1966:

We found a vein today. Of course, we were at the coffee shop again. Some workers from Velvet Avenue came to get coffee and they were talking about how they were so excited because a new shipment of clothing came in this Saturday. You'll never believe it, they even said the location. Well, not the exact location but they gave enough context clues for us to figure it out. It's at the port closest to the best deli, the bakery with the best bagels, and next to the biggest park. I think we're going to take a stroll by when everything comes in. Something suspicious is going on, but we just don't know what. Stay tuned, diary."

December 2nd, 1966:

"I'm almost afraid to write this down. We're going to the police station first thing in the morning. We went to the port early, and around one in the morning. Velvet Avenue started unloading their

cargo. Everything looked fine and normal, but then we saw the two guys who beat us along with a handful of other guys who we didn't recognize come in. Velvet Avenue workers were unloading clothes, but the tough guys were unloading much heavier, more protected cargo. We got a closer look, and both of us could've died when we saw it. Crates full of guns, cocaine, and I'm sure plenty of other illegal substances were being unloaded too. Velvet Avenue was an irrelevant fashion company in New York, but they were supplying black market guns and drugs. The reason why they could afford all their expensive materials was because they were laundering money and paying for it with their drug and gun money! That big warehouse overseas is supplying tons and tons of drugs and guns to New York, and this whole discovery will bring it down. Not only will it make New York safer, but it will put Silhouette Society on top. We are shaking with adrenaline. There won't be much sleep tonight, diary."

I turned the page with a shaky hand, and there were no more entries. I was quiet with awe.

"Someone must've seen them." Declan mumbled.

"But who?"

"I don't know…I'll go into work early and bring this up to Blackwell. This is absolutely crazy."

"I bet Max and Vee couldn't figure out who beat the girls so they didn't go anywhere with it. They probably didn't think anything of it after the fact, either. Alex and Gianni aren't mentioned by name, which blows. Maybe Vee's been obsessing because of that. He knows there's a connection between their disappearance and the beating and he can't figure it out."

"Very well could be. This will change everything. I mean, it makes complete sense The Black Lotus Syndicate is intertwined so complexly with Allegra running Velvet Avenue. I almost guarantee Enzo was the one trying to warn Goose and Sally, too." I slapped the journal shut with his conclusion. I couldn't be more positive The Black Lotus Syndicate killed Goose and Sally. "I'll tell Blackwell what we found, and tell him we need to stakeout for the next shipment from Velvet Avenue."

I placed the notebook on the ground next to my side of the bed, and I flopped back with a sigh.

"This is a big break for you. Not only are you solving a missing persons case, but it's actually a potential double homicide that ropes into bringing down a huge crime family along with a drug and gun bust."

Declan propped himself up on his left elbow, rolling himself right towards me. "You know, I couldn't have done it without you." He smirked, leaned in and kissed me deeply. Then he pulled away.

"I just wish it wasn't ending in their probable murder. I wanted a fairytale ending." I added. Declan pondered his response carefully before answering, understanding this was a subject that hits close to home.

"You know, traditional fairy tales had a dark endings? You can still have your traditional, perfect, fairy tale, but with its ups and downs."

"Yeah. Yeah you're right. I feel like I'm in a fairy tale now. A weird, twisted, fucked up one—but I'm in it."

"How so?"

I wanted to tell him everything. Tell him so badly and melt like butter into him. But I just couldn't. "I can't tell you right now. I will another time."

"That's not fair."

"Life isn't fair." I poked his nose. I then eyed up his body, yet again. And traced inked patterns along his arm. I saw his muscles clench when I reached the inside of his elbow, and goosebumps rise all over him, like a crowd of sports fans doing the wave.

Declan turned off the lamp next to him, and snuggled up underneath the covers. I felt an arm snake around my torso and rotate me towards him. He pulled my face closely to his, and whispered huskily.

"I'll protect you, Ivy. Nobody will ever hurt you again."

His tender lips pressed against mine, and he lifted himself on top of me. The comforting pressure of him acted like a welcoming weight, shielding me from the outside. I felt a bulge rub against my thigh, and I slowly slid my thighs open to welcome him, and he pressed himself against me. His slow, passionate, caring kisses became shorter and full of lust and desire. His primal instincts led him to interlace his fingers in mine and hold me where I lay. He broke his kiss, and held his forehead against mine, breathing hastily.

"Miss Ivy, my thoughts towards you are considered less than gentlemanly right now. Frankly, I'd like to ravish your body entirely and do things to you that you couldn't imagine without moaning. But I don't feel right now is the right time for that. You need to heal and you need sleep, and I want you to know I'll be here to assure you get the secure rest you need." I smiled, and turned away from him. He pulled me into a lovely little spoon, and held my body against his so tightly that I could feel his heart pulsing against me, let alone something else pulsing against me…

Chapter Twelve

I woke up the next morning, and rolled towards Declan. When my wanting hands hit an empty bed, I shot my eyes open. Declan wasn't there. I walked out into the kitchen, where I saw Elsie nursing a cup of coffee. She grew a grin faster than a bougainvillea could sprout a new leaf.

"Excuse my language but please tell me you climbed him like a fucking tree? In the least weird way, I couldn't stop thinking about it. He is so hot, and so into you." I laughed.

"No no, I didn't. But the sexy tree is absolutely plastered in tattoos. Isn't that sexy?" Her jaw dropped.

"So sexy. You know, I've always wanted one but I'm so scared. They're very taboo and I bet they hurt so badly! Declan was rushing out for work when I woke up this morning, but he did tell me you guys made some interesting discoveries you would tell me about."

I caught Elsie up with our findings, and near the end her eyes welled up with tears.

"Obviously, I'm sad because The Black Lotus Syndicate more than likely killed them. However…is it weird I'm also happy because we might have an answer?" She asked, almost rhetorically.

"No, not weird. I think closure in any sense is relieving. Like a weight lifted off of you. Better than not knowing." She wiped tears away, and nodded in agreement.

"So what's next?"

"He reports to his sergeant this morning about his/our findings and we get approved for a stakeout of the port they get shipments into. We bust them for the drugs and guns, and then bring up the disappearances of the girls."

Elsie sighed. "So there's nothing we can do to help the development of the case?" I shook my head. "Let's go check out the amazing bagel place. The one Sally and Goose mentioned in the diary that's close to the port."

"They didn't mention much? Just that it's by the best deli and a thickly forested park."

"We ask downstairs. I bet Donna would know."

Sure enough, Donna did know. And quickly enough we were on the road there. I was far less swollen today, but the bruises seemed to darken to their full form. I'll take that over the puffiness, I suppose.

I drove and Elsie navigated, per usual. Bob's Bagels looked like nothing special, but as soon as we got of the car out front, we smelled the delicious, yeasty smell of fresh baked bagels. The line out front confirmed that they were the probably busiest and the best, too.

We scampered to the back of the line, and breathed harshly watching our breath condense and create a cool, steamy condensation in front of us. As we got inside the door, we saw bustling workers scampering about. Spreading shmear, toasting bagels, handing out orders, pulling bagels out of the oven. Everything.

Something older Elsie taught me, was that the best bagels needed to be boiled for a minute or two max on each side in sugar water before they are baked. I was happy to see that they were boiled in bulk before baked. I was also excited to see that all of their bagels were sourdough as well. Gut healthy, guilt free, and the yummiest. It made me reflect on a version of old Elsie.

She ordered a blueberry bagel with cinnamon vanilla cream cheese, and I ordered a garlic bagel with vegetable cream cheese. We figured we would split the sweet and savory and get the whole feel. We collected our togo bag and headed outside, where we swapped half and half. I was happy to taste the snap and pop of the fresh blueberries and punch of the fresh grated cinnamon. The savory bagel had the bite of the fresh, roasted garlic and the crunch of the cream cheese packed with carrots, celery, scallions, and red pepper. Both were so delicious, I couldn't decide which one I liked more.

Once we finished, we took our coffees and went on a stroll alongside the sidewalk. Elsie grabbed my arm fiercely enough to stop me enough in my steps. I looked at her confused.

"I want to do something crazy, Ivy." I looked at her confused, wondering where this was coming from. I peered around our surroundings, and up ahead was a tattoo shop. I had a feeling where this was going. I glanced at her, suggestively.

"Let's get a tattoo." I didn't reply, anticipating a follow up. "Let's get a matching tattoo." Her enthusiasm made me laugh.

"Fuck it. Let's do it." I grabbed her hand tightly, and squeezed. She dominantly took my hand and led us to the door. Neon red "we're open" signs led us in. The loud buzzing of tattoo machines led us inside. Flash strung upon the walls caught our eye, but nothing was speaking to us.

Eventually, once an artist was done with his human canvas, he peeled off his skin tight gloves and flung them in the trash. The freshly inked client handed the artist a wad of cash and they parted their own ways.

"Be with you ladies in a minute." A plump man with coke bottle glasses and a Fu Manchu mustache shouted as he stood from his chair and began cleaning down his station. He went to the back to presumably use the bathroom. When he waddled up front to where Elsie and I were planted by the flash, he asked us the million dollar question. "What are we thinking about?"

"Do we have to get something from these sheets?" He shook his head no.

"I can draw you two up something. What do you have in mind?" We both pondered this question silently, given we hadn't even talked about it let alone think about it before walking in. Then it came to us both, almost at the same time.

"Cupcake." We both exclaimed in tandem.

"Color?" He asked us, less than enthused.

"Uh, I don't know about her but I just want a black outline of one." I answered.

"Yeah, me too. Same as hers." Elsie tagged on. Fu Manchu nodded and told us to give him a few minutes to put a stencil together.

Soon enough, he presented us with a minimalistic, simple, elegant, line work cupcake. We nodded in agreement and then took us over to his station. Cluttered with sketches, ink bottles, different packaged needles, all sorts of things I couldn't make out, but it was clean.

"What spot are you guys thinking?" I looked at Elsie, and without hesitation, she made her decision.

"My butt cheek. I want it on my butt cheek."

"Why there?!" I exclaimed.

"Well I don't want anyone to see it."

"Then why get it?"

"The memory, the experience. Something for Ernest to gawk at." I nodded. I couldn't fault her.

"Alright. Let's do it, I'll do it there too."

"Drop your pants to the side, ladies. We will put the stencil on, let it dry and we'll get started."

He placed stencils on the side of our butt cheeks. Her left and my right.

"Ivy, you go first." Elsie tagged on while we were drying.

"Why me?"

"Because you're the brave one in this relationship. This is how it works for us." She laughed and I rolled my eyes.

"Fine." Fu Manchu patted the bench and told me to lay on my stomach. He gave me a pillow and even handed me a stress ball to make me comfortable. Elsie sat next to me on a red, worn out, padded leather stool. As he got his machine assembled and working, I saw her eyes grow at the volume of the machine, and the needle approaching my skin.

"Don't look like that Elsie, you're freaking me out."

"Sorry, sorry. I've just never seen it up close." I felt him stretch my skin, and I squeezed my eyes shut tightly anticipating the needle. Then the seven round liner hit my skin.

Maybe it was because it was so small, but it didn't hurt that badly. It was like running your nail over a fresh sunburn. Annoying and uncomfortable, but doable.

"It's not that bad, Els. You'll be fine. You can stop holding your breath now." She closed her eyes and looked at me anxiously with pale skin.

About ten minutes later, I was done. Fu Manchu was cleaning up and setting up again for Elsie.

"You're gonna have to stop shaking if you want a clean tattoo. Nobody likes a squiggly cupcake."

"I'm sorry, I'm sorry. I'm trying." Elsie began taking deep breaths, trying to center herself.

"Don't pay attention to the tattoo, just talk to me about…cupcakes or something."

Elsie began rattling off cupcake combinations, which made all three of us laugh. Once he started tattooing, you could see Elsie relax. Her anticipation was worse than the actual tattoo. Same with mine, I suppose. I guess a lot of things in life the anticipation is worse than the actual thing.

He wrapped us up, I handed him a small fee and 20% tip for his work. He thanked us, told us he liked our spunk, and held the door for us. He was on his way out too, to smoke a cigarette.

"Hey can we get one of those off of you?" He pointed at the lit cigarette in his mouth to confirm, and she nodded. He slipped us two, and tossed us his lighter. She looked down at it, and fumbled it in her hand.

"Keep it. It has the shop information on it. Tell your friends about us."

"Thanks!" She replied, and we waved at him as we went our separate ways.

"You're a smoker now?" I asked her.

"No, never. But I figured today is a day of firsts." She struggled trying to light the cigarette in her mouth with the force of the wind coming at her. She eventually did, and lit mine for me too. We coughed almost in sync. "God, these are horrible tasting."

"Yeah, no kidding." My head began to buzz slightly from the drag. I've actually never smoked a cigarette before, either. I have used to a vape in my time, but that was different. I laughed to myself imagining trying to explain what a vape was to Elsie. Or a smartphone. God, it's crazy how different things were. "Well, now what?" I asked as I took another drag.

"I guess go back to the apartment, wait to hear from Declan. Lay low." I nodded.

"Sounds like the best plan."

We were both more than shocked to see Declan pacing in the alley the door to our apartment was in on the side of Doughy Joey's.

"What are you doing here so early?" I shouted to him as I got out of the car.

"I got fucking benched." He yelled back rubbing his temples and fidgeting, clearly upset. Elsie and I scampered over to him.

"What?!" We asked him, shocked.

"You'll never fucking believe it." He spit out. "First thing this morning, Blackwell arrested Max. They got an anonymous tip about Max, and Blackwell got a search warrant for Max's house and found his insane bug out room. Low and behold, in that room was a key to the girl's Chrysler Newport. Max claims he had an extra set to the car when he dated the girls in case of emergencies, but no other set of keys was recovered. Apparently, the anonymous tip also said where to find the car, which of course was covered in Max's fingerprints. The shop said Max dropped it there after the girls went missing, and Max says no way in hell he did that. He claims to know nothing about the whereabouts of the car and that he was looking for it, too. In his own investigation." Declan let out a frustrated sigh. "I told Blackwell I think he has the wrong guy. I told him what we found and that The Black Lotus Syndicate more than likely offed the girls. When he asked why they would kill them, I told him about the drug and gun smuggling theory. How Goose and Sally stumbled upon it and to keep Velvet Avenue number one and keep the syndicate safe, they silenced the girls so nobody would get exposed. Of course, I had to tell him how I came about this information, and because I got two civilians involved and illegally got the journal, I endangered the public and it probably wouldn't hold up in court. Plus, I guess there's more proof to arrest Max and close the case rather than investigate our lead. I'm suspended until further notice."

"But that doesn't make sense. Yeah, Max has some screws loose, but why wouldn't he at least follow your lead? Get proof along the way?"

"I'm just as confused as you. I told him we could not only solve what happens to the girls, but bring down The Black Lotus Syndicate and stop a large amount of illegal drugs and weapons from being imported and distributed here."

"What was his attitude when you told him?" Elsie asked an intriguing question.

"I…uh…huh. Weird. I guess it actually wasn't shock. It almost seemed more like annoyance."

"Why would he be annoyed? Shouldn't he be more than excited? This would make him look like a superstar if he exposed all of this." Elsie followed up. We all stood silent.

"Oh my god…" I mumbled, and they looked at me, wanting to know what was going through my head. "How didn't we see this before?!" I shouted at them, assuming they had the same realization.

"What are you talking about, Ivy?"

"Think about it. Look how far we got into this case. Just Elsie and I, at first. We have no experience, no contacts, don't know the area, and went into this blind. How didn't incredibly experienced Bates make a dent in this case in over a year's worth of time?" I asked, waiting for one of them to have an epiphany. "Bates worked under Blackwell, so Blackwell could steer him. Declan, you being new, Blackwell probably didn't think you were any good. If Bates couldn't solve it, he probably thought you wouldn't either. That's why he let you do things yourself. He didn't think you'd bring in outsiders with new information." I paused, still no comments. "Blackwell has got to be working with the syndicate. He tried to cover it up with Bates, maybe even blackmail him into retiring. That's why he's pushing your findings to the side and trying to pin this whole thing on Max. Max is his scapegoat." Their jaws dropped.

"You're so right. I've always had an off feeling about him, but didn't know what or why. I've got to go to the chief. But this is a big accusation." Declan added.

"You're on suspension. What's to lose now? If you bring us in with what we know, he'll at least listen to you and maybe let us stake out the port. The worst we can be is wrong. It's better than arresting an innocent man. I'm sure the chief would love to have bringing down The Black Lotus Syndicate, a double homicide, and stopping illegal gun and drug traffic under his belt." Elsie hyped him up.

"You're so right. We have to go in. Now. But I think in order to pitch this we need to have an idea of when the next import is."

"Easy." I pulled the journal out of my purse and flipped through the pages.

"You brought it with you this morning?" Elsie asked.

"Yeah, maybe I'm paranoid, but I don't want it out of sight." She nodded.

"Yeah, where were you guys this morning, by the way? I've been waiting here for like an hour."

"Yes, we're crime solving sleuths but we're also on vacation." I added with some sass. Him and Elsie laughed.

"She has a surprise for you later." Elsie nodded with a wink, and I elbowed her.

"Here it is. The date of the shipment was the first Saturday of the month. If things are the same, that's tomorrow. Tomorrow is the first Saturday of the month."

"Alright guys, let's pack up in the squad car. We have to go see the chief."

Chapter Thirteen

Declan marched us right into the station, past the front desk troll, who he gave a nod to. Then he led us to Chief Cutler's office. Declan rapped a few times, and a gruff voice from inside yelled for him to enter.

All three of us went inside, and Declan shut the blinds.

"What the hell is going on here?"

"Chief, I'm so sorry for this ambush. But you need to listen to us."

We told him everything about the case, excluding the details about Blackwell, and we included what our conclusion was.

"That's great work, Detective. That sounds pretty rock solid and will be a huge break for you, and this department. I don't like that you brought civilians in, but besides that, this is amazing police work. Why are you here though? Why aren't you with Blackwell establishing how to survey the port, though?" Cutler replied. The three of us went silent.

"This is where it gets a little messy, Chief." I announced.

"Blackwell arrested Max this morning and suspended me for everything I told you…we think Blackwell is working for the syndicate, Chief." Declan finally dropped the bomb, and the chief went silent.

"Think about it." I started, and his rocky gaze now shifted and pierced my eyes. "Two civilians with no experience that got further than him and Bates did in a week, than they did in a year. We have a literal diary from the girls with this information." I slapped it on the table. "Max is Blackwell's scapegoat so he doesn't get caught, too!" I jumped up from the table, not realizing how loud and passionate I was getting. The Chief just nodded. He let out a deep sigh.

"I had questions about Bate's sudden retirement. I questioned a lot of things, but not Blackwell. Maybe I should've. If you're right, Blackwell will alert the syndicate very fast, but probably not fast enough to stop the drop tomorrow night. Maybe they'll change the port. However, if it's the first Saturday every month, they'll definitely be in New York tomorrow. I'll reach out to some friends in other syndicates and we'll all stake out the ports. This needs to stay quiet. We don't want Blackwell to know we're onto him. This took major balls coming here, from all of you. And I appreciate it. Even if you're wrong, you had a very solid reason to doubt your superior, and that should never happen. Not in this force. Captain Sullivan and I will go with you three tomorrow night to stake out the port in the journal, the other precincts will cover the other." Elsie and I smiled gleefully, and it was hard to contain our excitement.

"Meet us at Doughy Joey's tomorrow night." Elsie added. "Er, that wasn't an order. If you want to, sir. Chief. Chief sir." He laughed.

"Blackwell can't know we're onto him, so I'm throwing you guys out. Go along with it." He stood up slowly from his desk, the bright lights above bouncing off his bald head. He opened the door and shoved us all out.

"Get the fuck out of here!" He barked so fiercely that he spat everywhere. I didn't think a man that old looking could be so menacing.

All of us ran out with our tails between our legs, looking pissed off, defeated, and sad.

We returned to Doughy Joey's where we picked up a pizza and split it upstairs in the apartment, full of adrenaline.

"I can't believe it. We solved it." Elsie said, eyes full of tears.

"Essentially, but don't get ahead of us. We still don't know who exactly it was." Declan tried to ground her.

"But we know why, and we know the group. The evidence is technically irrefutable."

"I know, but we can't charge a group of people with a murder. Someone will break, though."

"What if we offer Enzo a deal? If he spills the tea, he doesn't get charged." I let out my idea.

"That's brilliant, Ivy." Elsie clapped.

"Yeah, but we can't get ahead of ourselves. Calm down, you two." Declan laughed.

"That's Detective You Two, to you." Elsie remarked.

"What should we do tonight now?" I asked the crew.

"Well, Ernest and I have a phone date tonight. A sexy phone date. A sexy phone date that requires me to be alone here. So, I know what I'm doing, I just don't know what you're doing."

"Oh la la! Look at you go, Elsie. Didn't peg you for a phone sex girl." She laughed.

"We thought it would be fun to try. I don't have any toys…but I can make it work." Declan nearly choked on his pizza.

"Woah woah woah, I don't need to hear this." Declan waved his hands as if to silence girl talk.

"Did you tell him anything yet?" I asked Elsie. The smile melting from her face told me the answer.

"I will when we're home." She answered and brushed it off.

"With that being said. Miss Ivy, can you spend the evening with me?" He stood up and reached for my hand. "No talk of the case, either." I took his hand.

"I would love that." I stood beside him and kissed him on the cheek.

"Good." Elsie began cleaning up our mess. "You guys get out of here. I have to get ready." Declan and I laughed.

We decided to take his car, and leave mine here for Elsie in case she needed in.

"Where are you taking me?" I asked him.

"Well, we just ate so I was thinking we have a drink at a bar next to my house. If we're hungry maybe I'll cook dinner for us after and continue having some drinks at my house?"

"Sounds great. You aren't embarrassed of me looking like this?" I wasn't a self conscious person but in this moment, I felt like I was.

"No, it'll show people I mean business. I'll keep my lady in my place, and them in place." We both laughed, I'm glad he was so funny. "No babe, you're beautiful. Of course not."

"I'm sorry, I heard nothing except you calling me babe and your lady." I could see him blushing, but he didn't reply.

We pulled up to a bar on the corner of a street. It was all window, and wasn't swanky. Thank god. Wasn't fancy, but not a dive.

"I live right above it. It's a pretty nice place, too." He slid out of the car, and came around and opened my door before I had time to.

"Thank you." I smiled and took his arm. He moved my arm down and took his hand and interlaced his fingers in mine. The brisk air chilled my body and made me shiver. The air blew my hair around and exposed my face to the wind, which I could feel make my nose and cheeks pink. We rushed over to the door of the bar and he opened the door from me.

We took a seat at the far end of the bar, facing the door. Mahogany wood lined the bar, chairs, shelves, floors, everything. Black accents framed the woodwork and padded the chairs we sat upon. It smelled of musk, oak, and cigars. Classical music played, and chatter of many folks filled the air.

"I'll have a glass of Sauvignon Blanc, please."

"Make that a bottle, actually." Declan corrected to the young bartender. Very smiley, friendly looking guy. Doesn't look like a worn out, service industry, fella. He looked happy to be there. He returned quickly with a full bottle and two polished glasses.

"If you guys need anything, give me a holler. My name is Ernest." We said our thanks and he walked away.

"What a funny coincidence. That's Elsie's husbands name, if you didn't catch that."

"I did." He laughed, as he poured us both a glass half full.

"He's a very sweet guy. I like him. Those two are fated to be together, if I've ever seen it. It gives me hope." I smiled and ran my ring finger around the rim of my wine glass.

"What about you? Any husbands in your closet?" Declan asked me.

"No no, not at all. Chronically single, actually. And you?"

"I was actually engaged, about ten years ago. When I was engaged. That was my last relationship." I needed a big gulp of wine after that.

"She died shortly after. She was actually murdered." I didn't know how to follow it up.

"Can I ask what happened?" He fell silent for a moment.

"She was training to be a nurse. When she got off work, I was busy getting drunk underage with my friends and couldn't pick her up, so she walked home. Some guys robbed her, she told them no and fought back. They shot and killed her." Silence filled the space between us.

"I honestly don't know how to reply to that. I don't want to give you some basic I'm so sorry speech, so I won't. I am so fucking sorry for your loss. Easier said than done…but you can't blame yourself."

"I did for a while. Then I realized I can't live in guilt and shame and the shadow of that anymore, that's not what she would've wanted. Then I joined the force to help those in need. Hopefully prevent what I couldn't have at the time."

"Whether or not we see it at the time, but things happen for a reason. In her path…she was supposed to go. I know it sounds fucked up and I'm not sure what you believe in, but maybe it was her time. She was supposed to serve a higher purpose or get reincarnated to something more beautiful. Maybe her purpose was to teach you something. I'm not sure. But what I do know is that she would want you to live your life free of that punishment. Happy, content, and fulfilled. It seems to me like you're on a good path for that."

"You have any dark secrets you want to share?" I've been begging to come clean. To Elsie, to him, to someone about my story. This was my chance.

"Yes…I do. But it's not something I can tell. I'll have to show you, one day soon. If you'll stick around with me."

"I definitely plan on sticking around." He leaned in and gave me a gentle peck on my lips, and we both gulped up the rest of our glass of wine. Declan poured us another.

We made light of things, and carried the conversation more positively. We shared a lot about our childhood, excluding my timeline difference. He really made me feel a way I haven't felt before.

By the time we finished our third bottle, we cashed out and made our way upstairs.

Very bachelor pad, again. No wall decor, no decorations at all really. Just kitchen, bedroom, bathroom, living room. Nothing.

Declan cracked open a bottle of wine for us, I was already feeling pretty good.

"What do you think of the place?" He asked, almost rhetorically if I had to guess.

"It's nice. Kind of boring, though. Do you have any paint?" He laughed and nodded, surprised of my response.

"I actually do. My niece loves to paint so I have a lot of paint here."

"Can we give you an accent wall or something? You need a little pizzazz in here." He nodded, and ran away to a closet and returned with a ton of acrylic paints and a bed sheet.

He laid the sheet along a white wall in the living room, and he began squeezing tubes of paint out onto it.

"What do we paint?" He asked.

"I don't know, just feel it."

"I don't know where the brushes are." He tagged on, riffling through his paint supplies. "We have perfectly good brushes right here." I wiggled my fingers at him.

We covered our hands in paint, and began making abstract designs and shapes on the wall with no rhyme or reason. We laughed and drank plenty of wine throughout the process. It was beautiful. The painting and the time we had together. When the wall was full, we just looked at each other.

"I can't believe we did that." Declan declared.

"I can't believe you let me talk you into that so easily."

"What do you say about a shower?" He asked me, and I nodded gleefully.

"Show me the way." He grabbed my hand and dragged me towards the master bathroom. The paint on our hands swirled together to create different shades and patterns I hadn't seen before. It was very white in there, so I was careful with what I touched. He flipped the shower on, and turned to me, grabbing me at my sides gently.

He pulled my shirt above my head, leaving rainbow fingerprints on my sides and belly. Declan flung my shirt to the side. I did the same to his, smearing bright colors along his dark black tattoos. I traced my fingers along them, leaving bright colors in my wake. The pain, the hours, everything that went into them.

"Did you get these for a new start? To cover the old you up, cover the trauma up?" He shrugged.

"Yes and no. It was more beneficial than therapy. Made me feel better in my own skin. He pulled his pants down, leaving him only in his boxer briefs. My eyes widened at the bulge. I've never seen one that thick, that long.

Declan pulled me in deeply for a kiss, releasing my hair from the claw clip that in sat in. Letting it tumble down my back and knot into his colored fingers. His hands pushed my pants down below my butt, and they fell gracefully down my legs. I kicked them off. He pulled himself a few inches away.

Staring at me, vulnerable in my bra and underwear. Nothing very cute either, let I just state that for the record. I wasn't planning for this.

He slowly wrapped his arms around my back, touching the clasps on my bra. I looked in the mirror facing us, and viewed myself. So wanting. So needing. So eager. Steam began fogging up the mirror, clouding my beautiful view.

I felt him unclasp my bra. And I slowly threw it to the side. He placed his hands on my face and slowly dragged them down my neck, my collarbones, and to my tender breasts. He gently rubbed my nipples while making intense eye contact with me, and I let out a subtle moan. Nipple play normally didn't do much for me, but I suppose when you want someone or something so badly it does.

Hearing me moan must've let out a beast in him. He kissed me hard and pulled me tightly against him. I felt his throbbing member pulse through his underwear and against my thigh. He slipped my underwear down my thighs and to the ground, and I did the same to him.

Without breaking the kiss, he rotated us both into the walk in shower. My body was quaking with a need for him.

Hot water trickled down my hot body, and brought me a blanket of comfort. He began kissing my neck, then breasts, stomach, and then to my thighs. He looked up at me with want and desire in his eyes, and I obliged with a smile. He took my lips in his mouth, and dove a tongue in my core. I threw my back against the shower and moaned in satisfaction. Once the colored water ran clean, he ran a hand up my thigh and into my center. I opened my thighs, begging more of him. He plunged two fingers into my center and shoved his mouth against the part of me that was begging for his attention. The amount of suction he was providing and the rubbing from his tongue that he was giving me made me feel hot tingles rise throughout my body. I pushed myself down onto his face, and down onto his fingers, which only intensified my pleasure. My legs began shaking, feeling myself close to my breaking point. Like a rubber band with the most amount of tension, ready to snap. Finally, a white hot surge of fire burned throughout me, and I pushed down hard grinding into and onto him. I tightened around his thick fingers and I felt myself squirt over his face, which he more than happily tried to gulp up.

He raised himself to my face and pushed himself into me in a deep kiss, tasting myself on his lips and mustache.

I fumbled with his member, trying to get it close to my entrance as I raised my leg above his arm so he could help support me up.

Suddenly, I felt pressure in my already tightened center. I threw my head back in utmost pleasure. Declan let out a deep moan as well. As I raised my head forward, we made eye contact and met each other again in a deep kiss. My tight walls hugged him so tightly we both broke the kiss with moans of ecstasy. He began thrusting faster, and harder, making me sweat even under the droplets of water from the shower head. I pulled him so tight that my head was cradled between his neck and shoulder, and we both began screaming in ecstasy. I bit down hard on him, and he began pulsing into me so fast I couldn't even hold my composure. My legs wrapped around him tightly holding him into me, and I could feel his primalistic nature setting in. Romance wasn't there anymore, it was just our natural desire for pleasure and to finish. I threw my head back and he pinned it against the shower wall with his hand, lightly choking me.

"I'm gonna go." He moaned huskily in my ear, and I tightened automatically by him saying that, which made the pressure build in me. All I wanted was for him to finish, and I was hoping I would again too. I clung to him, and one of his hands shot down to me, almost hearing my silent wish to finish again. He fiercely began rubbing in circles, and I clung my legs against him heavenly.

"Please cum, for me." I squeaked out, and he did. We did. I came again and tightly encircled him inside of me. I felt warmth build inside my core, from him also finishing. My legs wrapped even tighter against him to hold me up as weakness fell over me, and I began to feel him shake with pleasure.

I panted and kissed his neck. His lips met mine, and we kissed passionately while we both slowly caught our breath in the steam of the shower.

We eventually got out, and he led me to his bed, where he brought me a full glass of white wine.

"Do you have a cigarette?" I asked him.

"Weirdly, I actually do. I don't smoke, but sometimes when I'm overwhelmed I do."

He handed me a pack of cigarettes and I pulled one out. He lit it while it was in my mouth. He then pulled one out for himself and lit it, too.

We sat together in bed on top of the sheets, naked, ashing into an empty wine glass

"Nice butt tattoo." Declan winked at me.

"Oh, you like that?" I laughed. "We got matching ones today."

"Very fitting. Tattoos are hot. Even if it's a mini cupcake." He teased.

"I haven't been this happy in a very long time." I put out there, vulnerably.

"I haven't either." He smiled at me and pulled me into a kiss. I leaned away and stood upright to use the bathroom. I pulled an oversized NYPD shirt that was lying on the floor over my head. When I came back from the bathroom, I heard a faint clawing noise. I knew he did too, because we were both looking around. I walked to the window to look outside, and sure enough on the small ledge by the window, there was a stray cat. My stray cat.

I opened up the window, and let him inside. ZZ pawed in like he owned the place, letting out a huge meow, showing Declan who was in charge.

"Don't freak out, this is my cat, ZZ. He likes to follow me around." I introduced him to Declan. ZZ hopped onto the bed and curled himself into a happy ball on my side of the bed. I joined the two, and Declan pulled me close into him as his baby spoon. He kissed the back of my neck, and the top of my back, while holding me so close to him that all I could feel was safety. ZZ readjusted, and positioned himself between the middle of our feet. Quickly, the three of us drifted into a comfortable slumber.

I woke up and adjusted myself. I peered down and realized ZZ wasn't there anymore. He must've snuck back out the window. Me moving around must've woken up Declan, because he started moving soon as well. I looked at him, and he gave me a huge, toothy smile. I turned around to him completely, and leaned in for a kiss.

"I'm sorry, I have morning breath." I broke the kiss to exclaim.

"Give me all of your morning breath." He added and rolled on top of me. I found his ruffled, messy hair so attractive. He began kissing me so passionately, I could feel myself dampen. I slowly began opening my legs to him. He ground himself into me, arousing me even more.

Declan briefly broke our kiss to spit on his hand and rub it on his member. He carefully guided himself slowly into me, erupting pleasure while stretching my tight walls. We kissed fiercely, full of desire. Hungry for one another. I wrapped my thighs around him, welcoming him into me as deep as he could go. I could feel heat build between us and we both began to sweat.

Declan kissed my throat and I arched my back. He traced his hands up from my waist and along my arms, interlacing his fingers in mine and pinning me down. The rhythmic pumping became a beat our bodies danced to, and suddenly I began moaning in ecstasy and he joined in completion.

He rolled over beside me, and I tucked myself back into the blankets and rolled into his chest. He rubbed my body back into a restful sleep.

When I awoke, Declan was looking at me lustfully and playing with my hair. I smiled and blinked the sleep away. He kissed me sweetly, and rolled me on top of him and hugged me closely. I felt so comfortable in his arms, so warm. So safe.

He slipped out underneath me. "Pancakes?" He asked. I nodded gleefully.

Declan strolled into the kitchen, and I went towards the bathroom. I took a real shower this morning, stepped out and got ready for our long day ahead. By the time I was done, breakfast was ready.

We sat down at his quaint dining room table and ate breakfast together over smiles, laughs, and kisses. Once I cleared the table from breakfast, Declan picked me up gracefully, and told me he wanted dessert to follow his breakfast this morning. He laid me back on the table, got on his knees, and went to work.

Chapter Fourteen

Most of the day was spent making love to each other, and talking about life. The one thing we avoided talking about is what would happen when the case was solved and I was to return home.

Declan packed us some dark hoodies to wear in the car for the stake out, and told me to hydrate now because the last thing we wanted was to have to take a potty break mid stake out.

On our way to the apartment, we stopped and grabbed a variety of sandwiches for the five of us to snack on at a corner store we passed. Around seven we rolled up to the apartment, and Declan told me he would wait outside in case the Chief and Captain pulled up.

Oddly enough, the door to our apartment wasn't locked. It was closed, though.

"Elsie! Ready for our big night!" I yelled as I took the steps, two at a time. Adrenaline was already racing through my veins and pumping my heart faster. No answer.

Once I got to the top of the stairs, my stomach dropped. Something was wrong, very wrong. Couch cushions were overturned, kitchen cabinets were out of array and their contents splayed about and shattered on the ground. The boxes of Sally and Goose's were dumped on the ground and picked through. Bedrooms were torn apart, some loose floorboards were even ripped up.

I knew she was gone, but I needed to make sure. I was careful not to touch the things that were disheveled, but I checked each closet, nook, and cranny, just to be sure.

I barreled down the stairs and burst through the door, almost taking out Chief Cutler.

"She's gone. The apartment is completely torn apart and she's gone." I spat out so quickly I didn't know if they comprehended me. Tears welled in my eyes. Captain Sullivan drew his gun and ran up the stairs. The Chief and Declan followed him.

About five minutes later, they returned.

"There's blood splatter in the bathroom. They must've got the jump on her when she couldn't hear them come up the stairs." Declan informed me.

"It's gotta be The Black Lotus Syndicate. What are the odds Blackwell knows we're onto him because of Elsie and I, and the day of or the day after he finds that out, our apartment was ransacked and she's gone."

Captain let out a sigh. "I know this is against protocol but honestly, I think we should wait to call it in. We're already busting the syndicate tonight and if they get word from someone corrupt at the station, like Blackwell, and they know we're onto them for the kidnapping as well, and they know that we're coming soon. Then Elsie might not have as great as a chance of survival as she would if we left it alone."

"I think you're right. I don't think they're going to kill her that fast. They're probably trying to get intel out of her. I doubt they realize we're going to bust them tonight. The syndicate probably thinks they have until the next shipment before we track down their schedule, and by then they'll change it." The guys nodded.

"The less people who know, the better off we are. We have the other ports covered, right?"

"Yeah. Lieutenant Penn is going with some guys from Precinct 11 to cover north port, Precinct 10 is covering mid port, and we're covering south port."

"Well, we have a long night ahead of us. Let's head over." Captain added, we all nodded and followed him.

"I'll drive us." Chief led us to his personal car. I wasn't sure what it was but it didn't look like a cop car. The windows were blacked out, though.

Declan and I sat in the back, Captain sat shotgun. Declan inconspicuously slid his hand over to mine, and gave it a tight squeeze. I looked at him and gave him an anxious smile. I was so worried about Elsie. I knew she would be fine though. I also knew no matter what, she wouldn't tell them we were coming tonight. She at least will have peace of mind knowing we're coming to rescue her.

It was dark when we got to the port. Dull, yellow street lamps illuminated the lot, but we still had to stay far enough away to keep our cover. Cargo bins were stacked and lined up against each other like an industrial maze. They were organized in rows, excluding a big middle space where shipments were offloaded. A tall, rusty iron gate with a padlock blocked out front, keeping everything inside secure. Starting at the gate down the left side of the road coming towards us were all the stores, and everything to the right was the heavily forested park.

No cargo ships were in sight, but there were some people walking by on and off. None of the guys recognized them as being mafia related, so we chocked it up to the homeless population. Maybe workers checking on the lot.

As time passed by, I didn't realize it but I must have dozed off. I awoke with a start and a big gasp of air, that made everyone jump.

"Jesus, kid. You can't scare an old man like that." Chief sighed out.

"Sorry, I didn't realize I fell asleep. What time is it?"

"Quarter to midnight." Captain added.

I began squirming, not realizing I must've drank a ton of fluids before the stake out. I had to pee.

"What?" Declan acknowledged my shifting.

"I have to use the bathroom." I added. Captain and Chief sighed. There wasn't much action going on around us still, so the Chief nodded.

"Go ahead." Chief waved me out.

"Where?"

"Behind a tree in the park or something." He gestured to the forested area to the right.

"I don't want to pee behind a tree."

"All the shops are closed." Captain pointed to the stores lining the left.

"I have an empty bottle you can use." Chief Cutler laughed at his own joke.

I sighed and trudged out of the car, checking my surroundings to make sure nobody was watching. I bolted to the fence line, making sure I was out of the overhead street lights, fast. Probably would've been less suspicious if I walked, but whatever.

A short chain link fence was wrapped around the park, so I braced my foot in a small hole and hoisted myself over to get over to a thick area of trees so I could pee in peace. I followed the fence back to a little privacy circle of trees. I hated peeing outside, men have it so easy.

I slipped my pants down, and squatted. I grabbed some low hanging branches to brace myself so I wasn't wrecking my quads.

No birds were chirping, the wind wasn't whistling, no creatures were exploring the moonlit woods, it was silent.

Until I heard the screaming. Screaming that made my blood thicken and run cold. A scream of a voice I knew well, Elsie.

I quickly stood up and peered around. It was certainly not coming from the woods, but the other side of the fence, the shipping yard.

I pulled up my pants while running out of the woods, nearly tripping on myself. I waved to the guys until I was sure they saw me. Then I gestured to the shipping yard, before I took back off into the woods, towards where I heard the screaming. I hopped over the small fence again that wedged me into a small space between the back of the cargo units. I carefully trekked behind the industrial metal boxes, placing my ear against them to listen inside. I moved stealthily and was careful to stay out of the light, and stay incognito.

The containers were all sorts of dim, unwelcoming colors. Mushroom brown, dirty olive green, burnt clay orange, muted maroon. All of them were silent now as well. As I crept along the backside, I reached one a little bit past the middle towards the back of the port. Or the front. I guess it depends where you're standing. It was closer to the water. There was no screaming, but I heard a whimpering inside, or a cry. I looked around, not seeing Declan, Chief, Captain, or anyone else anywhere. There was a very slim space between that storage container, and the one next to it. So slim I didn't think I could fit, but I know I needed to try.

I sucked in, and began squeezing between the two units. I felt sharp, shards of rust cut through my clothing and pierce my skin, probably drawing blood. Thankfully, I wasn't due for a tetanus shot. I kept pushing through, finding it hard to catch my breath because I was getting squeezed so tightly. As I reached the exit, I cautiously checked, and double checked the surroundings. Not one person was in sight. I pried myself out, almost nervous my hips would break from the pressure, and I fell to the ground with the force I had to use to unstick myself. I leaned my ear against the container, and was certain I was hearing the crying come from this one. I went to open the door, and it was padlocked. Of course. I looked around for anything I could use to break it, and the only thing I could see without venturing too far away was a broken piece of concrete, like a rock.

It was so heavy I could almost not pick it up. With both hands, I brought it over to the lock and began bashing it, over and over. Catching my knuckles on the metal surrounding it and cutting them open as well. One crack caught my finger so horribly I knew the bone was broken. I tried not to let a whimper escape my lips, but it did. On the tenth or so smash, the lock finally cracked off, defeated. I dropped the bloodied boulder and grabbed the door to open it. My open wounds burned with the rushes of cold, New York winter air. I looked upwards, and saw snow began falling lightly, in flurries. Maybe this will be a Christmas miracle.

As it creaked open a little too loudly, the smell was the first thing that hit me. I wretched involuntarily all over my shoes, unable to stop without plugging my nose. My eyes began to water, and I was so glad the lights were dim because I didn't want to see the horrors inside any more clearly than I already could make out.

In the middle of the container, Elsie was chained up by her wrists so tightly, the tips of her toes were the only thing touching the ground. She was bloodied and beaten. I couldn't tell if her face was swollen from crying, or from getting hit. The real horrors were what lay behind her. I was so glad she wasn't facing towards it.

Crumpled heaps of bones and dried goo were shoved in the corner. Maggots had mostly eaten the skin and muscle that remained on the bones, but flies still swarmed and buzzed around the stench of the decomposing bodies and their insides that had dried out. Hair coated patches of the broken skulls. Skulls that I believe once resembled Goose and Sally.

I rushed over to Elsie, and looked at how she was being held up. A chain was wrapped around a handle inside, and I began to unwind it. Elsie fell from the ceiling, and her legs fell out beneath her, making her collapse to the ground. I unwound the chains around her wrists until they were free.

"You're okay, you're safe. I'm breaking you out of here, Els. Come on." She nodded slowly, and struggled to her feet. I wrapped her arm over my neck and pulled her up. As we turned around, I stopped us dead in our tracks.

Blackwell.

"Well, well, well. I tried to keep you both out of it. Arrest Max, give you an answer, put this fucking case to rest. But you dumb bitches couldn't keep your fucking noses out of it." Blackwell sneered and spat at us with disgust.

"You weren't doing what was right, and you aren't doing what's right. You took an oath and you're blatantly disobeying it—for what? Allegiance to a fucking crime syndicate?" I yelled at him.

"Yeah, maybe I took an oath. But that job doesn't pay as well as the syndicate does. Sometimes you have to adjust your morals for the greater good." Blackwell gloated. I heard a gun click, and Blackwell stiffened.

"You call this the great or fucking good? You used to be a great cop, that's why I made you a sergeant. Now you're nobody. A waste of fucking space that's going to jail." Chief Cutler's aggressive voice yelled from out of our line of sight. Blackwell pondered his next move.

"I'll give you a chance. If you help us finish this, we'll be lenient with your sentencing." Blackwell slowly raised his hands, and turned around slowly.

"You think an old man with a little gun scares me?" He slowly replied back before smacking the Chief's gun out of his hands. Before he could make another move, Declan ran out behind him and ripped him off of the Chief, tackling Blackwell to the ground.

"You sorry son of a bitch." Declan began hitting him in the face, over and over, until Captain Penn pulled him off. Declan spat down at him.

"You're helping us break this wide open or I'll kill you right fucking now." The Chief stated menacingly behind gritted teeth, raising his weapon.

Blackwell was in and out of consciousness, filling coming all the way to. He slowly nodded, and the Captain threw him a hanky to hold on his wounds to help stop the bleeding.

Blackwell pointed out to the water. A large, barely lit up cargo ship was in sight.

"Shipments coming in now, the syndicate is going to start showing up soon if they haven't already." Blackwell added, defeated.

The Chief and Captain hooked him up to some sort of radio or recording device, underneath his shirt. Then they straightened him up a bit. Declan came to our rescue and made sure we were doing okay. I nodded, and he took the weight of Elsie off of me, giving her a brief once over and checking her injuries. Blackwell showed us all a good place to stand out of the line of sight, and Captain Sullivan carried Elsie and ran back to the car to radio to other units to show up here now. He tucked Elsie in with his jacket in the back seat, and then returned to us quickly. Plenty of faces I didn't know, but everyone else did, began to pack the lot. Then I saw Enzo, Alex, and Gianni, who was out on bail. I was also stunned to see Allegra, who appeared with a very large Italian looking man. I'm assuming her husband, and Enzo's dad. They opened the gargantuan iron gate out front, and began packing unmarked vans inside and opening the doors. Ready to load up with the deliveries and go.

Our inside rat, Blackwell, rolled up and approached Allegra and her husband. We began hearing his mic kick on and pick up noises from around him.

"What the fuck happened to you?" She looked at Blackwell, appalled.

"Oh, that girl fought me hard first. But I got her, don't worry. She'll meet the same fight as her sister." He lied. I clenched Declan's elbow as we all listened to that. Allegra looked suspicious.

"Enzo!" Allegra yelled. "Go check and make sure the girls in there still. We need information out of her."

The four of us looked at each other, hair standing on end, as Enzo reached the cargo container that held Elsie. By the look on his face, he knew something was wrong. He saw the destroyed lock on the ground in a puddle of my vomit. Enzo disregarded it and he peered inside, shut the door securely, and slowly turned around.

"She's passed out in there, mom." Enzo confirmed for us. We were all so shocked.

"Is he in on it with us?" I whispered. All the men looked at each other and shook their heads no. Even Blackwell looked surprised.

Enzo walked over to where Blackwell stood, and clapped him hardly on the back. "Nice job, for once." Enzo stated. It was almost like he had a sense of what's going on here.

"Mom, this isn't right." She rolled her eyes.

"Shut the fuck up, Enzo." She barked angrily. "You would be nothing without our empire."

"The empire is one thing. But kidnap? Murder?" Enzo argued.

"Those two idiots deserved to die. They were going to bring down my entire company, and the syndicate. I couldn't let that happen. That's why I put a bullet in their fucking skulls. That's why I had to kidnap the other dumb bitch who was onto us. Thankfully, the pig cops arrested Max, so this should all be put to rest finally." She spat.

"Do you even know what their names were?" Blackwell asked, trying to get her confession out.

"How could I forget? Ugly, uncouth names. Goose and Sally. I'll put a bullet in the skulls of those other two girls, too. I'll kill Elsie once we get the information she has, and I'll kill Ivy just for the thrill." The coldness in her voice made me shiver.

"That's all the information we need to put her away for the murders and kidnapping." Chief Cutler whispered to us.

Soon enough, the boat was anchored down and they began unloading wooden crates. The workers started cracking the boxes open with a crowbar, and they looked normal. They pulled out extravagant clothing, and we all didn't know what to think. That was until all the clothing was pulled out, and we saw palettes of guns and bricks of cocaine lining the bottom underneath where the clothes were.

"This does it, right?!" I asked, a little too excitedly. Before anyone had a chance to answer, an arm grabbed me from behind, which made me gasp loudly. A calloused hand covered my mouth and Declan pulled a gun on the person who snatched me.

Enzo.

"Be fucking quiet." He whispered aggressively. "Is Blackwell wired?" The three of them went silent, Declan still locked on him. "Put that the fuck down, Declan. I want to help."

"Yes he's wired." Declan replied, but not dropping his target.

"I can get her to admit to stashing the car. Do you need that?" The three of them nodded, and Enzo slowly released his hand from my mouth, gently caressing my body and letting his hand hold my side. I could feel rage build inside Declan, and project outwards in his aura.

"Why are you helping us?" Declan asked, annoyed. Enzo rolled his eyes.

"Listen. You and I have been brothers, Declan. Just because I didn't go straight like you, doesn't mean I want to be crooked. I'm tired of living my life the way the family wants me to. I'm not ready to be a cop or nothing, but I am ready to cut ties with that evil bitch. I swear to god I didn't know she killed those two girls, I just thought she paid them off to go out of town. I found out after you two started snooping around and Gianni drugged you. I just wasn't sure the next step I should take, because if it was the wrong one they'd kill me, too. Or I'd get arrested." His whiskey soaked breath burned my nose, but his firm grasp warmed me, in a good way. My skin melted where he touched. "Ivy, I'm so fucking sorry about what happened to you. I'll make Gianni pay. You are so beautiful inside and out, and that wasn't fair. I shouldn't have left you there. I was just so scared your cover would get blown, and the syndicate would realize I was figuring out a way to scheme against them. I guess it was just fate that brought us together in that bar." He smiled wistfully, and I could feel Declan seething.

He released his grip on me, and he stalked back to Blackwell. He blowed him in the side of his head. "Fucking narc!" Blackwell crumpled to the ground, lights out.

"What the fuck?!" Allegra interjected.

"I just got a call that he's feeding our information to the police. Mom—what did you do with the keys to the girl's Chrysler Newport that you took after you stashed it at the shop? I have to steal it back."

"The safe in the office, under the desk." Enzo nodded, and faked a phone call for someone to go get them.

"Hurry the fuck up!" She barked orders, and her husband stood patiently aside her, waiting for his shipment of art to be unloaded. I was so surprised to see a crime boss who was a woman in 1966. Her husband just seemed like her obedient pet.

Flying in too fast to count, cherries and berries rolled in surrounding the place. Declan, Captain Sullivan, and Chief Cutler ran into the field first, guns drawn, telling everyone to freeze. Occupants of the cop cars leapt out, guns drawn, following their lead.

I was expecting a gunfight, but I think the syndicate knew at this time they were overmatched, and caught red handed.

All the cops approached and began arresting the members, one by one.

Declan approached one of the guys I didn't recognize, pulling out handcuffs to arrest him. The Chief stopped him in his tracks. "You get the big fish." He gestured for him to arrest Allegra and Blackwell. Even from a hundred feet away I saw his eyes light up. Police cars kept rolling in, and members of the syndicate kept packing up into squad cars and were transported out.

I noticed, Enzo wasn't taken down yet. I walked over to him, and he let out a sigh before turning to me.

"I know I'll have to do time for this, but I'm grateful. After I do, I'll be free. I'll have a fresh, clean start. At least away from my parents and the syndicate." I smiled and gave him a hug.

"Thanks for trying to protect me that night." His smile faded, and he searched the crowd of syndicate members waiting to get taken away, until his eyes locked on Gianni.

"Here's a charge I don't mind adding onto my rap sheet." He pulled his shoulders back, and stalked towards Gianni, like he was Enzo's prey. I swear, he wound his arm up like Popeye and socked Gianni as hard as he could. He didn't stop either until cops pulled him off and restrained him. Gianni wasn't even recognizable.

Once all the members of the syndicate were arrested and all the contraband was secured, my brain started running in all sorts of directions. Crazy to think this syndicate went free originally, for all those years, and still had a vendetta so powerful against Goose and her family, that they ended up killing Elsie over it. Still afraid of getting exposed one day by potential loose ends they hadn't tied up. I'm surprised it took them that long to kill Elsie. I wonder if they killed anyone in Sally's family, too. I wonder how many lives we really did save today. My train of thoughts was derailed when Declan came over to me, and scooped me up in a deep kiss.

"You fucking did it." I congratulated.

"No. We fucking did it." He corrected with a smile

Chapter Fifteen

The next couple of days, Elsie and I began packing up all of our belongings, as well as all of Goose and Sally's belongings. We needed to catch up on our sleep before the drive back.

Obviously we knew what happened to the girls, but it did help that Allegra admitted again while in custody that she shot and killed the girls for being onto Velvet Avenue and The Black Lotus Syndicate.

The bodies in the shipping container were unfortunately confirmed as being Goose and Sally's, but Elsie was really just more relieved she had an answer as to what happened.

Velvet Avenue was liquidated very quickly. With no money to be made on the black market, the fashion part of them practically disintegrated and disappeared. That shot Silhouette Society to number one avant garde fashion company. With Blackwell being arrested, Declan was actually promoted to being Sergeant De Luca. The youngest Sergeant in the state. He told us it would take a while to prosecute the whole syndicate, but there was no chance of them being out on bail with the severity of all of their crimes.

Declan showed up to help us load up the car, and you could tell he was colored with distress, as I was too. I didn't want to say goodbye to him. Once we were all loaded up, Elsie gave Declan a hug and sat in shotgun to give Declan and I some privacy.

His eyes seemed to well up with tears. "I don't want this to be goodbye." He told me solemnly.

"Maybe it isn't." I added. "Just a see you later." He smiled.

"Yeah, but it still doesn't feel very good."

"No. No, it doesn't." I looked down at my shoes, unsure of what to say.

He took my chin between his pointer finger and thumb, then he lifted my head to his. He kissed me so passionately and deeply, I believe it could have woken my ancestors. I wrapped my arms around his neck and cradled his face in my hands. He grabbed at my waist and pulled me up. I wrapped my legs around him. Once we broke for air, I made eye contact.

"Thank you for everything. You were an amazing detective, and I can't wait to see what you do as sergeant of the 12th precinct." I smiled and leaned my forehead against his chin.

"I'll call you. Elsie gave me your number." I smiled at him.

"Good. We should get rolling." He gave me a peck, and hesitated to let my hands go. I slid into the driver's seat, and soon enough Declan blended into the background behind us.

I felt myself begin to cry, and Elsie grabbed my hand with a squeeze. I smiled at her empathy.

"Elsie, you realize we did it? We solved it?"

"I wish we had a better outcome, but I'm glad we did. Now they and their story can be put to rest."

"And all of The Black Lotus Syndicate will be prosecuted and brought to justice, so this can't happen again."

"And if it happens again, we'll fucking solve it." Elsie tagged on with a joke.

The rest of the ride was awfully silent. Maybe because we were both tired, or maybe because there was nothing left to say. It wasn't an awkward silence, but more of a comfortable silence.

When we pulled into her quaint driveway and began unpacking, the kids were still in school. Ernest ran out with open arms, beyond excited to see his wife. His face twisted in horror as he saw her face— the beating she took was apparent.

"What the—" He began.

"I love you so much!" She flung herself into his arms and began crying. "I wasn't honest with you Ernest. Can you make Ivy and I some very strong drinks, please? I'll tell you everything." He nodded, took her hand, and began pulling her inside. I started unloading everything into their house.

By the time I was done, Elsie and Ernest were planted outside by the fire pit. He was enthralled by the story she just finished up telling him. I plopped beside her, and took a large gulp of whatever he made me.

"Why didn't you tell me, Els?" He asked, more hurt than upset. She let out a sigh.

"Honestly, I didn't think you'd let me. I thought you'd think it was too dangerous." He nodded.

"I guess you're right and I understand where you're coming from. And honestly—it does seem like it was too dangerous. But I'm so happy you guys did it. You got the answers you so desperately needed and you even brought down a whole damn crime family." We nodded.

"You show him your butt?" I added to break the silence, and she slapped my knee, giving me the shush signal. Indicating she didn't tell him yet. Elsie stood up and lowered the back of her pants just a bit, revealing her tattoo to Ernest. His jaw dropped.

"Elsie! No fucking way!" He wiped at it, trying to figure out if it was a tattoo, or maybe just sharpie.

"She did it, too!" She laughed, looping me into the blame.

"We did it together, actually."

"Well, I'm glad you two got some great bonding time. I'm very happy for you both." We sat satisfied, in silence. I fumbled through my purse. I had the letter old Elsie wrote for me in there, too. The one about me spreading her ashes and solving her, Goose, and Sally's murder. I pulled it out and played with it in my hands.

"I have something to confess." My voice broke and became shaky. "It sounds crazy and I don't know if I should say it." I gently unfolded the paper.

"I doubt it can be crazier than that story!" Ernest got out with a laugh.

"Oh, it is. Or at least it's up there." I laughed uncomfortably.

I was interrupted by the door bell. The kids wouldn't ring that?

Elsie popped up from her seat and headed inside. A few minutes later, she returned back outside to us.

"Ivy, it's for you." She couldn't hide her grin. I was more than confused. She came back outside and took a seat, whispering something to Ernest. I went inside the house.

Standing in the kitchen was Declan. My jaw dropped. Was this a dream?

"I'm so fucking stupid." He began.

"What…?"

"I'm so fucking stupid. I should have never let you walk away." He paced towards me confidently, and wrapped me into a kiss. "Ivy, I love you. I want to do life with you. Letting you leave without telling you that is probably the dumbest thing I've ever done."

"I love you, Declan." He smiled and pulled me into a hug.

"I want you to come back with me. Come back, live with me, be a police consultant as a detective. I'm begging you." My jaw dropped, I wasn't sure what to say and he knew it. "You can come back here all the time to see Elsie. It isn't a far drive. When you get sick of me just take a vacation and come back here. But I love you and you need to give us a shot, because we both know fate is real, and this is it." I couldn't argue. After all, I didn't have a place to live. "Your weird cat that stalks you can even stay with us. Babe, we have an accent wall now. I can't look at that without thinking of you." I threw my head back in laughter.

"Yes, yes, one thousand times yes! I'm all in." He swiped me up in a kiss.

"Go tell your boss." I followed his order, and ran outside.

"So?!" Elsie asked me full of anticipation, but I couldn't help but feel a little sad.

"I don't want to leave you…" I began solemnly.

"Shut up, you're the brave one, remember? Plus now, I can vacation in New York whenever I want to. And you can come here whenever. You have to go." I nodded, happy and longing tears filling my eyes.

"I know."

"What did you want to tell us, by the way?" Ernest added on, lost.

"Oh, nothing." I smiled sweetly, and Elsie ran to me and wrapped me in a big hug.

"I love you, Ivy."

"I love you too, Elsie."

"Now get out of here before I get too emotional." She scolded. I gave Ernest a hug, and Declan came out and said goodbye as well. We went to the motel I was essentially using as storage and packed up both of our cars. I paid the front desk, and followed Declan's car back to New York, excited for my new life.

I pulled my purse onto my lap, and began fumbling through it for some gum. I found the gum—but what I didn't find was Elsie's letter. Elsie's old letter, that I was playing with in young Elsie's back yard.

Oh god—the letter was still there. Elsie was going to find the letter.